魔鬼╳特訓

倍斯特出版事業有限公司
Best Publishing Ltd.

新托福
聽力120

韋爾◎著

兩大創新的學習法
分別同時滿足重視「**多元主題學習**」和
「**畢業即就業**」的兩類學習者

QRCODE
DOWNLOAD

「跨領域」主題的學習：
活化思考、迅速拆解變化多端的考題（短期巧取致勝）
納入高明之極的多元主題，面對變招靈活的單領域考場考題，輕而易舉地考取聽力
28分以上高分。

「考用＋職場」整合為一的學習：
百大企業錄取通知書和新托福高分一次GET（長期穩收實效）
各職場主題融入聽力試題中，即學即用，口說和聽力能力讓考官和外商HR都滿意，
迅速成為學校和職場贏家。

先前一本聽力書《新托福聽力 100+》確是力作，當中提到了許多富思考性的主題，包含像是《複利效應》等實用話題。考生在練習聽力之餘，亦能夠藉由這些話題同時在生活和工作等層面有所提升，迎向更好的未來。此外，參加新托福測驗的考生其報考年紀大約介在大學和研究生的年齡層，許多些微的思考、決定和改變都對於個人的未來影響甚鉅。當中，即使有些一畢業就順利找到高薪資工作的求職者，在面對許多事情時，仍缺少了能做出更好決定的能力，這些都深深影響 30 後的你/妳。

有鑑於此，這本書的規劃除了延續「具思考性主題」、「強化核心聽力能力」和「就業力」，額外增加了「跨主題」的學術演講內容。這也意謂著考題內容更為多元，且並不單一，這絕對有助於考生更靈活思考（因為考生亦不太可能期盼在考場時寫到完全一樣的主題，靈活應對考題的能力遠比考古題更為重要多了）。在思考能力和核心聽力能力提升的同時，考生在考試的成果上就會有顯著的進步。例如在第一個話題《科學怪人》中，包含了英國文學、社會和心理學和法律主題的融合。不可否認的是，這些經典的著作確實不是短期流行劇可以比擬的，它是永

垂不朽的。它包含了許多具深度的思考性話題，這些都能幫助每位考生在回答寫作和口說話題時，更具備深入探討一個主題的能力且不辭窮、腦力源源不絕，等同於一石三鳥，準備聽力亦能迅速在寫作和口說單項中有所斬獲。

這個學術講堂特別選取了包含英國文化和法律等結合的話題，比起單一的文學主題更具吸引力。從賈斯婷的自辯陳詞，就能有眾多的感受，法庭如此的要求更不利於賈斯婷脫罪。更之後事情的進展並未因為受殺害的小男孩的表姐伊莉莎白的協助辯護，而使得聽審的民眾和法官們對案情有所改觀，反而使人民對於賈斯婷更為反感，最後法官們秉持著「寧可錯判 10 個無辜者，也不放跑一個罪犯」的態度令人瞠目結舌，此舉更使得賈斯婷受到絞刑判決並含冤而死…。

第二個話題則是**《百萬英鎊》**，這是個結合美國文學和商管的一個有趣話題，關鍵在於這一百萬英鎊是無法找開的，主角亨利要如何在具有百萬英鎊的這段時間運用這個好機會獲取更大的財富呢？故事的橋段亦讓人想到關於**《Storynomics》**中講述到的名聲和品牌，這些都能協助考生在寫分析時，有不同的思考點。

第三個話題亦是跨領域的主題，講堂的描述是以學生在來上課前都已溫習過指定閱讀內容，所以會是以教授接連叫學生接續回答的方式呈現。在學術講堂的設計中，除了此篇章外，其實避開了這樣的題型設計，一來這樣的搭配對考生來說難度會太高，在不具備文學背景或閱讀過這篇作品的考生來說會較為困難，因為考生要在不熟悉的主題中聽出許多細節性資訊且快速完成試題。但如果是到外國上課，這樣的討論性課堂的學習方式則較為常見。故事中亦包含很多具討論的話題，在當中選取了主角夫妻對於「選婿」的有趣話題。不可否認的是，女主角確實具備生意頭腦也在故事一開頭就以儲蓄和被動收入增加了自己和丈夫的資產。但後來的三萬美元的遺產也打亂了他們簡單的生活（這部分不經讓人想起在許多商管書中都曾提到的一個問題，更多的金錢只會製造出更多的問題？）。在後期，隨著他們的資產以各種方式的提升，他們對於選婿的條件也日趨嚴格，從一開始看不起泥瓦匠和補鍋匠意欲追求自己一雙女兒，到後來認為牙醫和律師也不夠格，就這樣越挑越令人張口結舌…到後來甚至在 4 位公爵人選裡亦挑三揀四…。

第四單元亦是跨領域的主題，是廣為人知的**《亂世佳人》**，除了在螢幕上所看到的浪漫愛情故事，當中有太多可以討論的主題，包含金錢和友誼等等（這部分很常被忽略掉了）。在前期，女主角思嘉莉曾在富有的男主角瑞德的好意提醒下，回應了帶點傲慢又斬釘截鐵的話，亦即她認為自己並不需要擔心錢的問題。她父親是莊園主人，而她並不愛首任丈夫，但她丈夫留下了亞特蘭大的房產給她，她對瑞德的建議嗤之以鼻。哪知道後來一旦都變了，她甚至盛裝打扮到監獄去跟瑞德借 300 元以繳取租金等等。到後來她甚至對天發誓「她再也不讓自己餓著了」。在中期，她和瑞德的對話揭露了她所選擇的道路。是的，她要錢，為了錢她甚至可以不擇手段。這把她推往了一個極端的道路。但這是她的選擇。瑞德回應她，那麼妳就該要為此付出代價，那就是寂寞（這句話也深深打擊她的內心）。在亞特蘭大因為她的風評沒人願意跟她交朋友。也因為她母親在戰後因為疾病先過世，她不能像往常那樣靠在母親的膝上傾訴。最後，她不經詢問瑞德，那麼在世界上，我還有朋友嗎？（這就是這篇講堂中，教授所要探討的主題，這篇也是稍微難答的主題，它包含許多跳著敘述的部分，需要比較多的組織和整合能力）。

第五到十一單元的講堂話題則是以「**商管＋職涯規劃＋心靈成長**」為主題。這部分對考生來說更為直接且實用性高，也能對求職面試等提供更多的思考面向。求職面試是所有人都要面對的議題。一位畢業後順利經由面試找到工作者和一位歷經千辛萬苦花費一年，面試了 30 幾間公司的求職者。我想後者已經具備了一定的面試表達和關鍵掌握了。我相信對這位求職者來說，這樣的安排是幸運的。有些一開始順利就業但中年後突然換工作或轉行的求職者，反而卻因為面試的問題而卡關了。這也跟收錄的第五個話題有關。

這話題中，Libby 是位具有西南航空 13 年經驗的中高階主管，當她選擇跳脫舒適圈並離開西南航空時，浮現在她腦海中的是，她已經有多少年沒有面試過了。面試包含了太多其他因素（在雅思閱讀書中，就有寫到的準備面試基礎一百題是遠遠不夠的，或是甚至在《新托福口說 100+》中工作面試話題中也有提到面試建議，你至少需要練習完《knock'em dead》再投履歷並參加面試。或許這些還可能不太夠）。以這本聽力書中某個講堂一開始的話題切入來說，一位名廚具備數年的工作經歷，所以他認為自己具備工作經驗等等，理所當然自己面試和面試官閒聊後就會雀屏中選，但卻在他講述完自我介紹後，女老闆遞給他一張名片，並要求他準備好再給她電話，就這樣面試結束了。這也跟第十一個講堂所講述的話題有關，或許你需要的是跳脫面試基礎一百題和《knock'em dead》這樣的書籍，轉而借助像是《**44 Insider Secrets That Will Get You Hired**》這樣的書籍，直接了解面試官心裡。如同這本書所提到的一個關鍵，「**妳/你正在被淘汰**」。這就像是在美劇《謀殺入門課》中Connor所遇到的問題一樣，Connor 很幸運在第一季的開端被名律師和大學教授安娜莉絲挑中，協助處理法律事務，但在第四季隨著名律師放手讓他所挑的五位學生出去闖的時候（找律師事務所的實習工作），Connor 在面試的情況慘不忍睹（教授也替每個人寫好了推薦函），也會被認定是在背誦像面試基礎一百題那樣的回答，在一連串的回答後，面試官只說了 We both know you are not going to get the job.，Connor 甚至一間律師事務所都沒獲得錄取（而第十一講堂中所討論的書籍，是資深人資跳脫這些傳統和背誦回答，協助求職者找到工作）。

　　從名廚師的面試結果，又令人拉回到第八到第十個講堂的主題。所以找工作時要抱持的態度是什麼呢？像鄉民版等所提到的，認為有朋友介紹就不認真看待或認為不需要準備面試，又或是認為有學歷和證照，公司就該錄取你？（但是別忘了在另一本暢銷書中所提到的 Resumes are just lists, and lists are not compelling.）關於求職，具劍橋大學學歷，儘管剛畢業就找到工作《*The Skills*》的作者所提供的看法又是什麼呢？又或是像星巴克前執行長和董事長 Howard Schultz 當初大學剛畢業時的求職態度是怎樣呢？他又是如何進到像 Xerox 這樣的大公司呢？

另外，在第九個講堂也跟第五個講堂中有些重疊的部分：轉職。其實如果名廚具備像講堂五中的主角 Libby 一樣的洞察力，他就能馬上吸引老闆的注意並獲得錄取，因為 Libby 完全站在執行長的角度在思考所有事情。關於這部分《*Tip: A Simple Strategy to Inspire High Performance and Lasting Success*》這本書的主角 Brain 也曾遇到工作挫折，但在後期卻能自發性的講述出一個發自內心、並非背誦的答案且符合面試官的要求。不過這則講堂則是側重在另一個思考點上面。故事要回到 Brain 受到無預警的裁員，這跟新聞中常出現的裁員故事雷同。他也認為很突然，他在公司做得好好的，然後就被裁掉了。事實上，他在這間公司有 11 年的工作經歷。書籍中提供另一個思考點是，早在 Brain 工作 5-6 年左右，他就被公司標記成「對公司未來不會再有任何貢獻了」。（但是公司必須要營利，且需要做事情都超乎預期的員工不斷地帶來收益以維持營運）。公司其實多給他這麼多年了，但他的工作表現並未改變。受到裁員時，他亦不這麼想，甚至氣憤到連主管寄給他的信也沒讀。Brain 一直是個每件事情都只做到剛好的工作者，然後就下班了去從事他所要從事的休閒活動。他也一直認為他會在這間公司一直待下去。最後，他後期勉為其難的去從事了吧檯的工作（他和吧檯老闆都知道中年轉職有多不容易，他如果想要找到他心儀的白領工作確實也需要時間）。這份吧檯工作對他有很大的啟發。公司有個規定就是每天會結算一大桶吧檯一整天所收取的小費，而公司老闆、員工 Kelly 和 Brian 會均分這些錢，即每個人都會獲取 1/3 的金額。Brain 剛來什麼都不懂，也都還在學習，且還打破酒杯等等，但是仍均分這些小費。Kelly 很直截了當地說，如果是原先沒離職的員工在的話，他們每天可以比現在多賺多少錢。也因為 Kelly 的抱怨，他開始思考自己在前公司的價值，而開始發憤更努力工作等等，最後離開這份工作時，他像脫胎換骨般，這些都幫助他找到了他最後的理想工作。

第十個講堂則是關於蘋果工程師 Ken 和 Don。時間要回到他們被裁員而且在找工作。Don 則掛保證要他不用擔心，其實 Ken 甚至不具備寫程式等能力，但也因為 Don 而進入蘋果。這時候蘋果的智慧型手機還沒開始研發。就只有 Ken 和 Don 兩個人在摸索，但算是毫無頭緒。Don 甚至還敢向公司要求要請假去旅遊。Don 和 Ken 是很具革命情感的工作夥伴和朋友。時間很快到了後期，Don 當了部門主管，甚至得到蘋果的另一次升遷，於是部門主管的空缺就空出來了。Ken 非常想要這份工作，但是不可否認的是，部門中其他工作能力出色的工程師也想要得到這份部門主管的工作，最後 Don 並沒有選擇 Ken，而是將部門主管的職務交給部門裡的另一位同事，這當然使 Ken 很不好受。於是 Ken 投了履歷，也收到 Google 的邀約，迎接而來的挑戰是 Google 內部工程師們接連詢問他一連串艱難的問題，並要求他在白板和平板上作答。這不經又令人想到了，Ken 具備足夠的硬實力以獲取 Google 這份工作呢？還是 Don 並沒有評估錯他，Ken 其實不夠優秀到可以成為部門主管呢？還有進入工作後是否就該不斷持續累積實力呢？（這本書當初有全部看完，這個是其中一個吸引點。扣除討論和製作手機的部分，其實還有幾個值得令人思考的點，包含 Don 在公司已經升遷兩次了，贏在起跑點的他，會一直贏著 Ken 嗎？等等的，有興趣的可以看看這本，可能對理工科系學生會蠻有吸引力的）。

另外要說的是關於「成功」的話題，講堂六就提到了追尋自我，Rebecca 從爬聖母峰的目標中找到自我，亦或是爬高山的人背後都有個故事。而成功和獲取財富也跟運氣脫不了關係，這也呼應了講堂七的話題。最後要說的是，在前一本書中有收錄了海洋生物等生物類的話題了，這次關於生物類的話題就只收錄了生物學中幾種蜜蜂的比較。另外，在心理學方面則是包含了關於探討感情關係，故事中的男主角和第三者如願在一起了，但最後兩人卻過得不快樂，到底又是為什麼呢？簡言之，這本書的規劃，不管在主題上或是...，似乎都貫穿著「疑問」和「為什麼」，不論是亂世佳人中的，那麼我還有朋友嗎？或是第十三個講堂中探討的，為什麼如願在一起了卻又彼此都感到不愉快呢？最後要祝所有考生都能獲取理想成績並且都有更璀璨的未來。

韋爾 敬上

Instructions

使用說明

美國文學＋商管

UNIT 3　《The 30,000 Bequest》更多的金錢只會產生更多問題嗎？瘋狂投資夫妻檔，這回又淘汰掉哪些女婿人選了呢？

▶▶ 聽力試題 (MP3 003)

1. What are the professions of Bradish and Fulton?
   (A) tinner and plasterer
   (B) the governor and the Congressman
   (C) lawyer and dentist
   (D) the earl and the duke

2. After the couple shelves the pork-packer's son and the village banker's son, who are their next considerations?
   (A) the earl and the duke
   (B) lawyer and doctor
   (C) viscount and marquise
   (D) the governor's son and the son of the Congressman

3. What does the author mean by saying..." Vast wealth, to the person unaccustomed to it, is a bane; it eats into the flesh and bone of his morals."?
   (A) to discourage people from getting wealthy
   (B) to warn a certain age group of the danger of wealth
   (C) to show the insensitivity phenomenon
   (D) to indicate the body condition getting torn apart

---

4. The following table lists the item that Sally takes.
   Click in the correct box

Item
A. chocolate
B. maple-sugar
C. apples
D. candles
E. soap

5. The following table lists the holdings that will get extra credits.
   Click in the correct box

Item
A. Ocean Cables
B. Klondike
C. Standard Oil
D. Steamer Lines
E. Tammany Graft
F. the Railway Systems
G. Diluted Telegraph
H. De Beers

文學跨領域

商管跨領域

其他

強化「細節性資訊」答題
精益求精，跨越門檻，達到理想成績

- 在邁向新托福聽力**27-30**的高分門檻中，能否答對細節性考題是關鍵。在《三萬美元遺產》話題中，涵蓋更多樣的細節性資訊考點，協助考生一次性掌握更多細節性資訊答題，應考時更無往不利。

涵蓋多元跨領域主題

迎向未來，擴充知識廣度

提升考生綜合答題實力

· 納入跨領域主題，例如：法律＋英國文學等，有效擴充考生知識面，每篇均在檢視考生的綜合答題實力，寫一篇等同演練無數考題，優化考生學習效率，事半功倍考取新托福佳績。

▶▶ 新托福聽力解析

1. 選項 A，only by the accused 是錯的。選項 B，聽力訊息僅提到 smart moves。選項 C，The conviction is not overturned，這個敘述比較難些，但是可以根據文中的 acquitted 得知最後是判無罪，所以是 overturned。選項 D，從獲判無罪和跟科學怪人的主角相比等，可以得知是 happy ending。

2. 選項 A，Justine 並沒有因為肖像而殺害小男孩。選項 B，聽審的民眾並未這樣想，而是在自我辯護時，她思考到如此推測對聽審的法官和民眾來說都是不具有說服力。選項 C，事實上，她並未要求，根據聽力訊息，她可以做出此要求，而非殺人（且以她跟小說男主角家的關係，他們也很願意贈送肖像給她，她根本不可能為了這個物品犯下殺人罪）。選項 D，符合這個段落所講述的，且為同義改寫，沒有證據能表示她的清白。

3. 選項 A，Elizabeth 知道 Justine 的人格而選擇替她辯護，並未如選項所述，要在法官面前營造自己高尚的人格，但是對聽眾而言，他們反而覺得 Elizabeth 人格高尚。選項 B，Elizabeth 的辯護未能替 Justine 洗脫罪嫌。選項 C，Elizabeth 認為自己的辯護「願意贈送肖像」能夠說明 Justine 不需去偷取此物品，但是她的辯護卻未能解釋「東西為何在 Justine 身上」，所以反而產生了料想不到的效果，答案要選 C。選項 D，是證詞讓大家覺得，而非她想讓 Justine 看起來很糟和不知感恩圖報。

4. 選項 A，惡魔其實本質不壞，是因為後來發生的事件而轉變，答案要選 A。選項 B，Justine 是被迫認罪的。選項 C，惡魔確實是因為被小男孩的言語激到而衝動犯行。選項 D，是惡魔將肖像放到 Justine 口袋裡的。

UNIT 1 《科學怪人》伊莉莎白的辯護、賈斯婷自辯陳詞、受到絞刑判決

5. 這題要選 B，教授提到這三個引述的主因是因為想要學生知道前因後果，從惡魔是如何變壞的，還有到底是誰將肖像嫁禍給 Justine。

答案：1. D 2. D 3. C 4. A 5. B

影子跟讀練習 MP3 001

做完試題目後，除了對答案知道錯的部分在哪外，更重要的是要修正自己聽力根本的問題，即聽力理解力和聽力專注力，聽力專注力的修正能逐步強化本身的聽力實力，所以現在請根據聽力內容「逐個段落」、「數個段落」或「整篇」進行跟讀練習，提升在實際考場時專注聽完每個訊息、定位出關鍵考點和搭配筆記回答完所有題目。Go!

This is English Fiction 101. And I believe all of you got an email from my assistant during the summer vacation to learn that you have to finish reading at least from chapter 1 to 15 prior to the class. And I will ask questions from these chapters at the end of the class today. You will be judged on how well you respond to each question. So let's get started. We will fast forward to chapter 8 and finish this classic in two weeks.

這是英文小說 101 課程。而我相信在暑假期間，你們都有收到

文學跨領域 商管跨領域 其他

生物學

UNIT 12 ▶ 幾種蜜蜂的比較：澳洲泥蜂、道森蜂、蜜蜂和大黃蜂

▶▶ 聽力試題 MP3 012

1. The following statements list traits of dirt daubers and their category
   Click in the correct box for each category

	dirt daubers	wasps
A. desensitize the prey		
B. encounter less obstacles		
C. tunnel-shaped nests		
D. indiscriminately build the nests		

2. The following statements list traits of honey bees and hornets
   Click in the correct box for each category

	honey bees	hornets
A. paralyze the prey		
B. kill sizable insects		
C. ability to pogrom		
D. use heat to defend		

3. The following statements list traits of dawson's bees
   Click in the correct box for each category

	female	male
A. high competition		
B. panmictic		
C. construct the nest		
D. remain unchanged after the sexual discourse		

4. The following statements list traits of honey bees and dawson's bees
   Click in the correct box for each category

	honey bees	dawson's bees
A. gregarious		
B. tunnel-shaped nests		
C. kill hornets		
D. sacrifices are made during mating season		

5. Listen again to part of the lecture. Then answer the question.
   (A) to show that honeybees will pretend to be larger when attacked.
   (B) to demonstrate that physique is the key to win in the insect world.
   (C) to explain those major weaknesses are inborn.
   (D) to show that they are still capable of reversing its disadvantageous situation.

文學跨領域

商管跨領域

其他

聽力模擬試題

納入加長題目，協助考生應對「加試題」

以更佳的**attention span**應戰，獲取更佳成績

· 「更高的專注力＋聽到更全面的重點」來應對應考，面對長度更為短的新托福實際考題，更能輕鬆應對，輕而易舉獲取理想成績。

⇉ 新托福聽力解析

1. 第 1 題的答案是 **C**，Bradish 和 Fulton 分別是律師和牙醫。
2. 第 2 題的答案是 **D**，the governor's son and the son of the Congressman。
3. 第 3 題的答案是 **C**，從作者講的話和學生的回答中可以推論出，這是要表達出一種麻木不仁和無感的現象，這些情況都導因於財富和逐漸累積的小事情，久了之後就不覺得有什麼了。財富也腐蝕了這對夫妻的心。
4. 第 4 題的答案是 **BCDE**，Sally 沒有拿巧克力，其他都有拿，故 A 不能選。
5. 第 5 題的答案是 **DF**，從 remaining items 中得知要選汽船公司和鐵路系統。
6. 第 6 題的答案是 **D**，編輯因為要感謝冰淇淋公司贈冰而將空位騰給了冰淇淋公司。
7. 第 7 題的答案是 **B**，從教授口中得知冰淇淋是草莓口味。
8. 第 8 題的答案是 **C**，富翁被目睹在街上乞討，所以他成了窮光蛋。

答案：1. C 2. D 3. C 4. BCDE 5. DF 6. D 7. B 8.C

70

🌫 影子跟讀練習 MP3 003

做完題目後，除了對答案知道錯的部分在哪外，更重要的是要修正自己聽力根本的問題，即聽力理解力和聽力專注力，聽力專注力的修正能逐步強化本身的聽力實力，所以現在請根據聽力內容「逐個段落」、「數個段落」或「整篇」進行跟讀練習，提升在實際考場時專注聽完個訊息、定位出關鍵考點和搭配筆記回答完所有題目。Go！

| Professor |

If you think, I'm doing all the talking like what we did last week... you are wrong... today we are going to talk about *The 30,000 Bequest*, a famous tale from Mark Twain.

| 教授 |

如果你們認為，我們會像上週一樣，課堂的進行都是由我從頭講到尾...那你們就錯了...今天我們將會談論《三萬元遺產》，馬克·吐溫的一篇著名的故事。

| Professor |

So Eric Winter? Who are among the first two pursuers for Electra's daughters?

| 教授 |

所以艾瑞克·溫特？伊萊克特拉兩個女兒最一開始的兩位追求者是誰呢？

71

生物類等主題
涵蓋更多的圖表題
建構更強、更全面的聽＋讀實力

· 充分運用聽和讀之間的關聯性，收錄更多圖表題所檢視的考點，考題中包含各類對比和描述性等的表達，能迅速歸類各項類別之間的差異就能迅速脫穎而出，獲取比其他考生更佳的分數。

摘要試題規劃

大幅提升考生簡報實力

畢業即就業，一次性獲取企業主青睞

- 內含檢視能否具備聽一大段訊息後，能夠轉換成口說式的摘要內容，這部分是更高階的語文檢視能力，具備此能力即能有效獲取新托福口說高分，並且在企業英語面試時具備一定的評價，獲取更佳的工作機會。

▶ 摘要能力

| Instruction | MP3 007

除了閱讀測驗外，其實培養能在聽完一大段訊息後，口述剛才聽到的聽力訊息是學習語言和表達很重要的一件事，讓自己養成並具備這樣的能力，除了能在聽力測驗中獲取高分外，也能在新托福寫作跟口說的整合題型上大有斬獲喔！所以快來練習，除了書中提供的參考答案外，自己可以試著重新聽過音檔一遍後，摘要出英文訊息並朗讀出來。

▶ 參考答案

During hiring processes, anything can happen, and hiring can be more complicated than we imagine. There are multiple factors that will influence how one gets hired, including luck. How luck works in the hiring can be further illustrated in two bestsellers and the sitcom.

Luck can also be the personality and charm that you exude. However, luck has also been linked to wealth, and other aspects, not just looking for a job. One's friendship is important in our career development.

The concept of the weak tie has been revealed, and it stands in sharp contrast to that of the close friend. You need to break the status to have more opportunities. The idea can be proved in the book like *How Luck Happens*.

Aside from the friendship, inheritance is the quickest way to wealth. You will be inherently lucky than others. Inheriting a large sum of money can also be attributed to luck, but like what is stated in the book, *The Wealth Elite*, you still need the genius to harness the amount of wealth handed to you; otherwise, the depletion of wealth will soon happen. Furthermore, "Wealthy individuals tend to ascribe their wealth overwhelmingly to personal qualities." It's an indication that pure luck isn't enough to make it last. To the person who is not inherently wealthy, it is actually good news. If you have the rich DNA or exact personal traits, you are still able to attain wealth.

文學跨領域　商管跨領域　其他

her job search was smooth... almost like it was handed to her... and she didn't seem to like it... she wrote "My **13.** _____ wasn't in the **14.** _____ news in which Bloomberg had made its reputation, but my time there allowed me to develop skills which I realized later would never have been possible had I gone straight from university to somewhere like the BBC."

... I understand some of you still haven't got the book... you can see the quote from the PPT slide... I think that says it all... plus when you are looking for the next job... most of the **15.** _____ about you stem from how well you do from your first job... you should be like a **16.** _____... absorbing everything there and make utmost of your time... something that can take you to the next job... and hopefully getting a higher salary... this also makes us think... a great job comes from your first job... people are doing so well so they get **17.** _____ by a great company in the same industry... that also reminds me of the book I read... but don't worry I'm not asking you to write a report on that book.

It's true some people get to work at a great company right out of colleges. The **18.** _____ still has to be based on your first job in order to be recognized as great. And if you are so great, you will be just fine in almost every place...

198

Let's take a look at the first job of the previous CEO of **19.** _____ and what was his thinking back then when he graduated... "I had no **20.** _____, no role models, no network that showed me how my education and **21.** _____ skills **22.** _____ into a working life." so how did he get a job at Xerox, one of the most admired companies back then... he obviously didn't get so **23.** _____ on getting hired by Xerox... he had a start at APECO, a small company, whose **24.** _____ was Xerox... he had a great job performance at APECO... then was recruited by Xerox... that also corresponds to the content of our topic today.... to have a great job...you need to have the work experience of the first job...and after the break, we are having a business guest speaker at the music hall... make sure you all put your clinical masks on...

│ **參考答案** │

1.	factors	2.	negotiating
3.	underpaid	4.	education
5.	range	6.	downside
7.	offers	8.	jobless
9.	accumulated	10.	lackluster
11.	drawback	12.	bachelor's
13.	heart	14.	financial
15.	evaluations	16.	sponge
17.	poached	18.	majority

199

文學跨領域
商管跨領域
其他

聽力筆記和填空測驗規劃
補足許多考生只寫官方試題但成績裹足不前的盲點
大幅提升聽力分數5-10分的成績

· 僅演練官方試題只是增加面對考試的熟悉度，但面對考試則需要更全面的檢視所有備考點，當中就包含了，聽到訊息後記筆記的能力和能否掌握每個填空題的考點。要寫新托福TPO的前提是要先具備這些能力再演練考題，才能發揮功效。

And it's astonishing to find that blue mud daubers feed on black widows. ... and for those of you who are having questions of how these mud daubers paralyzes the spider. We can begin by mentioning traits of these wasps. Wasps have the ability to paralyze the prey by using the sting to repeatedly sting the prey, such as tarantulas. And mud daubers also belong to the wasp's family, so they too are equipped with this ability. The injection of the neurotoxic venom on tarantula's body will only make them temporarily lose consciousness. The tarantula will be a zombie and it gets dragged to the larder of the wasp. The key difference between the wasp and the mud dauber is that the latter will encounter more hurdles. Predators are able to kill a group of the mud daubers at the same time, since the nest of the mud daubers is immensely close or adjacent to one another. Wasps, on the other hand, randomly build the larders in the habitat.

而令人感到震驚的發現還有藍色澳洲泥蜂以黑寡婦為食...然後你們之中有些人有著關於這些澳洲泥蜂是如何癱瘓蜘蛛的問題。我們可以藉由提及這些黃蜂的特性開始講述。黃蜂有個能夠癱瘓其獵物的能力，藉由使用螫針反覆地螫獵物，像是狼蛛。而且澳洲泥蜂也是屬於黃蜂家族的，所以他們也配有這項能力。注入神經毒素到狼蛛的身體將會使其短暫的失去意識。狼蛛會成了殭屍，而且被拖到黃蜂的巢穴裡。黃蜂和澳洲泥蜂最關鍵的不同在於後者會遭遇到更多的阻礙。掠食者能夠同時殺死一群澳洲泥蜂，因為澳洲泥蜂的巢穴極其靠近或是彼此緊鄰。在另一方面，黃蜂則在棲地上隨意地建構巢穴。

字彙輔助

1 astonishing 令人驚訝的
2 paralyze 癱瘓
3 repeatedly 重複地
4 injection 注射
5 neurotoxic 毒害神經的
6 venom 毒素
7 temporarily 暫時性地
8 consciousness 意識
9 immensely 巨大地
10 adjacent 鄰近的

In addition to the remarkable ability of wasps, the close relative of the wasp, hornets, are also fascinating. Hornets are able to take down large insects, such as mantises, which provide their offspring with a large source of protein. They contain larger venom than typical wasps. They are considered as quite incredibly cruel predators since hornets stage a large battle to other bee colonies, carrying with them larvae and adults for their young. The massacre can destroy an entire bee colony. It is not an individual fight like what a wasp does to a tarantula. The fight involves hundreds of corpses. It is the example of the cannibalization about what hornets can not only do to other insects, but species of the similar kind, such as honey bees.

除了黃蜂卓越的能力之外，黃蜂的近親，大黃蜂也是吸引人的。大黃蜂能夠打倒大型昆蟲，例如螳螂，以提供牠們後代大量的蛋白質。比起黃蜂，牠們包含較大量的毒液。牠們也被視為是相當驚人的殘酷掠食者，因為黃蜂可以策劃與其它蜂群的大型戰鬥，將牠們的

聽力主題亦涵蓋更多學術文句
有效強化新托福寫作實力（「寫作」和「聽＋寫」）
兩種新托福寫作的考試均獲取佳績

· 許多聽力講堂更包含了五花八門的學術長句，在反覆使用書中聽力學習規劃時，也無形中內建語感和相關的學術文句表達，快速強化面對新托福寫作時的應對能力，在兩個新托福寫作測驗中均獲取佳績。

商管＋職涯規劃

UNIT 11 ▶▶ 《44 Insider Secrets That Will Get You Hired》面試到底還需要注意些什麼呢？

▶▶ 聽力試題 MP3 011

1. How does the professor present the idea to the class?
   (A) a combination of books and documentaries
   (B) copying the teaching materials from last semester.
   (C) inviting outside HR experts.
   (D) a combination of her own experience and other forms.

2. Listen again to part of the lecture. Then answer the question.
   (A) She wants to point out Connor's incompetence.
   (B) She wants to point out the inadequacy of preparing basic interview questions
   (C) She wants to attract student's attention by making Connor look bad.
   (D) She loves a legal thriller.

3. Listen again to part of the lecture. Then answer the question.
   (A) to strengthen the usefulness of the idea
   (B) to craft your own story
   (C) to cater to other bestsellers
   (D) to make your storytelling impeccable

4. Listen again to part of the lecture. Then answer the question.
   (A) Recreating the impression is not necessary.
   (B) Let interviewers know you love the job at the end of the interview.
   (C) Interviewers will neglect your excitement if they like you.
   (D) Interviewers are able to tell one's enthusiasm right from the start.

5. Listen again to part of the lecture. Then answer the question.
   (A) You have to remain doubtful for whatever the interviewer says.
   (B) Doubts will only inflict people's mind.
   (C) You have to pretend that you know the secret code.
   (D) Every question is designed to rule out the candidate who is not fit for the job.

暢銷類書籍的納入

更完備的思考，有更好的態度和觀點

迎向更好的人生

· 30後會站在哪裡，是許多在大一就該思考的問題，許多主題納入了更全面的過來人觀點，讓考生面對未來不盲從且不茫然，邁向更好的畢業生活。

CONTENTS 目次

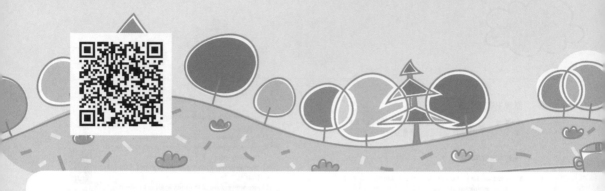

01

文學跨領域

篇章概述

這個篇章收錄了幾個著名有趣的文學主題,許多討論的內容更可用於新托福口説和寫作話題中,有效強化論點説服力和講話的深度,三倍化攻略三個單項。

UNIT 1 ▶▶ 《科學怪人》伊莉莎白的辯護、賈斯婷自辯陳詞、受到絞刑判決

▶▶ **聽力試題** MP3 001

1. What can be inferred about *A Tale of Two Cities*?

   (A) The defense is made only by the accused.

   (B) The protagonist has slim in picking moves.

   (C) The conviction is not overturned.

   (D) It's a happy ending.

2. Listen again to part of the lecture. Then answer the question.

   (A) Justine did kill the little boy for the precious picture.

   (B) People attending the hearing surmise that someone else puts the picture in her pocket to frame her.

   (C) There is proof that she had asked for the picture before the murder was committed.

   (D) There is no evidence to back up Justine's innocence.

3. Listen again to part of the lecture. Then answer the question.

   (A) She wants to present to the judge that she has a grandiose character.

   (B) Elizabeth's statements are so powerful that Justine will get acquitted.

(C) Her elucidation has produced an unexpected effect.

(D) She wants to make Justine look bad and ungrateful.

4. What is untrue about *Frankenstein*?

(A) The devil is evil in nature.

(B) Justine is forced to confess.

(C) The devil acts on impulse and kills the little boy.

(D) The devil puts the picture into Justine's pocket.

5. Why does the professor mention three quotes of what the devil says at the end of the class?

(A) to strengthen the wicked conduct of the devil

(B) to understand the cause and effect

(C) to demonstrate the devil's appreciation of the portrait

(D) to demonstrate the devil's appreciation of the lesson given by Fliex

▶▶ 新托福聽力解析

1. 選項 A，only by the accused 是錯的。選項 B，聽力訊息僅提到 smart moves。選項 C，The conviction is not overturned，這個敘述比較難些，但是可以根據文中的 acquitted 得知最後是判無罪，所以是 overturned。選項 D，從獲判無罪和跟科學怪人的主角相比等，可以得知是 happy ending。

2. 選項 A，Justine 並沒有因為肖像而殺害小男孩。選項 B，聽審的民眾並未這樣想，而是在自我辯護時，她思考到如此推測對聽審的法官和民眾等顯然是不具有說服力。選項 C，事實上，她並未要求，根據聽力訊息，她可以做出此要求，而非殺人（且以她跟小說男主角家的關係，他們也很願意贈送肖像給她，她根本不可能為了這個物品犯下殺人罪）。選項 D，符合這個段落所講述的，且為同義改寫，沒有證據能表示她的清白。

3. 選項 A，Elizabeth 知道 Justine 的人格而選擇替她辯護，並未如選項所述，要在法官面前營造自己高尚的人格，但是對聽眾而言，他們反而覺得 Elizabeth 人格高尚。選項 B，Elizabeth 的辯護未能替 Justine 洗脫罪嫌。選項 C，Elizabeth 認為自己的辯護「願意贈送肖像」能夠說明 Justine 不需要去偷取此物品，但是她的辯護卻未能解釋「東西為何在 Justine 身上」，所以反而產生了料想不到的效果，答案要選 C。選項 D，是證詞讓大家覺得，而非她想讓 Justine 看起來很糟和不知感恩圖報。

4. 選項 A，惡魔其實本質不壞，是因為後來發生的事件而轉壞，答案要選 A。選項 B，Justine 是被迫認罪的。選項 C，惡魔確實是因為被小男孩的言語激到而衝動犯行。選項 D，是惡魔將肖像放到 Justine 口袋裡的。

5. 這題要選 B，教授提到這三個引述的主因是因為想要學生知道前因後果，從惡魔是如何變壞的，還有到底是誰將肖像嫁禍給 Justine。

答案：1. D 2. D 3. C 4. A 5. B

 影子跟讀練習 MP3 001

做完題目後，除了對答案知道錯的部分在哪外，更重要的是要修正自己聽力根本的問題，即聽力理解力和聽力專注力，聽力專注力的修正能逐步強化本身的聽力實力，所以現在請根據聽力內容「逐個段落」、「數個段落」或「整篇」進行跟讀練習，提升在實際考場時專注聽完每個訊息、定位出關鍵考點和搭配筆記回答完所有題目。Go!

This is English Fiction 101. And I believe all of you got an email from my assistant during the summer vacation to learn that you have to finish reading at least from chapter 1 to 15 prior to the class. And I will ask questions from these chapters at the end of the class today. You will be judged on how well you respond to each question. So let's get started. We will fast forward to chapter 8 and finish this classic in two weeks.

這是英文小說 101 課程。而我相信在暑假期間，你們都有收到我的助理所寄送的電子郵件，在開課之前，你們都必須要至少完成第一章至第十五章的閱讀。以及，我將會在今日的課堂結束之前詢問關於這些章節的問題。你們對於每個問題的回答得體程度會影響到你們的表現評估。所以，讓我們開始吧！我們會快速跳至第八章，然後在兩周內完成這本經典作品的討論。

This is not a story of the happy ending that some of you might expect from the defense in *A Tale of Two Cities* in which the accused gets successfully acquitted from the crime by the attorney. In *A Tale of Two Cities*, there are certainly some smart moves that are employed by the protagonist. It makes us see the silver lining in things. Simply put, the main character does not commit the crime, whereas in *Frankenstein*, Justine unbelievably suffers. She is innocent on all accounts, but multiple mysterious things blended. That makes her the culprit of the crime. She deems that there is a glimmer of hope for her to get acquitted.

這個故事不同於《雙城記》那樣，被告成功地藉由律師的辯護而獲判無罪，而是有著一個不美滿的結局。在《雙城記》中，主角確實使用上了一些聰明的對策，使我們在困境當中看到了一絲曙光。簡言之，主角並未犯罪，而在《科學怪人》裡頭，賈斯婷卻令人難以置信地蒙受其害。無論如何，她是無辜的，但是卻有許多神秘的事情攪和在一塊了。這使得她成了罪案中的刑事被告。她認為自己能脫罪的希望是渺茫的。

字彙輔助

1 assistant 助理

2 respond 回應

3 expect 期待

4 defense 辯護

5 the accused 被告

6 acquit 宣告...無罪

7 attorney 律師

8 protagonist 主要人物

9 unbelievably 難以置信地

10 glimmer 微光、少許

What's worse, she has to defend herself on the stand, the kind of place where she is vulnerable to attack, and it's a strategy frequently employed by several TV programs to make it riveting for the audiences. Audiences love to see the interaction between the prosecutor and the accused. Her explanations for what happened that night as to why the picture was in her pocket fail to convince people at the court. It's inexplicable, and the picture actually belongs to the little boy who gets killed. Apparently, there is no evidence as to why Justine would steal the picture and killed the boy. She can simply ask for it rather than commit the crime of this magnitude and puts herself in so much trouble. But it is groundless to make a conjecture that someone else puts the picture in her pocket to frame her.

更糟的是,她必須要在庭上自我辯護,這使得她更易於受到攻擊,這類的策略被幾個電視劇頻繁地使用著,因為這樣能讓觀眾覺得饒有興味。觀眾喜愛看到被告和檢察官之間的互動。她對於當晚所發生的事情所進行的解釋，關於為什麼那幅肖像會在她的口袋裡，無法說服在法庭內聽審的民眾。這件事情是無法解釋的，而那幅肖像是所被殺害的那位小男孩所持有的。顯而易見的是，沒有證據顯示出為什麼賈斯婷會竊取那幅肖像，並且殺害小男孩。她可以直截了當地要那幅肖像，而非犯下如此重的罪刑，並致使自己蒙受眾多的困擾。但是如此推測說，是有其他人將那幅肖像放入她的口袋中陷害她卻又毫無根據。

字彙輔助

1. defend 替...辯護
2. vulnerable 易受...攻擊
3. riveting 饒有興味的、引人入勝的
4. prosecutor 檢察官
5. explanation 解釋
6. inexplicable 無法解釋的
7. evidence 證據
8. magnitude 強度、重大、嚴重性
9. conjecture 推測、猜測
10. frame 陷害、捏造

As the story progresses, for fear of the crime, several witnesses are reluctant to defend her character. Luckily, Elizabeth, the little brother's cousin, is unexpectedly willing to take the stand when she notices that Justine's character is to no avail to move the judges and others. She addresses on how well she has known Justine for years by living with her and sees firsthand the treatment she does for her own mother and Justine's care for the little boy as her own son. Elizabeth does talk about something important.... she is willing to give the picture as a present to Justine... so there is no reason for Justine to steal the picture. Still Elizabeth fails to explain why the picture is in Justine's pocket. These statements make Justine an ungrateful person, and Elizabeth, a person of noble character.

隨著故事的進展，幾位證人因為對於此犯罪的恐懼感，而不願意替賈斯婷辯護。幸運的是，伊莉莎白，也就是這位小男孩的表姊，當她注意到賈斯婷的品格無法使法官們和其他人對案情的看法有所動搖時，出乎意料之外地願意在審訊時出庭作證。她提及這幾年來跟賈斯婷同住的這段時間，她有多了解賈斯婷這個人，以及親眼目睹賈斯婷為她母親治療和賈斯婷對這位小孩的照顧，就如同自己親兒子般地對待。伊莉莎白確實講到了些重點處……她願意將那幅肖像當作禮物贈送給賈斯婷…所以賈斯婷更沒有偷竊那幅肖像的理由。伊莉莎白仍舊未能解釋出為何那幅肖像會在賈斯婷的口袋裡頭。這些陳述讓賈斯婷成了不懂得感恩圖報的人，而反襯出伊莉莎白的高尚人格。

字彙輔助

1 progress 進展

2 witness 目擊者、證人

3 reluctant 不情願的、勉強的

4 character（人的）品質；性格

5 unexpectedly 未料到地、意外地

6 avail 效用、利益、幫助

7 treatment 對待、待遇

8 picture 肖像

9 ungrateful 忘恩負義的，不領情的

10 noble 高貴的、高尚的

Then comes the sentence. All judges unanimously agree that **"ten innocent should suffer than that one guilty should escape."** It is Justine's confessor that makes her confessed, and all judges make the decision based on the fact she confesses. On the morrow, she dies on the scaffold.

緊接著就是判決。所有的法官均一致性地同意「寧可錯判 10 個無辜者，也不放跑一個罪犯」。是賈斯婷的懺悔神父逼她招供，而所有的法官們是根據賈斯婷坦承犯行這點而做出決定。在翌日，她在絞刑架上死去。

Yet the question remains... who put the picture in the pocket... let's turn to chapter 16... we will see how the devil has changed from a kind person who saves other people's life to a horrific, merciless person who frames Justine and commits multiple heinous crimes. The devil just wants to be not left out from the crowd. Then he approaches the little boy and gets agitated by words the little boy says. In an instant the little boy gets murdered.

然而，問題仍舊存在著...是誰將那幅肖像放入口袋的...讓我們翻至第 16 章...我們將會看到惡魔是如何從一位救人性命的良善的人，變成一位可怕、殘酷且陷害賈斯婷的人，並且犯下多起令人髮指的罪。惡魔只是不想被群眾遺棄。接著，他接近小男孩，然後因為小男孩所講述的話，而感到激動。迅雷不及掩耳的情況下，小男孩被謀殺了。

Let's take a look at what the devil says... **"As I fixed my eyes on the child, I saw something glittering on his breast. I took it; it was a portrait of a most lovely woman. "** The devil then encounters Justine... the feelings of exclusion make him mad... what's on the devil's mind... redemption. Let's take a look at what the devil states... a few sentences from the bottom of this paragraph... **"Thanks to the lessons of Fliex and the sanguinary laws of man, I had learned how to work mischief."** This is exactly the reason why the devil goes estrange and even wants to frame someone else... a sharp contrast to what we have read in chapter 8 when Justine says... **"I believe that I have no enemy on earth, and none surely would have been so wicked as to destroy me wantonly."**

　　讓我們來看一下惡魔所陳述的部分…「我凝眸注視這孩子，突然發現有件東西在他胸前閃閃發光。我解下一看，原來是個非常漂亮的女人肖像。」惡魔緊接著遇到賈斯婷…被人們排除在外的感覺讓他感到憤怒…在惡魔的心頭處…有著救贖的念頭。讓我們看一下惡魔的陳述…在段落底部往上幾行的地方…。「多虧菲利克斯給我上過的課，也多虧了那些血淋淋的人類法則，我現在也學會了陷害別人。」這就是惡魔走入歧途的原因，並且甚至想要陷害其他人…跟我們已經讀過的第八章的內容中，當賈斯婷説道…「在這個世界上，我相信自己沒有任何敵人。沒有誰會如此惡毒，竟無端加害於我。」有著強烈的對比。

文學跨領域

商管跨領域

其他

1. confessor 懺悔者；告解的神父   2. confess 坦白、供認、承認

3. morrow 翌日   4. scaffold 絞刑架

5. merciless 無情的；殘酷的   6. heinous 令人髮指的

7. agitate 使激動；使焦慮   8. exclusion 排斥、排除在外

9. redemption 挽救；贖救   10. sanguinary 血腥的；好殺戮的

▶▶ 試題聽力原文

1. What can be inferred about *A Tale of Two Cities*?

2. Listen again to part of the lecture. Then answer the question.

   Apparently, there is no evidence as to why Justine would steal the picture and killed the boy. She can simply ask for it rather than commit the crime of this magnitude and puts herself in so much trouble. But it is groundless to make a conjecture that someone else puts the picture in her pocket to frame her.

   What can be inferred about the incident?

3. Listen again to part of the lecture. Then answer the question.

   Elizabeth does talk about something important.... she is willing to give the picture as a present to Justine... so

there is no reason for Justine to steal the picture. Still Elizabeth fails to explain why the picture is in Justine's pocket. These statements make Justine an ingrateful person, and Elizabeth, a person of noble character.
What can be inferred about Elizabeth's statements?

4. What is untrue about *Frankenstein*?

5. Why does the professor mention three quotes of what the devil says at the end of the class?

N O T E

▶▶ 記筆記與聽力訊息

| Instruction | `MP3 001`

　　新托福聽力與其他聽力測驗不同，可以於聽力的紙上記筆記，除了寫試題外，更重要的一點是訓練自己能夠在聽完一段訊息後，將重要的聽力訊息都記下。也可以將自己聽到跟記到的重點訊息跟試題做比對，因為試題考的就是長對話跟講座中出現的重點，能修正自己選取聽力訊息重點的能力。

| 聽力重點 |

- 記筆記有很多方式，包含符號跟自己習慣的縮寫字等等，可以找出最適合自己的模式，一定要自己重複聽音檔作練習數次。
- 這篇是關於英國文學和法律的結合主題，**段落中很多論述都能用於新托福口說和寫作中。**

NOTE

▶▶ 參考筆記

Main idea ❶	
A Tale of Two Cities	gets successfully acquitted
Frankenstein	culprit of the crime

Main idea ❷	
Justine	• defend herself on the stand • it is groundless to make a conjecture that someone else puts the picture in her pocket to frame her
Elizabeth	• take the stand for Justine's integrity • fails to explain why the picture is in Justine's pocket

Main idea ❸	
All judges	**"ten innocent should suffer than that one guilty should escape."**
Justine's confessor	makes her confess

Main idea ❹	
Cause and effect	• exclusion from the crowd and getting accepted • frame Elizbeth and kill the little boy

文學跨領域

商管跨領域

其他

▶▶ 填空測驗

Instruction | MP3 001

現在請再聽一次音檔，並做下列的測驗，檢視自己能否完成此填空測驗和強化自己聽力能力和拼字能力，降低自己漏聽到聽力訊息的機會，大幅提升應考實力。

This is not a story of the happy **1.** _____ that some of you might expect from the **2.** _____ in *A Tale of Two Cities* in which the accused gets successfully **3.** _____ from the crime by the **4.** _____. In *A Tale of Two Cities*, there are certainly some smart moves that are employed by the **5.** _____. It makes us see the silver lining in things.

Simply put, the main character does not commit the crime, whereas in *Frankenstein*, Justine **6.** _____ suffers. She is innocent on all accounts, but multiple **7.** _____ things blended. That makes her the culprit of the crime. She deems that there is a **8.** _____ of hope for her to get acquitted.

What's worse, she has to defend herself on the stand, the kind of place where she is **9.** _____ to attack, and it's a strategy frequently employed by several TV programs to make it **10.** _____ for the audiences. Audiences love to see the interaction between the prosecutor and the accused. Her **11.** _____ for what happened that night as to why the picture was in her pocket fail to convince people at the court.

It's **12.** _____, and the picture actually belongs to the little boy who gets killed. Apparently, there is no **13.** _____ as to why Justine would steal the picture and killed the boy. She can simply ask for it rather than commit the crime of this **14.** _____

and puts herself in so much trouble. But it is **15.** _____ to make a conjecture that someone else puts the picture in her pocket to frame her.

As the story progresses, for fear of the crime, several **16.** _____ are reluctant to defend her character. Luckily, Elizabeth, the little brother's cousin, is **17.** _____ willing to take the stand when she notices that Justine's character is to no avail to move the judges and others. She addresses on how well she has known Justine for years by living with her and sees firsthand the **18.** _____ she does for her own mother and Justine's care for the little boy as her own son.

Elizabeth does talk about something important.... she is willing to give the picture as a **19.** _____ to Justine... so there is no reason for Justine to steal the picture. Still Elizabeth fails to explain why the picture is in Justine's pocket. These statements make Justine an **20.** _____ person, and Elizabeth, a person of the noble character.

Then comes the sentence. All judges unanimously agree that **"ten innocent should suffer than that one guilty should 21.** _____.**"** It is Justine's **22.** _____ that makes her confessed, and all judges make the decision based on the fact she confesses. On the morrow, she dies on the **23.** _____ _____.

Yet the question remains... who put the picture in the pocket... let's turn to chapter 16... we will see how the devil has changed from a kind person who saves other people's life to a horrific, **24.** _____ person who frames Justine and commits multiple heinous crimes. The devil just wants to be not left out from the crowd. Then he approaches the little boy and gets **25.** _____ by words the little boy says. In an instant the little boy gets murdered.

Let's take a look at what the devil says... **"As I fixed my eyes on the child, I saw something glittering on his breast. I took it; it was a 26.** _____ **of a most lovely woman."** The devil then encounters Justine... the feelings of **27.** _____ make him mad... what's on the devil's mind... redemption. Let's take a look at what the devil states... a few sentences from the bottom of this paragraph... **"Thanks to the lessons of Fliex and the 28.** _____ **laws of man, I**

had learned how to work mischief."

　　This is exactly the reason why the devil goes **29.** _____ and even wants to frame someone else... a sharp contrast to what we have read in chapter 8 when Justine says... **"I believe that I have no enemy on earth, and none surely would have been so wicked as to destroy me 30.** _____ **."**

│ 參考答案 │

1. ending	2. defense
3. acquitted	4. attorney
5. protagonist	6. unbelievably
7. mysterious	8. glimmer
9. vulnerable	10. riveting
11. explanations	12. inexplicable
13. evidence	14. magnitude
15. groundless	16. witnesses
17. unexpectedly	18. treatment
19. present	20. ungrateful
21. escape	22. confessor
23. scaffold	24. merciless
25. agitated	26. portrait
27. exclusion	28. sanguinary
29. estrange	30. wantonly

▶▶ 摘要能力

| Instruction | MP3 001

除了閱讀測驗外，其實培養能在聽完一大段訊息後，口述剛才聽到的聽力訊息是學習語言和表達很重要的一件事，讓自己養成並具備這樣的能力，除了能在聽力測驗中獲取高分外，也能在新托福寫作跟口說的整合題型上大有斬獲喔！所以快來練習，除了書中提供的參考答案外，自己可以試著重新聽過音檔一遍後，摘要出英文訊息並朗讀出來。

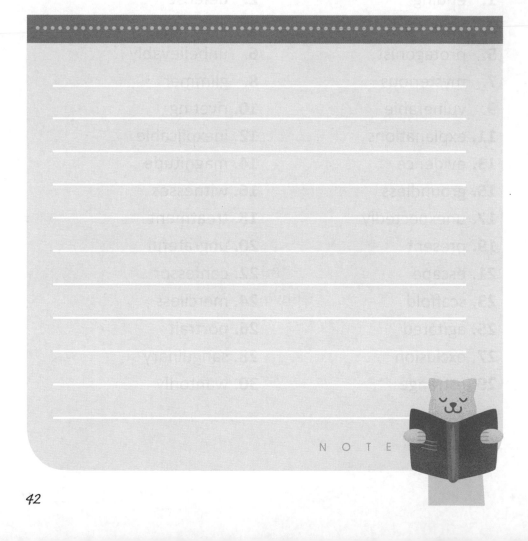

NOTE

▶▶ 參考答案

Frankenstein stands in sharp contrast to *A Tale of Two Cities* in which the accused does not get successfully acquitted from the crime.

What's worse, Justine has to defend herself on the stand, the kind of the place where she is vulnerable to attack. Apparently, there is no evidence as to why Justine would steal the picture and killed the boy. It is groundless to make a conjecture that someone else puts the picture in her pocket to frame her. Luckily, Elizabeth, the little brother's cousin, is unexpectedly willing to take the stand to defend her, but Elizabeth fails to explain why the picture is in Justine's pocket. Justine suffers form unjust ruling and dies.

At the end of the novel, we get to see how the devil has changed from a kind person who saves other people's life to a horrific, merciless person who frames Justine and commits multiple heinous crimes. If there had been more love given to the devil, things would have turned out so differently.

美國文學＋商管

UNIT 2 ▶▶ 《The 1,000,000 Bank Note》這個打賭最後是誰會贏呢？Henry 要如何運用百萬英鎊賺大錢呢？《Storynomics》名聲和品牌影響消費者決定？

▶▶ **聽力試題** MP3 002

1. Listen again to part of the lecture. Then answer the question.
   (A) The guy is destined to get despised by others.
   (B) The guy will starve to death.
   (C) The guy needs new clothes to change people's perceptions of him.
   (D) Superficiality is unfair to the poor.

2. Listen again to part of the lecture. Then answer the question.
   (A) Because the Bank Note is very difficult to get
   (B) Because he is the friend of the rich
   (C) Because the Bank Note is too large for the change
   (D) Because the Bank Note is invisible

3. Listen again to part of the lecture. Then answer the question.
   (A) Because he creates the cash flow
   (B) Because he wants to see the foreign crank with the bank note
   (C) Because his fame turns the restaurant into earnings
   (D) Because Harris has a strong faith in him

4. What is untrue about the lecture?

(A) Rich Londoners will believe Henry's name.

(B) The heroine in *The 30,000 Bequest* knows how to use passive income to multiply her income.

(C) Advertising companies grab the chance to hire youtubers to boost the sales.

(D) Lloyd's Gould and Curry Extension doesn't need any capitalists.

5. Listen again to part of the lecture. Then answer the question.

(A) to stress the importance of the attitude

(B) to highlight the significance of the law of the attraction

(C) to encourage people to be an expert in the stock

(D) to make a clarification about Henry's eventual success

新托福聽力解析

1. 選項 A，the guy is destined to get despised by others，他會因為衣著受到輕視，但是並不代表注定是如此。選項 B，the guy will starve to death，聽力訊息中出現一樣的敘述，但不是這段陳述要表明的主要意思。選項 C，The guy needs new clothes to change people's perceptions of him，男子確實需要新的衣著來改變別人對他的觀感，故答案要選**選項 C**。選項 D，Superficiality is unfair to the poor，或許根據我們的認知或惻隱之心會覺得是如此，但敘述中也有提到不該因此歸咎責任到人們身上。

2. 聽力訊息中有提到因為面額過大而無法找開，再加上大家覺得他很富有，也不急著討這筆錢（後面的聽力訊息還有提到現金流，讓他更不缺這筆錢了），所以答案要選**選項 C**。

3. 聽力訊息中表明 Henry 的名氣讓小食館人潮絡繹不絕，故創造了現金流，故答案要選**選項 C**。

4. 聽力訊息中有提到 Lloyd「需要」投資客的幫助（題目是問 untrue），故答案要選**選項 D**。

5. 小說一開始和聽力訊息中都有提到 Henry 對人生的滿足感，若非這樣的機遇，他大概也只會是個一般人，也不會去投資等等而成為富翁。是機遇造就了他現在的人生，教授提到這點的原因是要澄清，故答案要選**選項 D**。

答案：1. C 2. C 3. C 4. D 5. D

影子跟讀練習 MP3 002

> 做完題目後，除了對答案知道錯的部分在哪外，更重要的是要修正自己聽力根本的問題，即聽力理解力和聽力專注力，聽力專注力的修正能逐步強化本身的聽力實力，所以現在請根據聽力內容「逐個段落」、「數個段落」或「整篇」進行跟讀練習，提升在實際考場時專注聽完每個訊息、定位出關鍵考點和搭配筆記回答完所有題目。Go!

The 1,000,000 Bank Note... what would you do if you had that note... but it's more about what the guy in the story would do, than what you will do...

一百萬英鎊…如果你擁有一百萬英鎊的鈔票，你會拿來做什麼用途…但是比起你會如何使用這本資金，更重要的是故事中的男子又會如何使用這筆錢…

Let's take a look at what's written in the letter.... **"Enclosed you will find a sum of money. It's lent to you for thirty days, without interest."**

讓我們看一下在信中的描述…「信裡有一筆錢，是借給你的，期限是 30 天，不用利息。」

The bet between brother A and brother B is on... **"The 1,000,000 Bank Note"** does work in the advantage of the guy... in the materialistic society, you simply cannot blame people for their superficiality. As a saying goes, **"clothes make a man."** The guy is bound to be judged by how well he dresses... the ragged cloth he dresses presents the image of poorness in the eyes of the clerks, and he has no money. It's like what's been predicted by one of the brothers... he will starve to death...

兄弟 A 和兄弟 B 的賭注就此開打了...《百萬英鎊》確實時來運轉般地替男子帶來優勢...在物質社會，你無法責究人們之所以膚淺的原因。俗話説，「人要衣裝。」這位男子勢必會因為他穿著得如何而受到評價...他所穿著的破舊的衣服，在店員們的眼中就呈現出貧窮的意象，而且他沒有錢。這個現象就像是其中一位兄弟已經作出的預測一樣...他將會餓死...。

字彙輔助

1 Enclosed 被附上的

2 interest 利息

3 advantage 有利條件、優點、優勢

4 materialistic 唯物主義的；實利主義的

5 superficiality 表面性；表面情況；淺薄

6 ragged 破爛的；衣衫襤褸的

7 poorness 貧窮、缺乏

8 starve 餓死；挨餓

However, the 1,000,000 bank note is actually an invisible hand that will turn things around. The key here is that nobody is able to get the change for that kind of money. 1,000,000 is simply too large for anything, such as clothes. He can conspicuously live on his lives without costing a dime. The image of the eccentric millionaire is rooted in the mind of those clerks and his later encounters. It can be used as a way to boost the fame of Harris's humble feeding house. People want to see the foreign crank with million-pound bills. Frequent customers in the feeding house have led to a never-ending loan from Harris to Henry, creating a flow of cash for Henry to live a rich life. Increasing notoriety facilitates courteous treatment he is going to get.

　　然而，《百萬英鎊》實際上是個隱形的推手而將改變機運。在這裡的重點是，像這樣大額的金錢是沒有人能夠找零的。一百萬對任何東西，像是買衣服來說，顯然過於鉅額。他可以以此引人注目地過生活而不需要花費一毛錢。這位古怪的百萬富翁的印象從此就深植於那些店員和他後來遇到的人的心中。此能用於增進哈里斯的勉強餬口的小食館。人們想要親眼目睹有著百萬英鎊的怪人。小食館內絡繹不絕的顧客讓亨利因此有了哈里斯提供的源源不絕的借款，替亨利創造了能過上富有生活的現金流。日益增長的名聲促成了他所能獲得的禮遇。

1. invisible 無形的；不顯眼的
2. conspicuously 顯著地；超群地
3. image（心目中的）形象；印象
4. eccentric 古怪的、反常的
5. encounter 邂逅；撞上
6. boost 提升
7. crank 怪人
8. notoriety 惡名昭彰；聲名狼藉
9. facilitate 促進
10. courteous 有禮貌的

There is a surprising turn when he meets Lloyd. Using Henry's name can convince capitalists to believe him.

在他遇見勞艾德時，事情有了驚人的轉變。使用亨利的名字能夠讓資本家們相信他的話。

The 1,000,000 Bank Note... has also linked to the use of money. In *Storynomics*, it mentions "**consumers only debate brands in the mental minute just before they make purchase.**" That is, they don't discuss any company brands until they are making a purchase decision. In real life, we rely so much on others to make the decision for us. The charts of the bestsellers. The charts of the bestsellers help us screen out the one from numerous options which overwhelm our mental capacity. In life, you have so many things to do that you don't necessarily have the time to figure which brand is actually useful. Some do spend time studying every detail so that they won't spend a dime on the wrong products. Nowadays, we have youtubers from every walk of life to share products they find useful. A comparison is constantly made to the same product with a different brand. It also has a lot to do with the fame of the youtuber. Advertising companies are using this opportunity to let those youtubers to broadcast their products so that a significant improvement in the product sales can be reached.

百萬英鎊...也與使用金錢有著連結。在《故事行銷聖經》，它提及「消費者僅在要作出消費決定時，腦中才會考慮到商品品牌。」也就是説，消費者們直到他們正要作購物決定時，才會論及任何公司的品牌。在現實生活中，我們過度仰賴其他人替我們做決定。暢銷品的排行。暢銷品的排行幫助我們，從超過腦部容載的眾多選擇中篩選出唯一的選擇。在生活中，你有太多事情要做了，以致於你不必然有時間去了解哪個品牌實際上更有用。有些人確實花費時間去研究每個細節，這樣他們就不會浪費任何一分錢購買到錯的產品。現今，我們有各個行業的 Youtube 影音網站的網路紅人分享他們認為有用的產品。不同品牌的同類商品不斷地被比較。這也關乎到影音網站的網路紅人的名氣。廣告公司正利用這個機會讓那些網路紅人宣傳自家的產品，這樣一來，就能達到顯著的商品銷售。

1. capitalist 資本家　　2. consumer 消費者
3. purchase 購買　　4. numerous 為數眾多的
5. option 選擇　　6. overwhelm 壓倒
7. capacity 容納的能力　　8. comparison 比較

Back to the story... Henry's excogitation of using the name to save Lloyd's Gould and Curry Extension is a great idea. Henry won't have to spend a dime to reap the immense value created by his own name. Rich Londoners' belief in Henry's name are surely enough. They will soon gather and contend for the stock. At the end of the month, Henry and Lloyd already have a million dollars each in the London and County Bank. Investing money in any field is too risky a move than using money this way. You might lose everything. The story is in a sharp contrast to that of *The 30,000 Bequest*. It starts well with the 19 year-old heroine's clever strategy of using her savings to buy an acre of land, and she manages to save the money and uses the money and the passive income to multiplies her fortune. However, it goes unexpectedly bad at the end... I guess you will probably learn what actually happens in another literature course...

回到故事...亨利構想出使用名字來拯救勞艾德的古爾德和加利

礦業公司是極棒的點子。亨利甚至不必花費一毛錢就能藉由自己的名字創造出驚人的收益且因此而受惠。倫敦闊佬們對亨利名字的信念就足以成事了。他們會迅速聚集並且爭奪股份。在月終時，亨利和勞艾德在倫敦銀行已各自擁有一百萬元。將金錢投資在任何領域比起以此方式運用金錢都更具風險。你可能會損失一切。這個故事和《三萬元遺產》的故事是大相逕庭的。故事起始於一位 19 歲的女主角，運用了聰明的策略以她的存款購得一畝地，而她設法存下錢並運用金錢和被動收入使她的財富倍增數倍。然而，最後卻出乎意料地出了差錯…我想你們可能會在另一個文學課堂中了解實際上到底發生了什麼事情…

And back to the story of *The 1,000,000 Bank Note*, it's a chance event that alters the fate of Henry... even though he is an expert who specializes in the stock, his attitude and contentment about where he is now is not going to make him rich. He is so unlike others who also work as brokers who are ambitious and will use so many things, such as the law of the attraction, to get what they want... especially getting extremely wealthy... by the way we won't be having essay homework this week... but I'm going to ask questions for the remaining 30 minutes...

回到百萬英鎊的故事，是機遇的事件改變了亨利的命運…即使他是個精通股票的專家，他對於本來身處的環境所抱持的態度和滿足是不可能讓他致富的。他不像其他股票經紀人那麼野心勃勃且會使用許多事物，例如吸引力法則，以獲取他們所想要的…特別是變得非常有錢…順帶一提，這週我們不會有小論文回家作業…但是在最後剩下的 30 分鐘，我會問問題。

字彙輔助

1. excogitation 構想
2. immense 巨大的；廣大的
3. Investing 投資
4. risky 危險的；冒險的
5. heroine 女主角
6. manage 設法
7. passive 被動的
8. fortune 財產，財富
9. contentment 滿足
10. ambitious 野心勃勃的

▶▶ 試題聽力原文

1. Listen again to part of the lecture. Then answer the question.

   In the materialistic society, you simply cannot blame people for their superficiality. As a saying goes, "clothes make a man." The guy is bound to be judged by how well he dresses... the ragged cloth he dresses presents the image of poorness in the eyes of the clerks..., and he has no money. It's like what's been predicted by one of the brothers... he will starve to death...

   What can be inferred about these statements?

2. Listen again to part of the lecture. Then answer the question.

   He can conspicuously live on his lives without costing a dime.

Why can Henry make a living without spending any money?

3. Listen again to part of the lecture. Then answer the question.

It can be used as a way to boost the fame of Harris's humble feeding house. People want to see the foreign crank with million-pound bills. Frequent customers in the feeding house have led to a never-ending loan from Harris to Henry, creating a flow of cash for Henry to live a rich life. Increasing notoriety facilitates courteous treatment he is going to get.

How can Henry get the endless loan from Harris?

4. What is untrue about the lecture?

5. Listen again to part of the lecture. Then answer the question.

It's a chance event to alter the fate of Henry... even though he is an expert who specializes in the stock, his attitude and contentment about where he is now is not going to make him rich. He is so unlike others who also work as brokers who are ambitious and will use so many things, such as the law of the attraction, to get what they want... especially getting extremely wealthy...

Why does the professor mention the chance event?

▶▶▶ 記筆記與聽力訊息

| Instruction | MP3 002

　　新托福聽力與其他聽力測驗不同，可以於聽力的紙上記筆記，除了寫試題外，更重要的一點是訓練自己能夠在聽完一段訊息後，將重要的聽力訊息都記下。也可以將自己聽到跟記到的重點訊息跟試題做比對，因為試題考的就是長對話跟講座中出現的重點，能修正自己選取聽力訊息重點的能力。

| 聽力重點 |

- 記筆記有很多方式，包含符號跟自己習慣的縮寫字等等，可以找出最適合自己的模式，一定要自己重複聽音檔作練習數次。
- 這篇是關於美國文學和商管結合的主題，**段落中有穿插一本暢銷商管書和另一本短篇小說，其實仔細區分考點，還是能答好這篇。**

N O T E

▶▶ 參考筆記

Main idea ❶	
The letter	"Enclosed you will find a sum of money. It's lent to you for thirty days, without interest."
superficiality	the ragged cloth he dresses presents the image of poorness in the eyes of the clerks

Main idea ❷	
The bank note	• nobody is able to get the change for that kind of money. • live on his lives without costing a dime
fame	• a never-ending loan from Harris

Main idea ❸	
Storynomics	**"consumers only debate brands in the mental minute just before they make purchase."**

Main idea ❹	
surprising turn/ meeting Lloyd	Henry's excogitation of using the name to save Lloyd's Gould and Curry Extension

result	Henry and Lloyd already have a million dollars each in the London and County Bank
Main idea ❺	
The 30,000 Bequest	heroine's clever strategy of using her savings
chance event	That makes Henry rich

▶▶ 填空測驗

| Instruction | MP3 002

現在請再聽一次音檔，並做下列的測驗，檢視自己能否完成此填空測驗和強化自己聽力能力和拼字能力，降低自己漏聽到聽力訊息的機會，大幅提升應考實力。

The 1,000,000 Bank Note... what would you do if you had that note... but it's more about what the guy in the story would do, than what you will do...

Let's take a look at what's written in the letter.... **"Enclosed you will find a sum of money. It's lent to you for thirty days, without 1. _____."**

The bet between brother A and brother B is on... **"The 1,000,000 Bank Note"** does work in the **2. _____** of the guy... in the **3.** _____ society, you simply cannot blame people for their **4.** _____. As a saying goes, "clothes make a man." The guy is bound to be judged by how well he dresses... the **5.** _____ cloth he dresses presents the image of **6.** _____ in the eyes of the clerks, and he has no money. It's like what's been predicted by one of the brothers... he will starve to death...

However, the 1,000,000 bank note is actually an **7.** ____ hand that will turn things around. The key here is that **8.** _____ is able to get the change for that kind of money. 1,000,000 is simply too large for anything, such as clothes. He can **9.** _____ live on his lives without costing a dime.

The image of the **10.** _____ millionaire is rooted in the mind of those clerks and his later encounters. It can be used as a way to **11.** _____ the fame of Harris's humble feeding house. People want to see the foreign crank with million-pound bills. **12.** _____ customers in the feeding house have led to a never-ending loan from Harris to Henry, creating a **13.** _____ of cash for Henry to live a rich life. Increasing **14.** _____ facilitates **15.** _____ treatment he is going to get.

There is a surprising turn when he meets Lloyd. Using Henry's name can convince capitalists to believe him.

The 1,000,000 Bank Note... has also linked to the use of money. In *Storynomics*, it mentions "**16. _____ only debate brands in the mental minute just before they make purchase.**" That is, they don't discuss any company brands until they are making a **17. _____** decision. In real life, we rely so much on others to make the decision for us. The charts of the bestsellers.

The charts of the bestsellers help us screen out the one from **18. _____** options which overwhelm our mental **19. _____**. In life, you have so many things to do that you don't **20. _____** have the time to figure which brand is actually useful. Some do spend time studying every detail so that they won't spend a dime on the wrong products. Nowadays, we have youtubers from every walk of life to **21. _____** products they find useful.

A **22. _____** is constantly made to the same product with a different brand. It also has a lot to do with the fame of the youtuber. Advertising companies are using this **23. _____** to let those youtubers to **24. _____** their products so that a significant improvement in the product sales can be reached.

Back to the story... Henry's **25. _____** of using the name to save Lloyd's Gould and Curry Extension is a great idea. Henry won't have to spend a dime to reap the **26. _____**

_____ value created by his own name. Rich Londoners' belief in Henry's name are surely enough.

They will soon gather and contend for the stock. At the end of the month, Henry and Lloyd already have a million dollars each in the London and County Bank. Investing money in any field is too risky a move than using money this way. You might lose everything. The story is in a sharp **27. _____** to that of *The 30,000 Bequest*.

It starts well with the 19 year-old heroine's clever strategy of using her savings to buy an acre of land, and she manages to save the money and uses the money and the **28. _____** income to multiplies her fortune. However, it goes unexpectedly bad at the end... I guess you will probably learn what actually happens in another literature course...

And back to the story of *The 1,000,000 Bank Note*, it's a chance event to alter the fate of Henry... even though he is an expert who specializes in the stock, his attitude and **29. _____** about where he is now is not going to make him rich. He is so unlike others who also work as brokers who are **30. _____** and will use so many things, such as the law of the attraction, to get what they want... especially getting extremely wealthy... by the way we won't be having essay homework this week...

1. interest
2. advantage
3. materialistic
4. superficiality
5. ragged
6. poorness
7. invisible
8. nobody
9. conspicuously
10. eccentric
11. boost
12. Frequent
13. flow
14. notoriety
15. courteous
16. consumers
17. purchase
18. numerous
19. capacity
20. necessarily
21. share
22. comparison
23. opportunity
24. broadcast
25. excogitation
26. immense
27. contrast
28. passive
29. contentment
30. ambitious

▶▶ 摘要能力

| Instruction | `MP3 002`

　　除了閱讀測驗外，其實培養能在聽完一大段訊息後，口述剛才聽到的聽力訊息是學習語言和表達很重要的一件事，讓自己養成並具備這樣的能力，除了能在聽力測驗中獲取高分外，也能在新托福寫作跟口說的整合題型上大有斬獲喔！所以快來練習，除了書中提供的參考答案外，自己可以試著重新聽過音檔一遍後，摘要出英文訊息並朗讀出來。

▶▶ 參考答案

The bet between brothers on "The 1,000,000 Bank Note" has shown that in the materialistic society, superficiality is unavoidable. You are bound to get judged by others on how well you dress. Nobody is able to get the change for that kind of money, so Henry can conspicuously live on his lives without costing a dime.

The image of the eccentric millionaire is rooted in the mind of those clerks and his later encounters. It can be used as a way to boost the fame of Harris's humble feeding house. People want to see the foreign crank with million-pound bills. Frequent customers in the feeding house have led to a never-ending loan from Harris to Henry, creating a flow of cash for Henry to live a rich life. Increasing notoriety facilitates courteous treatment he is going to get.

There is a surprising turn when he meets Lloyd. Using Henry's name can convince capitalists to believe him. Henry's excogitation of using the name to save Lloyd's Gould and Curry Extension is a great idea. Henry won't have to spend a dime to reap the immense value created by his own name. The story is in a sharp contrast to that of *The 30,000 Bequest*.

It's a chance event to alter the fate of Henry. Even though he is an expert who specializes in the stock, his attitude and contentment about where he is now is not going to make him rich.

▶▶ **聽力試題** MP3 003

1. What are the professions of Bradish and Fulton?
   (A) tinner and plasterer
   (B) the governor and the Congressman
   (C) lawyer and dentist
   (D) the earl and the duke

2. After the couple shelves the pork-packer's son and the village banker's son, who are their next considerations?
   (A) the earl and the duke
   (B) lawyer and doctor
   (C) viscount and marquise
   (D) the governor's son and the son of the Congressman

3. What does the author mean by saying..." Vast wealth, to the person unaccustomed to it, is a bane; it eats into the flesh and bone of his morals."?
   (A) to discourage people from getting wealthy
   (B) to warn a certain age group of the danger of wealth
   (C) to show the insensitivity phenomenon
   (D) to indicate the body condition getting torn apart

4. The following table lists the item that Sally takes.

   Click in the correct box

Item
A. chocolate
B. maple-sugar
C. apples
D. candles
E. soap

5. The following table lists the holdings that will get extra credits.

   Click in the correct box

Item
A. Ocean Cables
B. Klondike
C. Standard Oil
D. Steamer Lines
E. Tammany Graft
F. the Railway Systems
G. Diluted Telegraph
H. De Beers

6. Why doesn't the newspaper include obituary?

(A) Tilbury fears the couple will figure out the scam, so he tells the newspaper before he dies.

(B) Tilbury bribes the ice cream company.

(C) the Ice cream Parlors begs to have more exposure.

(D) newspaper's editor makes place for the Ice cream Parlors.

7. What is the flavor of the ice cream?

(A) Vanilla

(B) strawberry

(C) chocolate

(D) Cappuccino

8. What can be inferred from the historic crash?

(A) The millionaire's wealth remains impervious.

(B) The editor and proprietor of Sagamore successfully predicts the stock crash.

(C) The millionaire has become a beggar.

(D) Gilt-edged stocks fell 85 points.

文學跨領域

商管跨領域

其他

NOTE

▶▶ 新托福聽力解析

1. 第 1 題的答案是 **C**，Bradish 和 Fulton 分別是律師和牙醫。

2. 第 2 題的答案是 **D**，the governor's son and the son of the Congressman。

3. 第 3 題的答案是 **C**，從作者講的話和學生的回答中可以推論出，這是要表達出一種麻木不仁和無感的現象，這些情況都導因於財富和逐漸累積的小事情，久了之後就不覺得有什麼了。財富也腐蝕了這對夫妻的心。

4. 第 4 題的答案是 **BCDE**，Sally 沒有拿巧克力，其他都有拿，故 A 不能選。

5. 第 5 題的答案是 **DF**，從 remaining items 中得知要選汽船公司和鐵路系統。

6. 第 6 題的答案是 **D**，編輯因為要感謝冰淇淋公司贈冰而將空位騰給了冰淇淋公司。

7. 第 7 題的答案是 **B**，從教授口中得知冰淇淋是草莓口味。

8. 第 8 題的答案是 **C**，富翁被目睹在街上乞討，所以他成了窮光蛋。

....

答案：1. C 2. D 3. C 4. BCDE 5. DF 6. D 7. B 8.C

影子跟讀練習 MP3 003

做完題目後，除了對答案知道錯的部分在哪外，更重要的是要修正自己聽力根本的問題，即聽力理解力和聽力專注力，聽力專注力的修正能逐步強化本身的聽力實力，所以現在請根據聽力內容「逐個段落」、「數個段落」或「整篇」進行跟讀練習，提升在實際考場時專注聽完每個訊息、定位出關鍵考點和搭配筆記回答完所有題目。Go!

| Professor |

If you think, I'm doing all the talking like what we did last week... you are wrong... today we are going to talk about *The 30,000 Bequest*, a famous tale from Mark Twain.

| 教授 |

如果你們認為，我們會像上週一樣，課堂的進行都是由我從頭講到尾...那你們就錯了...今天我們將會談論《三萬元遺產》，馬克・吐溫的一篇著名的故事。

| Professor |

So Eric Winter? Who are among the first two pursuers for Electra's daughters?

| 教授 |

所以艾瑞克・溫特？伊萊克特拉兩個女兒最一開始的兩位追求者是誰呢？

| Eric Winter |

... hmm Adelbert, a tinner... and Hosannah Dilkins... a plasterer...

| 艾瑞克・溫特 |

...嗯嗯，阿德爾伯特，一位補鍋匠...，和小霍薩納・迪爾金斯...一位泥瓦匠...。

| Professor |

Excellent...

| 教授 |

好極了...。

| Professor |

Who are considered to be invited for the dinner, after Adelbert and Dilkins have shown interests in their daughters?...And If you think you are not going to get called on twice during my class, you are wrong... Eric Winter...

| 教授 |

在阿德爾伯特和迪爾金斯都顯示出對他們的女兒深感興趣後，誰被該對夫妻考慮邀請來家中吃晚餐？...而如果你們認為在我的課堂之中不會被叫到第二次，那麼你就錯了...艾瑞克・溫特...。

| Eric Winter |

... hmm Bradish and Fulton?

| 艾瑞克‧溫特 |

...嗯嗯，布萊迪斯和福爾頓？

| Professor |

Close your book now...What are their professions respectively?...Susan Vaughn...

| 教授 |

...現在都把你們的書闔上...他們的職業分別是什麼呢？...蘇珊‧沃恩...

| Susan Vaughn |

.... lawyer and doctor.... hmm... lawyer and dentist...

| 蘇珊‧沃恩 |

...律師和醫生...嗯嗯...律師和牙醫...。

| Professor |

... correct...

| 教授 |

...答對了...。

| Professor |

Since the couple has a high expectation for their own daughters, who are on the agenda after disqualification of both the lawyer and the dentist... Susan Vaughn...

| 教授 |

既然這對夫妻對他們的女兒有高度的期望，在律師和牙醫都失去資格後，誰在他們的下個議程上呢？...蘇珊·沃恩...。

| **Susan Vaughn** |

... the pork-packer's son and the village banker's son...

| 蘇珊·沃恩 |

...豬肉批發商的兒子和銀行老闆的兒子...。

字彙輔助

1. pursuer 追求者
2. tinner 補鍋匠
3. plasterer 泥瓦匠
4. profession 職業
5. expectation 期望
6. agenda 待議諸事項；議程
7. disqualification 取消資格；無資格；不合格
8. pork-packer 豬肉批發商

| **Professor** |

And after the couple shelves the pork-packer's son and the village banker's son, who are their next considerations? Vicky Summer

| 教授 |

在這對夫妻將豬肉批發商的兒子和銀行老闆的兒子都束之高閣後，誰是他們的下個考慮人選呢？維琪·夏天。

| Vicky Summer |

... hmm

| 維琪‧夏天 |

...嗯嗯嗯。

| Professor |

Vicky... for once... I'm expecting highly of you...

| 教授 |

維琪...這是第一次...我對你有很高的期望...。

| Eric Winter |

... the governor's son and the son of the Congressman...

| 艾瑞克‧溫特 |

...州長的兒子和國會議員的兒子。

| Professor |

Correct... but... that's very nosy...

| 教授 |

答對了...但是...這很多管閒事...。

| Professor |

And what does the author mean by saying... **"Vast wealth, to the person unaccustomed to it, is a bane; it eats**

into the flesh and bone of his morals."? Eric Winter...

| 教授 |

作者提到「鉅額的財富對窮人是一劑猛烈的毒藥，會連皮帶骨地吞噬著他的良心」，他所指的是什麼呢？艾瑞克·溫特...

| **Eric Winter** |

... it all starts with the little thing... and then you will feel like it's nothing... and you feel nothing about the stealing...

| 艾瑞克·溫特 |

...都是由小事情開始的...然後你就覺得沒什麼了...而且你對於偷竊也麻木不仁了。

| **Professor** |

... very well... and what does Sally take from the store... Vicky Summer..

| 教授 |

...非常好...而薩利從商店裡偷走了什麼？...維琪·夏天。

| **Vicky Summer** |

... chocolate, candles, soap...

| 維琪·夏天 |

...巧克力、蠟燭、肥皂...。

| Professor |

Who can help her... Susan Vaughn...

| 教授 |

誰能幫幫她...蘇珊・沃恩...。

| Susan Vaughn |

First, he took candles... then apples, soap, and maple-sugar...

| 蘇珊・沃恩 |

...首先，他偷取了蠟燭...然後是蘋果、肥皂和楓糖...。

| Professor |

Excellent.... let's continue... what are the holdings of this couple? Eric Winter

| 教授 |

好極了...讓我們繼續...這對夫妻所持有的股票有什麼呢？艾瑞克・溫特。

字彙輔助

1. governor 州長
2. Congressman 國會議員
3. nosy 好管閒事的；愛追問的
4. unaccustomed 不習慣的；不熟悉的
5. morals 道德上的教訓；寓意
6. maple-sugar 楓糖

文學跨領域

商管跨領域

其他

7 holdings 持股

| Eric Winter |
  ... Standard Oil, Ocean Cables, Diluted Telegraph...

| 艾瑞克・溫特 |
  ...標準石油公司、遠洋電報、微音電報公司...。

| Professor |
  and what else... Cindy Thrones...

| 教授 |
  還有什麼呢？...辛蒂・索恩...。

| Cindy Thrones |
  ... Klondike, De Beers, Tammany Graft...

| 辛蒂・索恩 |
  ...克朗代克金礦、德比爾斯鑽石礦和塔瑪尼貪賄公司...。

| Professor |
  and what else... Vicky Summer

| 教授 |
  還有什麼呢？...維琪・夏天。

| **Vicky Summer** |

... Shady Privileges in the Post-office Department...?

| 維琪・夏天 |

...郵政部的曖昧特權...？

| **Professor** |

and what else.... for the remaining items... you will get extra points for the mid-term...

| 教授 |

還有什麼呢...剩餘的部分...你會在期中考時多得到額外的加分。

| **Vicky Summer** |

... Steamer Lines... and the Railway Systems...

| 維琪・夏天 |

...汽船公司...和鐵路系統...。

| **Professor** |

... excellent... you will be getting additional two points for the mid-term.... let's continue... the sequence of four barons that the couple deems disqualified... 3 ponits... anyone...

| 教授 |

好極了...你期中會加額外兩分...讓我們繼續...那對夫妻認為不

符資格的四位男爵的順序...加三分...有人知道嗎？...

| Eric Winter |

... viscounts, marquises, earls, dukes...

| 艾瑞克・溫特 |

子爵、侯爵、伯爵、公爵...。

| Cindy Thrones |

... viscounts, earls, marquises, dukes...

| 辛蒂・索恩 |

子爵、伯爵、侯爵、公爵...。

| Professor |

... excellent... Cindy is correct...

| 教授 |

很棒...辛蒂答對了...。

| Professor |

Why does Sally say **"Money has brought him misery, and he took revenge upon us."** at the end of the story...?... two points...

| 教授 |

在故事尾端，為什麼薩利提到「金錢帶給他痛苦，他卻報復在我們身上。」…加兩分。

| Eric Winter |

... Money creates more problems than we can realize... it's a snare set by the relative...

| 艾瑞克・溫特 |

…金錢創造出比起我們所能意識到的問題還來的多…這是那位親戚所設的圈套…。

| Professor |

Correct... and what is the responsible guess from the couple about the absence of Tilbury's death notice in the newspaper? And why doesn't the newspaper include an obituary? Five points.

| 教授 |

正確無誤…而那對夫妻對於提爾伯里的死訊未出現在小報上頭，其合理的解釋為何？而為什麼報紙刊登時並未加入訃告？額外加五分。

字彙輔助

1 additional 附加的；額外的

2 sequence 連續；接續

3 barons 男爵（英國爵位最低的貴族）

4 disqualified 失去資格的

5 misery 痛苦；不幸；悲慘

6 revenge 報仇；報復

7 snare （捕捉鳥、獸等的）陷
   阱、羅網

8 reasonable 通情達理的；
   合理的

9 absence 缺少、缺乏

10 obituary 訃告；報導某人
   去世的消息

| **Vicky Summer** |

... they thought the rational explanation was that Tilbury was still alive, so they didn't put it in the newspaper... and in fact he died... and the newspaper's editor made room for the gratitude to the Ice cream Parlors, who generously gave them the ice cream.

| 維琪・夏天 |

…他們認為的合理解釋是，提爾伯里尚在人間，所以報社的人員並未將訊息加到報紙上頭…而實際上提爾伯里死了…而報社的編輯騰出版面把公布死訊的位置來刊慷慨地給予他們冰淇淋的冰淇淋店以示感謝。

| **Professor** |

... excellent... but what kind of flavor... you're going to get the extra two points... if you can answer this question...

| 教授 |

好極了…冰淇淋店是給他們什麼口味的冰淇淋呢？…你會額外加兩分…如果你能答對這題…

| Vicky Summer |

... chocolate?... Vanilla? Cappuccino?

| 維琪・夏天 |

...巧克力？...香草？...卡布奇諾？

| Professor |

... you can't just randomly guess, hoping you can get it right... it's strawberry...

| 教授 |

...你不能隨意亂猜，然後希望自己能夠矇對答案...答案是草莓口味...。

| Professor |

... How can the tragedy be prevented? Even that means they have to violate the agreement?

| 教授 |

...怎麼才能避免掉此悲劇的發生呢？即使這意謂著他們要違反這項合約？

| Eric Winter |

... attend the funeral... then they will know that Tilbury doesn't even have a cent to his name...

| 艾瑞克・溫特 |

...參加葬禮...那麼他們就會知道提爾伯里名下根本連一分錢都沒有...。

| Professor |

... And they eventually learned the news from a visitor.. And what's his profession? Three points

| 教授 |

...他們最終從一位訪客那裡得知這項消息...該訪客的職業為何？加三分。

| Eric Winter |

... the editor and proprietor of Sagamore...

| 艾瑞克・溫特 |

...薩加摩爾週報的編輯兼老闆...。

| Professor |

... excellent... what happens to the multimillionaire after the historic crash...? Three points

| 教授 |

...好極了...在歷史性暴跌後，千萬富翁發生了什麼事情？加三分。

| Cindy Thrones |

The multimillionaire is seen begging for his bread in the Bowery...

| 辛蒂・索恩 |

千萬富翁被看見在包華麗大道討飯...。

| Professor |

One last question? In five hours, how many points does gilt-edged stocks fall? Three points

| 教授 |

最後一個問題，在五小時內，金籌股跌了多少？加三分。

字彙輔助

1 rational 理性的、有理性的

2 gratitude 感激之情、感恩

3 Parlors【美】店

4 generously 慷慨地、不吝嗇地

5 randomly 任意地；隨便地

6 tragedy （一齣）悲劇

7 violate 違背、違反

8 proprietor 所有人；業主

9 multimillionaire 千萬富翁；大富豪

10 gilt-edged stocks 金籌股

| Vicky Summer |

... 95 points...

| 維琪・夏天 |

...95 點。

| **Professor** |

    ... I guess that's all for today's short quizzes... now I'm going to hand out the essay sheet... you will be asked to answer 3 questions from the 7 questions listed.... good luck...

| 教授 |

    ...我想今天的小測驗就到此為止...現在我要發佈小論文回答卷...你們要從所列出的 7 個問題中回答其中 3 題...祝好運...。

▶▶ 試題聽力原文

1. What are the professions of Bradish and Fulton?
2. After the couple shelves the pork-packer's son and the village banker's son, who are their next considerations??
3. What does the author mean by saying..." Vast wealth, to the person unaccustomed to it, is a bane; it eats into the flesh and bone of his morals."?
4. The following table lists the item that Sally takes.
   Click in the correct box
5. The following table lists the holdings that will get extra credits.
   Click in the correct box

6. Why doesn't the newspaper include obituary?
7. What is the flavor of the ice cream?
8. What can be inferred from the historic crash?

▶▶ 記筆記與聽力訊息

| Instruction | MP3 003

　　新托福聽力與其他聽力測驗不同，可以於聽力的紙上記筆記，除了寫試題外，更重要的一點是訓練自己能夠在聽完一段訊息後，將重要的聽力訊息都記下。也可以將自己聽到跟記到的重點訊息跟試題做比對，因為試題考的就是長對話跟講座中出現的重點，能修正自己選取聽力訊息重點的能力。

| 聽力重點 |

- 記筆記有很多方式，包含符號跟自己習慣的縮寫字等等，可以找出最適合自己的模式，一定要自己重複聽音檔作練習數次。
- 這篇是關於商業概念和美國文學的結合主題，**當中有很多細節考點要特別注意，還有這篇的呈現方式是教師問學生答的方式，對某些考生來說難度較高**，不過這樣的呈現比較貼近國外的上課模式。

NOTE

▶▶ 參考筆記

Main idea ❶

the first two pursuers for Electra's daughters	Adelbert, a tinner... and Hosannah Dilkins... a plasterer
second	Bradish and Fulton/ lawyer and dentist
third	the pork-packer's son and the village banker's son
fourth	the governor's son and the son of the Congressman

Main idea ❷

"Vast wealth, to the person unaccustomed to it, is a bane; it eats into the flesh and bone of his morals."	it all starts with the little thing

Main idea ❸

Sally take from the store	Candles, apples, soap, and maple-sugar
the holdings of this couple	Standard Oil, Ocean Cables, Diluted Telegraph, Klondike, De Beers, Tammany Graft, Shady Privileges in the Post-office Department, Steamer Lines, the Railway Systems

the sequence of four barons	viscounts, marquises, earls, dukes

Main idea ❹

Money has brought him misery, and he took revenge upon us."	Money creates more problems than we can realize
the reasonable guess from the couple about the absence of Tilbury' death notice in the newspaper	Tilbury was still alive, so they didn't put it in the newspaper
truth	the newspaper's editor made room for the gratitude to the Ice cream Parlors, who generously gave them the ice cream
Flavor/the ice cream	strawberry
violate the agreement	attend the funeral
the multimillionaire after the historic crash	begging his bread in the Bowery
gilt-edged stocks	fall 95 points

文學跨領域

商管跨領域

其他

▶▶ 填空測驗

| Instruction | MP3 003

現在請再聽一次音檔，並做下列的測驗，檢視自己能否完成此填空測驗和強化自己聽力能力和拼字能力，降低自己漏聽到聽力訊息的機會，大幅提升應考實力。

Professor: And what does the author mean by saying... "Vast 1. _____, to the person 2. _____ to it, is a 3. _____; it eats into the flesh and bone of his morals."? Eric Winter...

Eric Winter: ... it all starts with the little thing... and then you feel like it's nothing... and you feel nothing about the 4. _____...

Vicky Summer: ... 5. _____, candles, soap...

Susan Vaughn: first, he took candles... then apples, soap, and 6. _____...

Eric Winter: ... 7. _____, Ocean Cables, Diluted Telegraph...

Vicky Summer: ... Shady Privileges in the Post-office 8. _____...?

Professor: and what else.... for the remaining items... you will get extra points for the mid-term...

Vicky Summer: ... **9.** _____ Lines... and the **10.** _____ Systems...

Professor: ... excellent... you will be getting **11.** _____ two points for the mid-term.... let's continue... the sequence of four **12.** _____ that the couple deems disqualified... 3 ponits... anyone...

Cindy Thrones: ... viscounts, earls, marquises, **13.** _____...

Professor: Why does Sally say **"Money has brought him 14. _____, and he took 15. _____ upon us."** at the end of the story...? ... two points...

Eric Winter: ... Money creates more problems than we can realize... it's a snare set by the **16.** _____...

Professor: correct... and what is the **17.** _____ guess from the couple about the **18.** _____ of Tilbury' death notice in the newspaper? And why doesn't the newspaper include **19.** _____? Five points.

Vicky Summer: ... they thought the rational explanation

was that Tilbury was still alive, so they didn't put it in the newspaper... and in fact he died... and the newspaper's editor made room for the **20.** _____ to the Ice cream **21.** _____, who **22.** _____ gave them the ice cream.

Vicky Summer: .... chocolate?... Vanilla? **23.** _____?

Professor: ... you can't just randomly guess, hoping you can get it right... it's **24.** _____ ...

Professor: ... How can the **25.** _____ be prevented? Even that means they have to **26.** _____ the agreement?

Eric Winter: ... attend the **27.** _____ ... then they will know that Tilbury doesn't even have a cent under his name...

Eric Winter: ... the editor and **28.** _____ of Sagamore ...

Professor: ... excellent... what happens to the **29.** _____ after the historic crash...? Three points

Professor: one last question? In five hours, how many points does gilt-edged **30.** _____ fall? Three points

Vicky Summer: ... 95 points...

| 參考答案 |

1. wealth
2. unaccustomed
3. bane
4. stealing
5. chocolate
6. maple-sugar
7. Standard Oil
8. Department
9. Steamer
10. Railway
11. additional
12. barons
13. dukes
14. misery
15. revenge
16. relative
17. responsible
18. absence
19. obituary
20. gratitude
21. Parlors
22. generously
23. Cappuccino
24. strawberry
25. tragedy
26. violate
27. funeral
28. proprietor
29. multimillionaire
30. stocks

文學跨領域

商管跨領域

其他

▶▶ 摘要能力

| Instruction | MP3 003

　　除了閱讀測驗外，其實培養能在聽完一大段訊息後，口述剛才聽到的聽力訊息是學習語言和表達很重要的一件事，讓自己養成並具備這樣的能力，除了能在聽力測驗中獲取高分外，也能在新托福寫作跟口說的整合題型上大有斬獲喔！所以快來練習，除了書中提供的參考答案外，自己可以試著重新聽過音檔一遍後，摘要出英文訊息並朗讀出來。

N O T E

▶▶ 參考答案

The 30,000 Bequest is a famous tale from Mark Twain. The most intriguing part is the couple's increasing standard about those pursuers. Dissatisfaction happens when their imaginary wealth increasingly builds up. The bequest from the relative is the turning point for the family. The couple is not smart enough to notice that eccentricity of the rules set by the relative. This further has misled them into believing that there is actually money left for them. It is not until the editor and proprietor of Sagamore arrives in the town that they come to the realization that they have been fooled. The obituary was removed so that the editor could have room for the ice cream parlors. Tilbury doesn't even have a cent under his name.

文學跨領域

商管跨領域

其他

UNIT 4 ▶▶ 《Gone with the Wind》選擇金錢和富有，在人生道路上思嘉麗還有朋友嗎？

▶▶ 聽力試題 MP3 004

1. Listen again to part of the lecture. Then answer the question.
   (A) to show the significance of the aquamarine earbobs
   (B) to show little value about the admiration.
   (C) to show simplicity and innocence of the Gerald.
   (D) to demonstrate the scheming of the Scarlett.

2. Listen again to part of the lecture. Then answer the question.
   (A) to show her father is not a pauper
   (B) to show Charles is rich
   (C) to demonstrate she has nothing to worry about
   (D) to show Rhett's poor judgment

3. Listen again to part of the lecture. Then answer the question.
   (A) Ms. Wilkes will agree with whatever Scarlett does, except murder.
   (B) Ms. Wilkes will not condone Scarlett to commit the crime like murder.
   (C) Ms. Wilkes wants the murder to be right on target and in a short timeframe.

(D) Ms. Wilkes will condone Scarlett to murder someone with the right reason.

4. Listen again to part of the lecture. Then answer the question.

(A) to show how distant her relationship with Aunt Pitty

(B) to show how important Macon is to Aunt Pitty.

(C) to show India that Scarlett is desperate to go home.

(D) to show how much Scarlett has sacrificed for her.

5. What is untrue about Scarlett and Melanie?

(A) Melanie even concurs in Scarlett's killing.

(B) Melanie does not believe the rumor.

(C) Melanie is afraid of Aunt Pitty's increasing arrogance.

(D) Scarlett puts Melanie ahead of her mother.

▶▶ 新托福聽力解析

1. 這段敘述是藉由比較襯托出 Scarlett 對 Ashley 的愛就像那耳環一樣沒有太大的價值，所以答案**要選 B**。

2. 這段敘述是 Scarlett 被 Rhett 嘲笑後所作出的反擊，事實上，她也真的不缺錢，但是戰爭改變了一切，只能說世事難料。她講這句話是要證明她根本不用擔心，故答案**要選 C**。

3. 這段敘述是 Rhett 的對於 Ms. Wilkes 理解部分，不是 Scarlett 的回答，short of = except，所以答案**要選 A**。

4. 這段敘述是 Ms. Wilkes 反擊 India 對於 Scarlett 的指控，另一部分也說明了 Scarlett 對她的犧牲很大，連自己的親人 Aunt Pitty 都逃到小鎮躲避北方佬，Scarlett 只是她大嫂，相較之下 Aunt Pitty 更親才對，所以答案**要選 D**。Ms. Wilkes 就是 Melanie。

5. C 選項的部分，聽力訊息中並未出現，實際上也不是如此，故答案**要選 C**。

答案： 1.B 2.C 3.A 4.D 5.C

影子跟讀練習 MP3 004

做完題目後，除了對答案知道錯的部分在哪外，更重要的是要修正自己聽力根本的問題，即聽力理解力和聽力專注力，聽力專注力的修正能逐步強化本身的聽力實力，所以現在請根據聽力內容「逐個段落」、「數個段落」或「整篇」進行跟讀練習，提升在實際考場時專注聽完每個訊息、定位出關鍵考點和搭配筆記回答完所有題目。Go!

Gone with the Wind may seem like a romantic love story at first, but it is truly a combination of the love story and the friendship, or more than that. The friendship part has been marginalized by the selection and editing of the storylines in the movies, but a closer look at the fiction can reveal how important the friendship is. Scarlett might love Melanie more than she loves Ashley... I know some of you might not agree with me... but when you read the last part of the fiction... you will understand when Scarlett eventually knows that she loves Rhett instead of Ashley and she just doesn't know it. Let's take a quick look at chapter 61... near the very end... **"she could see so clearly now that he was only a childish fancy, no more important really than her spoiled desire for the aquamarine earbobs she had coaxed out of Gerald."** This part clearly shows Ashley means little to her. Her affection towards Melanie is even stronger than she realizes. Her feelings towards Melanie are deeper than those of Ashley...

　　《亂世佳人》起初可能似乎令人覺得是個浪漫愛情故事，但是它實際上卻是友誼和愛情故事的結合體，或者是更甚之。在電影中，情節受到編輯和篩選，而使得友誼的部分受到大幅削弱，但是較為仔細地查看小說時，可以顯現出友誼是多麼重要。思嘉麗對於梅蘭妮的愛甚至大過了其對艾希禮...我知道你們之中有些人在這個論點上可能不同意我這麼說...但是當你閱讀到小說最後的部分...你了解到當思嘉麗最終體會到她所愛的人是瑞德而非艾希禮，只是她自己並不知道。我們很快的看下第 61 章...在接近很後面的地方...「她現在可以清楚的看出，他僅僅是兒時愛戀，真正的重要價值不超過她因為慣壞的物慾哄騙傑拉爾德買的海藍色的耳環。」這個部分清楚地顯示出艾希禮對她來說有多麼不重要。她對梅蘭妮的感情甚至強過了她所能體會的。那些情感比起對於艾希禮的情感更為深...。

字彙輔助

1. romantic 羅曼蒂克的；多情的
2. combination 結合（體）；聯合（體）
3. marginalized 使局限於社會邊緣；排斥
4. storyline 故事情節
5. fancy 愛好；迷戀
6. aquamarine earbobs 海藍色的耳環
7. coax 用好話勸，哄誘
8. affection 影響；屬性

And what does Melanie mean to Scarlett? And what does Scarlett mean to Melanie? Let's go back to part two chapter thirteen... Scarlett says **"Do you think Pa is a pauper? He's got all the money I'll ever need and then I have Charles' property besides."** What does this have to do with the friendship of the two... we will have to jump to the middle part where Rhett jokes about Scarlett... earlier, Scarlett is so confident that she won't be needing Rhett's advice since she has plenty of money... but that all changes after the war... and now she is desperate for money... there is a part when she visits the jail to see Rhett in order to get 300 dollars so that she can save Tara. Hunger, war and lots of things have aggravated Scarlett's craving for money... she even vows that with God as her witness that she will never be hungry again... all these have led her down the path of avarice and decadency. However, she doesn't care and she only wants money...

　　而梅蘭妮對於思嘉麗來說意謂著什麼呢？而思嘉麗對於梅蘭妮來說意謂著什麼呢？讓我們回到小說第二部分第 13 章…思嘉麗説道「你認為我爸是個窮光蛋嗎？他的錢可足夠我花一輩子呢，而且我還有查理斯的財產。」這又跟兩人之間的友誼有什麼關聯性呢？…關於這點，我們要跳至小説中段，當瑞德於早先嘲笑思嘉麗時，思嘉麗極其自信，她並不需要瑞德的建議，而且她有很多錢…但是在戰後那些都隨之改變了…而現在她迫切需要金錢…書中有個部分提到她到監獄拜訪瑞德以獲取 300 美元，如此一來她才能保住塔拉。飢餓、戰爭和許多事情已經加劇了思嘉麗對於金錢的渴望……她甚至發誓，上帝為鑑，她絕不再讓自己餓著了…所有這些都導致她走向了貪婪和墮落之途。然而，她不在乎，而且她只要有錢…

1 pauper 窮人、貧民；乞丐　　2 property 財產、資產

3 confident 有信心的、自信的　　4 desperate 絕望的；孤注一擲的

5 aggravate 加重；增劇　　6 crave 渴望獲得；迫切需要

7 avarice 貪婪、貪慾　　8 decadency 衰落；墮落

In chapter 38, Scarlett says **"Yes, I want money more than anything else in the world."** and in exchange there are sacrifices... so Rhett responds **"but there is a penalty attached as there is to most things you want. It's loneliness."** The price is obviously too high. No women want to be friends with Scarlett, and she used to have her mother to console her and Melanie to accompany her. She begins to wonder do I still have friends?

在第 38 章，思嘉麗說道「這毫無疑問，我愛錢勝過愛世界上的一切東西」，而換取而來的就是這是要付出代價的…所以瑞德回應了「那麼這就是你唯一的選擇。不過這個選擇附帶著一種懲罰，就是寂寞。」這個代價顯然太過高昂。沒有女性想要跟思嘉麗交朋友，而她過去有著母親能夠安慰她，還有梅蘭妮可以陪伴她。她開始納悶，我還有朋友嗎？

Rhett says **"you forget Ms. Wilkes"** **"I dare say she'd approve of anything you did, short of murder."** To which

Scarlett responds **"she's even approved of murder."**

瑞德說道「妳忘記了威爾克斯太太了。」「我敢說，除了謀殺，妳幹什麼她都會贊成的。」對此，思嘉麗回覆著「她甚至連殺人也贊同呢！」

Scarlett and Melanie have been through so much, and they have endured so many hardships... let's take a look at the proclamation made by Ms. Wilkes... it's in chapter 27... she says **"We haven't lost each other and our babies are alright and we have a roof over our heads."**

思嘉麗和梅蘭妮一同經歷了這麼多，而且他們都已經忍受過那麼多的苦難...讓我們看一下，威爾克斯太太所發的宣言...是在第 27 章...她說道「畢竟我們沒有丟掉彼此，我們的孩子都還活著，而且還有房子住。」

字彙輔助

1. sacrifice 犧牲
2. penalty 處罰；刑罰
3. loneliness 孤獨、寂寞
4. console 安慰、撫慰
5. accompany 陪同、伴隨
6. approve 贊成、同意
7. endure 忍耐、忍受
8. hardship 艱難、困苦
9. proclamation 宣布、公布

Scarlett even chooses to stay in Atlanta to take care of Melanie when her mother is sick, and even aunt Pitty flees to Macon to avoid Yankees when Melanie is about to give birth to a baby. Scarlett has always been there for her.

當母親生病時，思嘉麗甚至選擇待在亞特蘭大照顧梅蘭妮，而且皮蒂姑媽逃至梅里以躲避北方佬時，梅蘭妮的小孩正剛要出生。思嘉麗總在她身旁陪著她。

In a later episode, when Scarlett is in trouble with the rumor about her affairs with Ashley, Melanie defends her and stands by her side...

在更後面的事件中，當思嘉麗蒙受她與艾希禮的謠傳所困擾時，梅蘭妮替她辯護並在她身旁陪著她。

Melanie even gets a confrontation with India. Melanie says **"she stayed with me through the whole siege when she could have gone home, when Aunt Pitty had run away to Macon..."**

梅蘭妮甚至與英蒂雅發生爭執。梅蘭妮說道「北方軍圍城時期，她本來可以回家的，就連皮蒂姑媽也逃往梅里…」

However, it is not until later when Melanie is dying that Scarlett realizes how much Melanie's friendship means to her. it's been Melanie, not Ashley or Rhett.

然而，一直到了很後期，當梅蘭妮快死去時，思嘉麗才意識到梅蘭妮的友誼對她來說是多有價值。一直以來都是梅蘭妮，而不是艾希禮或瑞德。

Let's also flip to chapter 61... **"she had relied on Melanie, even as she had relied upon herself, and she had never known it."**

讓我們翻至…也是第 61 章的地方…「原來她是那樣依賴梅蘭妮，如同她依賴自己一樣，可是她自己以前從來都沒察覺。」

So the answer is yes... even though Scarlett is on the path of pursing wealth, she still has a loyal friend, who is willing to stand by her side no matter what...

所以這個答案毫無疑問的…即使思嘉麗朝著追求財富之路前進，她始終有個忠誠的朋友，那位不論發生任何事情都在身旁陪她度過的人。

I think that pretty much covers the friendship between Melanie and Scarlett... and of course you have to read through other details by yourself and as for the mid-term... it's open book... and you will be tested on a combination of identification and essays.

我想這大概都涵蓋了梅蘭妮和思嘉麗友誼的部分了…而當然，你們必須要自己讀透所有其他的細節部分，而關於期中考的部分…是開書考試…測驗包含辨識名詞和論說文。

字彙輔助

1　choose 選擇；挑選　　　　2　Yankee（南北戰爭）北軍士兵

3　rumor 謠言、謠傳　　　　4　defend 防禦；保衛

5　confrontation 比較；對抗　　6　wealth 財富；財產

7　loyal 忠誠的、忠心的　　　　8　detail 細節；詳情

▶▶ 試題聽力原文

1. Listen again to part of the lecture. Then answer the question.

   "she could see so clearly now that he was only a childish fancy, no more important really than her spoiled desire for the aquamarine earbobs she had coaxed out of Gerald".

   Why does the professor mention the comparison?

2. Listen again to part of the lecture. Then answer the question.

   "Do you think Pa is a pauper? He's got all the money I'll ever need and then I have Charles' property besides."

   Why does Scarlett counter with this when Rhett jokes about her?

3. Listen again to part of the lecture. Then answer the question.

Rhett says "you forget Ms. Wilkes" "I dare say she'd approve of anything you did, short of murder."

What's Rhett's understanding about Ms. Wilkes?

4. Listen again to part of the lecture. Then answer the question.

"She stayed with me through the whole siege when she could have gone home, when Aunt Pitty had run away to Macon..."

Why does Ms. Wilkes mention Aunt Pitty's flee to another town?

5. What is untrue about Scarlett and Melanie?

▶▶ 記筆記與聽力訊息

| Instruction | MP3 004

新托福聽力與其他聽力測驗不同，可以於聽力的紙上記筆記，除了寫試題外，更重要的一點是訓練自己能夠在聽完一段訊息後，將重要的聽力訊息都記下。也可以將自己聽到跟記到的重點訊息跟試題做比對，因為試題考的就是長對話跟講座中出現的重點，能修正自己選取聽力訊息重點的能力。

| 聽力重點 |

■ 記筆記有很多方式，包含符號跟自己習慣的縮寫字等等，可以找出最適合自己的模式，一定要自己重複聽音檔作練習數次。

■ 這篇是關於美國文學和心理學，**當中穿插很多引述還有跳著篇章介紹，要注意這種呈現方式，但透過這樣的呈現方式很快就能掌握這本厚重的小說中兩個主角之間的情誼。**

▶▶ 參考筆記

Main idea ❶	
Gone with the Wind	a combination of the love story and the friendship
realization	"she could see so clearly now that he was only a childish fancy, no more important really than her spoiled desire for the aquamarine earbobs she had coaxed out of Gerald"./ Ashley means so little to her

Main idea ❷	
The quest for money/relation to the topic of friends	"Do you think Pa is a pauper? He's got all the money I'll ever need and then I have Charles' property besides."
Lending money	visits the jail to see Rhett in order to get 300 dollars
A path towards avarice and decadency	"Yes, I want money more than anything else in the world."
outcome	"but there is a penalty attached as there is to most things you want. It's loneliness."

reasoning	• "you forget Ms. Wilkes" "I dare say she'd approve of anything you did, short of murder." • "she's even approved of murder."

Main idea ❸

Scarlett and Melanie	• "We haven't lost each other and our babies are alright and we have a roof over our heads." • rumor about her affairs with Ashley • "she stayed with me through the whole siege when she could have gone home, when Aunt Pitty had run away to Macon..."

Main idea ❹

ending	"she had relied on Melanie, even as she had relied upon herself, and she had never known it."

Instruction | MP3 004

現在請再聽一次音檔，並做下列的測驗，檢視自己能否完成此填空測驗和強化自己聽力能力和拼字能力，降低自己漏聽到聽力訊息的機會，大幅提升應考實力。

Gone with the Wind may seem like a **1.** _____ love story at first, but it truly is a combination of the love story and the **2.** _____, or more than that. The friendship part has been **3.** _____ by the selection and editing of the **4.** _____ in the movies, but a closer look at the fiction can reveal how important the friendship is. Scarlett might love Melanie more than she loves Ashley... I know some of you might not agree with me... but when you read the last part of the fiction... you will understand when Scarlett eventually knows that she loves Rhett instead of Ashley and she just doesn't know it.

Let's take a quick look at chapter 61... near the very end... **"she could see so clearly now that he was only a childish 5.** _____**, no more important really than her spoiled desire for the aquamarine earbobs she had 6.** _____ **out of Gerald"**. This part clearly shows Ashley means little to her. Her **7.** _____ towards Melanie is even stronger than she realizes. Her feelings towards Melanie are deeper than those of Ashley...

And what does Melanie mean to Scarlett? And what does Scarlett mean to Melanie? Let's back to part two chapter thirteen... Scarlett says **"Do you think Pa is a 8._____ ? He's got all the money I'll ever need and then I have Charles' 9._____ besides."** What does this have to do with the friendship of the two... we will have to jump to the middle part where Rhett jokes about Scarlett... earlier, Scarlett is so confident that she won't be needing Rhett's advice since she has plenty of money... but that all changes after the war... and now she is **10._____** for money... there is a part when she visits the jail to see Rhett in order to get 300 dollars so that she can save Tara.

11._____, war and lots of things have **12._____** Scarlett's crave for money... she even vows that with God as her witness that she will never be hungry again... all these have led her down the path of **13._____** and **14._____**. However, she doesn't care and she only wants money...

In chapter 38, Scarlett says **"Yes, I want money more than anything else in the world."** and in exchange there are sacrifices... so Rhett responds **"but there is a penalty attached as there is to most things you want. It's 15._____."** The price is obviously too high. No women want to be friends with Scarlett, and she used to have her mother to **16._____** her and Melanie to accompany her. She begins to wonder do I still have friends?

Rhett says **"you forget Ms. Wilkes"** **"I dare say she'd approve of anything you did, short of murder."** To which Scarlett responds **"she's even approved of murder."**

Scarlett and Melanie have been through so much, and they have endured so many hardships... let's take a look at the **17.** _____ made by Ms. Wilkes... it's in chapter 27... she says **"We haven't lost each other and our babies are alright and we have a roof over our heads."**

Scarlett even chooses to stay in Atlanta to take care of Melanie when her mother is sick, and even aunt Pitty flees to Macon to avoid **18.** _____ when Melanie is about to give birth to a baby. Scarlett has always been there for her.

In a later episode, when Scarlett is in trouble with the **19.** _____ about her affairs with Ashley, Melanie defends her and stands by her side...

Melanie even gets a **20.** _____ with India. Melanie says **"she stayed with me through the whole siege when she could have gone home, when Aunt Pitty had run away to Macon..."**

However, it is not until later when Melanie is dying that

Scarlett realizes how much Melanie's friendship means to her. it's been Melanie, not Ashley or Rhett.

Let's also flip to chapter 61... **"she had relied on Melanie, even as she had relied upon herself, and she had never known it."**

So the answer is yes... even though Scarlett is on the path of pursing **21.** _____ , she still has a **22.** _____ friend, who is willing to stand by her sider no matter what...

| 參考答案 |

1. romantic
2. friendship
3. marginalized
4. storylines
5. fancy
6. coaxed
7. affection
8. pauper
9. property
10. desperate
11. Hunger
12. aggravated
13. avarice
14. decadency
15. loneliness
16. console
17. proclamation
18. Yankees
19. rumor
20. confrontation
21. wealth
22. loyal

▶▶ 摘要能力

| Instruction | `MP3 004`

　　除了閱讀測驗外，其實培養能在聽完一大段訊息後，口述剛才聽到的聽力訊息是學習語言和表達很重要的一件事，讓自己養成並具備這樣的能力，除了能在聽力測驗中獲取高分外，也能在新托福寫作跟口說的整合題型上大有斬獲喔！所以快來練習，除了書中提供的參考答案外，自己可以試著重新聽過音檔一遍後，摘要出英文訊息並朗讀出來。

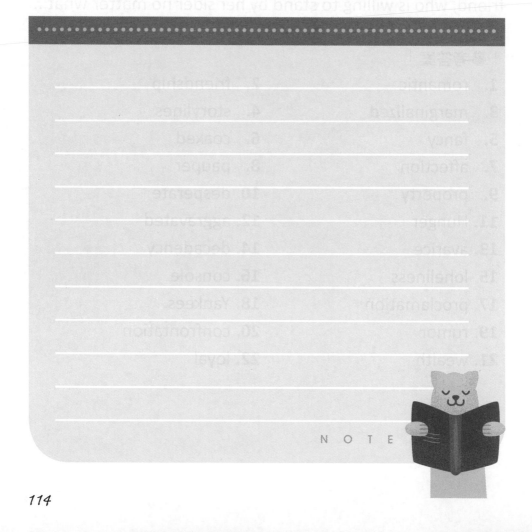

NOTE

▶▶ 參考答案

Gone with the Wind may seem like a romantic love story at first, but it is truly a combination of the love story and the friendship, or more than that. The friendship part has been marginalized by the selection and editing of the storylines in the movies, but a closer look at the fiction can reveal how important the friendship is. At the end of the novel, Ashley means so little to Scarlett.

Hunger, war and lots of things has aggravated Scarlett's crave for money. All these have led her to go down the path of avarice and decadency. Rhett kindly informs her that loneliness is what she will get in return. That's when she starts to think about friendship. Indeed, she still has Melanie, who even approves of her murdering someone. Scarlett and Melanie have been through so much from the birth of the child to the rumor. **"she had relied on Melanie, even as she had relied upon herself, and she had never known it."** So even though Scarlett is on the path of pursing wealth, she still has a loyal friend, who is willing to stand by her sider no matter what...

02

商管跨領域

篇章概述

這個篇章側重在商管、面試和職涯規劃，結合考用和求職的層面，提供了很多的切入點（很多學校不會教你的知識），有助於未接觸職場的考生了解和規劃未來，更認識自我等等的。

UNIT

5 ▶▶ 《Success on Your Own Terms》具 13 年西
南航空資歷的 Libby，如何成功轉職到科技業？
她是如何辦到的？

▶▶ **聽力試題** MP3 005

1. Listen again to part of the lecture. Then answer the question.
   (A) people with a stunning resume and sales records
   (B) people with dusty golden trophies
   (C) people with a growth mindset
   (D) people with a lot of foreign currencies

2. Listen again to part of the lecture. Then answer the question.
   (A) She aims to have a steady and natural transition.
   (B) She quits an unprosperous job.
   (C) Airlines are her only options.
   (D) She dreams big.

3. What is untrue about the lecture?
   (A) Jobs with great benefits and perks are not necessarily easy to get.
   (B) The chef just needs to work on what he can bring to the organization.
   (C) Libby's candor had a worse effect on her.
   (D) Libby has several offers from other Airlines.

4. Listen again to part of the lecture. Then answer the

question.

(A) Past experiences have become obsolete, so it won't have any effect any more.

(B) Libby visions her future work at Yahoo, while she was working at the Airline.

(C) Thinking in the shoe of the CEO is what gets her hired.

(D) Her experience of the past means so little to her now.

5. Listen again to part of the lecture. Then answer the question.

(A) to ask for help from a coach who resembles her personality

(B) to ask for help from an expert who knows how

(C) to ask for help from the CEO

(D) to have more interview experiences

▶▶ 新托福聽力解析

1. 聽力訊息中有提到，並非著眼於過去所獲得的成就，而是未來的學習力和成長，要選 C 較符合，故答案要選**選項 C**。

2. 聽力訊息中有提到儘管還有幾間航空公司向 Libby 招手，但她卻選擇跨出舒適圈，待在原來的航空業服務才是 have a steady and natural transition，故 A 不能選。B 和 C 亦不符合。**選項 D**，dreams big 等同於聽力訊息中的 is gallant enough to step out of the comfort zone。

3. 聽力訊息中表明 Her candidness in pursuing other options not only earned her the accolades from audiences, but also other opportunity，所以 worse effect 顯然是錯誤的描述，故答案要選**選項 C**。

4. 聽力訊息中有提到 her experience of the past still matters... she can still apply those to Yahoo...，故 A 和 D 不能選。B 選項則是無法從聽力訊息中做出判定，故也不能選。選項 C，think about a really big picture... things such as company's brand in the marketplace... 是 Thinking in the shoe of the CEO is what gets her hired 的同義改寫，故答案要選**選項 C**。

5. 這題要選 B，to ask for help from an expert who knows how，故答案為**選項 B**。

....

答案：1. C 2. D 3. C 4. C 5. B

影子跟讀練習 `MP3 005`

> 做完題目後，除了對答案知道錯的部分在哪外，更重要的是要修正自己聽力根本的問題，即聽力理解力和聽力專注力，聽力專注力的修正能逐步強化本身的聽力實力，所以現在請根據聽力內容「逐個段落」、「數個段落」或「整篇」進行跟讀練習，提升在實際考場時專注聽完每個訊息、定位出關鍵考點和搭配筆記回答完所有題目。Go!

Succeeding in an interview has not always been easy, especially when you crave an envious job. Jobs with great benefits and perks are not necessarily easy to get. Things can be quite unpredictable during an interview. Anything can happen. A great beginning can turn into a drastically bad ending if you say something that is unpleasant. For example, a great chef who has 10 years of experience and has prepared multiple interview questions, thinking that he is going to get the job... just like some of the job-seekers who have a prestigious degree and have written a great resume... deeming that they are going to get hired or the company should hire them because of that... things just don't turn out like that...

成功地完成一場面試一直以來都不是件容易的事情，尤其是當你渴望著一份令人稱羨的工作。有很棒的福利和津貼的工作也不是那麼容易就找到。在面試期間，情勢可能會相當難以預測，任何事情都有可能會發生。一個很棒的開端，也可能因為你說了一些不合時宜的話而急轉直下，導致糟糕的結局。例如，一位很棒的廚師，有著十年的經驗，並且已經準備了多樣的面試問題，認為他會因此而錄取該工作。像極了一些找工作的求職者，儘管有著亮眼的學歷並且已撰寫了很棒的履歷表...認為他們會受到聘用或是公司應該要因此而雇用他們...事情卻是不同他們所預期那樣的展開。

During the chef's interview, the interviewer asks him a simple question... then it ends right after that... then the boss says... give me a call when you are ready... that's it... I saw some of you back in the row look dumbfounded... what seems to be missing... perhaps the interview is not based on what he has done before... The chef just needs to work on what he can bring to the organization... and this actually resembles the viewpoint in *Success on Your Own Terms*... by Libby Sartain... she wrote... **"Today's success currency isn't about what you have achieved in the past; it's about your capacity to learn and grow in the immediate future."** ... that chef should probably have bought this book earlier... kidding...

在廚師的面試期間，面試官詢問他一個簡單的問題...然後緊接著面試就結束了...然後，那位老闆說道...，等你準備好的時候，再打通電話給我...就這樣...我看到你們後面那排有些人看起來很目瞪口呆...當中到底缺少了什麼呢？...或許這次的面試不是基於他以前所完成過的實績...他只需要把重點放在他能帶給這間公司什麼...而實際上在《符合自己所定義的成功》中，莉比的觀點就與這個情況相似…她寫道…「今日成功的資產不是關於你以前所達到的成就；而是在即將到來的未來，你的學習和成長的能力。」…那位廚師可能應該要早點買這本書才對…開玩笑的…。

字彙輔助

1 envious 嫉妒的；羨慕的
2 unpredictable 出乎意料的
3 drastically 徹底地；激烈地
4 unpleasant 使人不愉快的；不中意的
5 prestigious 有名望的
6 dumbfounded 驚呆的；目瞪口呆的
7 organization 組織，機構
8 resemble 像、類似
9 currency 通貨、貨幣
10 immediate 立即的、即刻的

The job market can change in a blink of an eye... many things can happen... a job once prosperous can be a disaster in the instant... so you really need to work on your future... since your professional skills can be obsolete and you will be looking for the next job in no time... or you happen to get fired... I think Libby here is a great example for your to learn from... to have a great mindset and be able to make a transition to another industry... I know it's not easy... an accountant who used to work in a renowned firm... loses a job... how is he going to find a job in other industry... and especially if he doesn't want to work an entry-level job or something laborious... but Libby did it...

就業市場可能在一瞬間就發生變化...許多事情都有可能會發生...一份曾是繁盛的工作可能在下個瞬間就變成了災難產業...所以你真的需要替自己的未來作打算...既然你的專業技能可能會過時，而你會馬上就需要找尋下份工作...亦或是你碰巧被解雇...我認為莉比在此就提供你很棒的例子來學習...要有著很棒的心態並且能夠轉瞬跳到另一個產業...我知道這並不容易...一名曾經在知名公司上班的會計師...丟了頭路...他要如何在其他的產業找尋一份工作呢...而特別是他又不想要從事基層工作或是一些勞力活的工作...但是莉比就做到了。

字彙輔助

1 blink 一瞥；一瞬間
2 prosperous 興旺的、繁榮的
3 obsolete 淘汰的；過時的
4 mindset 心態；傾向
5 transition 過渡；過渡時期
6 accountant 會計師
7 renowned 有名的；有聲譽的
8 laborious 費力的、吃力的

It somehow sheds some light on those who are undergoing the COVID period. People who get fired are due to the company's unnecessary workforces. What's more amazing is that Libby quits the job, when her industry is in the prime. And she has several offers from other Airlines. That will make her job a steady and natural transition, yet she is gallant enough to step out of the comfort zone... how did she pull it off?

這碰巧替那些因為新冠肺炎時期受到影響的求職者提供了解

釋。人們由於公司的冗員情況而被裁員。更驚人的是，莉比辭掉了這份工作，當她所處的產業還在其全盛階段時。而她從其他航空公司那裡也有幾個錄取通知。這會讓她在轉換跑道時更為穩固且順利，然而她卻膽大到跳脫了舒適圈…她又是如何辦到的呢？

There was a chance event after she gave the speech about leaving the company. Her candidness in pursuing other options not only earned her the accolades from audiences, but also another opportunity. A guy handed her a business card saying Yahoo is looking for the head of HR… she jumped on the chance…

在她發表演離職演説後，有個機遇。她要尋求其他工作機會的坦蕩不僅讓她從聽眾中贏得滿堂彩，也獲取了其他的機會。一位男子遞給她一張商業名片説道雅虎正在找人力部門的總負責人…她對此機會欣然承應。

字彙輔助

1. shed light on 闡明；解釋清楚
2. undergoing 經歷
3. unnecessary 不需要的
4. workforce 人力
5. prime 全盛時期
6. steady 穩固的、平穩的
7. gallant 英勇的；騎士風度的
8. candidness 率直
9. accolade 稱讚；盛讚
10. audience 聽眾、觀眾

But... you need to go on an interview to get a job... that's what most people will be facing... when they are jobless or when they are making a job hop... some are really lucky to have the first job.... and when they are looking for a next job... they panic... they don't have so much job interview experience and that can totally be a downside for them. It can hinder a really good opportunity.

但是…你需要參加面試以獲取一份工作…這也是大多數的人將要面對到的事情…當他們失業時或是要跳槽時…一些人真的很幸運有第一份工作…而當他們找尋下份工作時…他們驚慌失措…他們沒有那麼多的工作面試經驗，而這對他們來説很不利，可能阻礙他們獲取一個相當好的機會。

According to her, she hadn't been on a job interview for 13 years... what she eventually came up with was amazing.... she found a coach to articulate answers that would resonate with the CEOs... it's about the future and what we have said earlier. And what is the major concern for the CEO and why they should hire her... what solutions can she come up with to alleviate the burden of the CEO... definitely not her 13 years of experience working at South West... so when a simple question like "**tell me about yourself**"... talking about past glory at South West won't work... and it's the past... the great chef is not aware of this... and Libby is smart enough to come up with something great that will certainly get her hired... and undoubtedly she got the job... great candidates like Libby think about a really big picture... things such as a company's brand in the marketplace... but her experience of

the past still matters... she can still apply those to Yahoo...

　　根據莉比的說法，她已經有 13 年沒有參加工作面試過了…而她所想到的準備方法令人感到驚艷…她找了一位教練，使她的面試回答明確有力且能引起執行長的共鳴…這是關於未來，和我們先前所述一樣，還有對執行長來說的主要考量是什麼和為什麼他們要雇用她…她能想到什麼是能減輕執行長負擔的解決之道…當然並非她在西南航空的 13 年的工作經驗…所以當一個簡單的問題像是談論你自己…談論在西南航空過去的輝煌戰績不會奏效…這是過去式…名廚就沒有意識到這點…而莉比就聰明到想出一些很棒的事情，確信這樣會讓她獲得錄取…而無疑地，她獲取了該份工作…優秀的候選人像是莉比會考量到很大的方向上…像是公司在市場上的品牌這樣的事情…但是她過去的經驗仍舊是有用的…她仍可將那些經驗運用在雅虎工作上頭…。

字彙輔助

1. jobless 失業的
2. downside 不利；下降趨勢
3. articulate 明確有力地表達
4. solution 解答；解決（辦法）
5. alleviate 減輕；緩和
6. undoubtedly 毫無疑問地
7. marketplace 市場；集市
8. apply 運用

1. Listen again to part of the lecture. Then answer the question.

   this actually resembles the viewpoint in *Success on Your Own Terms*... by Libby Sartain... she wrote... "Today's success currency isn't about what you have achieved in the past; it's about your capacity to learn and grow in the immediate future."

   What is the determining factor that recruiters are looking for?

2. Listen again to part of the lecture. Then answer the question.

   What's more amazing is that Libby quits the job, when her industry is in the prime. And she has several offers from other Airlines. That will make her job a steady and natural transition, yet she is gallant enough to step out of the comfort zone.

   What can be inferred about Libby's job search?

3. What is untrue about the lecture?

4. Listen again to part of the lecture. Then answer the question.

   ... something that will certainly get her hired... and undoubtedly, she got the job... great candidates like Libby think about a really big picture... things such as a company's brand in the marketplace... but her experience of the past still matters... she can still apply those to Yahoo...

What can be inferred about Libby's job search?

5. Listen again to part of the lecture. Then answer the question.

According to her, she hadn't been on a job interview for 13 years... what she eventually came up with was amazing.... she found a coach to articulate answers that would resonate with the CEOs.

What is Libby's solution to the bottleneck?

N O T E

▶▶ 記筆記與聽力訊息

| Instruction | MP3 005

　　新托福聽力與其他聽力測驗不同，可以於聽力的紙上記筆記，除了寫試題外，更重要的一點是訓練自己能夠在聽完一段訊息後，將重要的聽力訊息都記下。也可以將自己聽到跟記到的重點訊息跟試題做比對，因為試題考的就是長對話跟講座中出現的重點，能修正自己選取聽力訊息重點的能力。

| 聽力重點 |

- 記筆記有很多方式，包含符號跟自己習慣的縮寫字等等，可以找出最適合自己的模式，一定要自己重複聽音檔作練習數次。
- 這篇是關於商業概念和職涯規劃，**提供了很多引人深省的部分，很值得參考，成功的人永遠會想到更好的方法。**

NOTE

▶▶ 參考筆記

Main idea ❶	
Succeeding in an interview	has not always been easy
outcome	unpredictable

Main idea ❷	
The chef	unprepared
Libby Sartain	"Today's success currency isn't about what you have achieved in the past; it's about your capacity to learn and grow in the immediate future."
others	professional skills can be obsolete

Main idea ❸	
Libby's path	• Libby quits the job, when her industry is in the prime • she has several offers from other Airlines • step out of the comfort zone • her candidness in pursuing other options

Main idea ❹	
problem	hadn't been on a job interview for 13 years

solution	found a coach to articulate answers that would resonate with the CEOs
big picture	company's brand in the marketplace
her experience of the past	can still apply those to Yahoo

▶▶▶ 填空測驗

| Instruction | MP3 005

　　現在請再聽一次音檔，並做下列的測驗，檢視自己能否完成此填空測驗和強化自己聽力能力和拼字能力，降低自己漏聽到聽力訊息的機會，大幅提升應考實力。

　　1. _____ in an interview has not always been easy, especially when you crave an **2.** _____ job. Jobs with great **3.** _____ and perks are not necessarily easy to get. Things can be quite unpredictable during an interview. Anything can happen. A great beginning can turn into a **4.** _____ bad ending if you say something that is unpleasant.

　　For example, a great chef who has 10 years of experience and has prepared **5.** _____ interview questions, thinking that he is going to get the job... just like some of the job-seekers who have a **6.** _____ degree and have written a great resume... deeming that they are going to get hired or the company should hire them because of that... things just don't turn out like that...

During the chef's interview, the interviewer asks him a simple question... then it ends right after that... then the boss says... give me a call when you are **7.** _____... that's it... I saw some of you back in the row look dumbfounded... what seems to be missing... perhaps the interview is not based on what he has done before...

The chef just needs to work on what he can bring to the **8.** _____... and this actually resembles the viewpoint in *Success on Your Own Terms*... by Libby Sartain... she wrote... **"Today's success 9. _____ isn't about what you have achieved in the past; it's about your capacity to learn and grow in the 10. _____ future."**... that chef should probably have bought this book earlier... kidding...

The job market can change in a **11.** _____ of an eye... many things can happen... a job once **12.** _____ can be a disaster in the instant... so you really need to work on your future... since your **13.** _____ skills can be **14.** _____ and you will be looking for the next job in no time... or you happen to get fired... I think Libby here is a great example for your to learn from... to have a great **15.** _____ and be able to make a transition in another industry... I know it's not easy... an accountant who used to work in a

16. _____ firm... loses a job... how is he going to find a job in other industry... and especially if he doesn't want to work an **17.** _____ job or something **18.** _____... but Libby did it...

It somehow sheds some light on those who are **19.** _____ the COVID period. People who get fired are due to the company's unnecessary **20.** _____. What's more amazing is that Libby quits the job, when her industry is in the prime. And she has several offers from other Airlines. That will make her job a steady and natural **21.** _____, yet she is **22.** _____ enough to step out of the comfort zone... how did she pull it off?

There was a chance event after she gave the speech about leaving the company. Her **23.** _____ in pursuing other options not only earned her the accolades from audiences, but also another opportunity. A guy handed her a **24.** _____ card saying Yahoo is looking for the head of HR... she jumped on the **25.** _____...

But... you need to go on an interview to get a job... that's what most people will be facing... when they are jobless or when they are making a job hop... some are really lucky to have the first job.... and when they are looking for a next job... they panic... they don't have so much job interview experience and that can totally be a **26.** _____

for them. It can hinder a really good opportunity.

According to her, she hadn't been on a job interview for 13 years... what she eventually came up with was amazing.... she found a coach to **27.** _____ answers that would resonate with the CEOs... it's about the future and what we have said earlier.

And what is the major **28.** _____ for the CEO and why should they hire her... what solutions can she come up with to **29.** _____ the burden of the CEO... definitely not her 13 years of experience working at South West... so when a simple question like "tell me about yourself"... talking about past **30.** _____ at the South West won't work... and it's the past... the great chef is not aware of this... and Libby is smart enough to come up with something great that will certainly get her hired... and undoubtedly she got the job... great candidates like Libby think about a really big picture... things such as a company's brand in the marketplace... but her experience of the past still matters... she can still apply those to Yahoo...

| 參考答案 | |

1. Succeeding	**2.** envious
3. benefits	**4.** drastically
5. multiple	**6.** prestigious
7. ready	**8.** organization
9. currency	**10.** immediate
11. blink	**12.** prosperous
13. professional	**14.** obsolete
15. mindset	**16.** renowned
17. entry-level	**18.** laborious
19. undergoing	**20.** workforces
21. transition	**22.** gallant
23. candidness	**24.** business
25. chance	**26.** downside
27. articulate	**28.** concern
29. alleviate	**30.** glory

▶▶ 摘要能力

| **Instruction** | MP3 005

　　除了閱讀測驗外，其實培養能在聽完一大段訊息後，口述剛才聽到的聽力訊息是學習語言和表達很重要的一件事，讓自己養成並具備這樣的能力，除了能在聽力測驗中獲取高分外，也能在新托福寫作跟口說的整合題型上大有斬獲喔！所以快來練習，除了書中提供的參考答案外，自己可以試著重新聽過音檔一遍後，摘要出英文訊息並朗讀出來。

▶▶ 參考答案

Succeeding in an interview has not always been easy, especially when you crave an envious job. Things can be quite unpredictable during an interview. Anything can happen. A great beginning can turn to a drastic bad ending if you say something that is unpleasant.

In the chef's case, the interview ends shortly after he answers the question.

Libby Sartain; however, offers a great solution to the problem. **"Today's success currency isn't about what you have achieved in the past; it's about your capacity to learn and grow in the immediate future."**

The job market can change in a blink of an eye... many things can happen. You need to think of an answer that echoes the future goal of the CEO. Thinking in the shoe of the CEO is what gets you hired. The boss always wants to hire someone who can solve his or her immediate problems. Great candidates like Libby think about a really big picture... things such as company's brand in the marketplace.

商管＋心靈成長

▶▶ 聽力試題 MP3 006

1. What can be inferred about Fran?
   (A) She didn't expect that one day she is going to be poor.
   (B) She used to gamble a lot.
   (C) She shouldn't have bought the China in the first place.
   (D) She was too diligent, so eventually she went broke.

2. What do Gaby and Fran have in common despite how things eventually turn out?
   (A) Their gambling problems
   (B) Their inability to cope with the setback
   (C) Their shallowness on expensive stuff
   (D) Their husbands all went through a difficult time

3. Listen again to part of the lecture. Then answer the question.
   (A) Because it enhances your physical fitness.
   (B) Because it diminishes risks
   (C) Because it helps build your knowledge of the psychology
   (D) Because it triggers mental characteristics to achieve one's goal

4. Listen again to part of the lecture. Then answer the question.

(A) You win some and you lose some. So she has to lose a job to climb the mountain.

(B) It helps her get her life on track.

(C) It greatly reduces her loneliness.

(D) It makes her aimless about her future.

5. Listen again to part of the lecture. Then answer the question.

(A) to strengthen her students' conviction of climbing the Everest

(B) She wants her students to be physically built.

(C) to help students find the purpose in life

(D) to reveal the secret of standing on the Everest longer than 10 minutes

1. 選項 A，Fran 從未預期自己會成為窮人，故答案要選**選項 A**。gambling 只是 Gaby 的猜測，故 B 不能選。或許她不該過得太奢華，買昂貴瓷器，但無法從聽力訊息中判定 Fran 不該如此，僅說因為她丈夫生病等因素。選項 D 亦不符合。

2. 這題是詢問兩人之間的共同點，儘管後來 Gaby 仍過上好的生活，而 Fran 卻淪為排隊領餐點的窮人。聽力訊息中有提到 Fran 的丈夫生病，而 Gaby 提到自己的丈夫曾經失明，患重病其實也就等同是有一段低潮期或有 difficult time，故要選**選項 D**（為同義改寫）。

3. 聽力訊息中表明 climbing the mountain might be the motivation to enhance the psychology inside them, so that a certain goal can be achieved，所以要選 it triggers mental characteristics to achieve one's goal，故答案要選**選項 C**，mental characteristics 跟 psychology 為同義改寫。

4. 聽力訊息中有提到 Rebecca 必須要辭掉工作去爬聖母峰等，但從她的 conviction 等可以得知她自己不覺得是損失，是找回自我，對其他人來說才有可能是 you win some you lose some。而找回人生目標，不再漫無目的等都剛好是**選項 B** 的描述，為同義改寫 helps her to get her life on track。

5. 教授提到 Rebecca 對成功的定義，很明顯是要協助學生找到人生的目標，故答案為**選項 C**。

答案： 1. A 2. D 3. D 4. B 5. C

影子跟讀練習 MP3 006

文學跨領域

商管跨領域

其他

> 做完題目後，除了對答案知道錯的部分在哪外，更重要的是要修正自己聽力根本的問題，即聽力理解力和聽力專注力，聽力專注力的修正能逐步強化本身的聽力實力，所以現在請根據聽力內容「逐個段落」、「數個段落」或「整篇」進行跟讀練習，提升在實際考場時專注聽完每個訊息、定位出關鍵考點和搭配筆記回答完所有題目。Go!

In *Desperate Housewives*, Gaby wants to teach her children to be grateful, so she takes them to a homeless shelter, only to find her friend, Fran, is waiting in line for a free soup. After the encounter, she then discusses with her husband as to why Fran can be in that kind of situation... she was so wealthy and had so many tiffany Chinas... and of course Gaby makes numerous conjectures, such as gambling problems, but those do not seem convinced by her husband... eventually, her increasing curiosity drives her to the shelter house. There she finds Fran, and Fran responds, I'm still poor... Gaby finds a not so direct way to probe into the reason behind her destitution... Fran recalls her husband suddenly lost a job and followed by a cancer... and they were completely wiped out. Then Fran answers, an accident or a tumor can turn you into waiting in line for a free soup. However, Gaby doesn't buy what she says... so she counters with her situation by saying that her husband went blind and they were nearly broke, and still they made it back...

在《慾望師奶》裡，蓋比想教導她小孩要懂得感恩，所以她帶孩子們到遊民收容所，卻發現她的朋友，芙蘭正排隊等著免費的湯。在那天的相遇後，她緊接著和她老公討論關於芙蘭處於該處境的可能原因…她曾那麼的富有而且有那麼多蒂富妮中國瓷器…而當然蓋比做了數不清的猜測，例如賭博問題等，但是那些推測並未說服她的老公…最後，她與日俱增的好奇心驅使她到了庇護之家。在那裡，她發現了芙蘭，而芙蘭回應說，我仍舊是個窮人…，蓋比發現一個較不那麼直接的方式去探查她變窮背後的原因為何…芙蘭回憶著她老公突然失去工作且伴隨著得到癌症…他們所有財產也因此都賠上了。然後，芙蘭回答，一場意外或是一個腫瘤就能讓你成為排隊等一碗免費湯的人。然而，蓋比並不相信她所說的話…所以她以自己的情況回應芙蘭，說道她丈夫曾失明，然後他們幾乎破產，但是他們還是拯救回來了…。

字彙輔助

1 grateful 感謝的、感激的　　**2** shelter 躲避處；避難所

3 situation 處境、境遇　　**4** conjecture 推測、猜測

5 curiosity 好奇心　　**6** probe 探索；徹底調查

7 destitution 窮困；缺乏　　**8** tumor 腫瘤；腫塊

To this day, this scenario still has a lot for me to think about... not just about saving money or a meticulously researched retirement plan... but more about life. Anything can happen and all of a sudden... it's been taken away... truly... an airplane crash takes the life of your loved one, who claims that he or she is going to spend the rest of his or her life with you for better or for worse... the fickleness of the life actually makes those who have suffered to start a journey to find themselves... or a person who feels adrift... and that's why people would often say... there's always a story behind those who choose to climb the highest cliff... their purposes are definitely not for showing off... and they all have undergone a lot; therefore, they have a lot of things to share... some are truly heartbreaking...

直到今日，這個情景仍讓我有很多思考的地方…不僅僅是存錢或是小心翼翼研究的退休計畫…而是生活。任何事情都可能發生，而突然之間…一切都被奪走了…真的…一場飛機失事的意外可以奪走你的摯愛，他或她曾說過要陪你度過餘生，不論人生是好或壞…生命變化無常實際上讓那些已經受苦之人開啟了找尋他們自我的旅程…或是一位覺得人生飄忽不定毫無目標的人…而這也就是為什麼人們常會說…那些攀爬最高懸崖的人背後總是有個故事…他們的目的絕不是為了要炫耀…而他們都經歷了許多，因此，他們有很多事情可以分享…有些確實很令人感到心碎…。

And let's cut to the chase... back to our textbook... *Success on Your Own Terms*... It's in chapter 5... Rebecca goes on a journey of climbing Mount Everest... to find who she is... it's also one of the reasons why people would like to go on such a journey... to find who they are...

而讓我們言歸正傳…回到我們的課本《符合自己所定義的成功》在第五章…蘿貝卡展開了一趟爬聖母峰的旅程…以找尋她自我…這也是人們想要展開那樣的旅程的原因之一…以找尋自我…。

字彙輔助

1. scenario 情節；劇本
2. meticulously 一絲不苟地
3. retirement 退休；退職
4. airplane 飛機
5. fickleness 浮躁；變化無常
6. purpose 目的、意圖
7. heartbreaking 令人心碎的
8. journey 旅程、行程

It all started when she worked for the *Financial Times*... the assignment triggered her to find out why those climbers would dare to take such a risk to go there... but it's true that if you truly want to accomplish something... a certain risk is required... climbing the mountain might be the motivation to enhance the psychology inside them, so that a certain goal can be achieved.

事情源於她在財經時報工作的時候…該任務驅使她去了解那些攀爬者為什膽敢冒險到那樣的地方…但千真萬確的是，如果你想要完成一些事情…冒特定的風險是必須的…爬山可能是增進他們體內的心理的動機，如此一來特定的目標就能夠達成。

To her it was more than writing a story... like what we have stated so far... she falls into the category of being aimless in life... she said **"I had never sought out anything**

with such conviction as I did to climb Everest."

　　對她來說，這不僅僅是寫一則故事...像是我們目前所説過的...她落入了生活中漫無目的生活範疇...她説道「她未曾做過任何一件事有著像攀爬聖母峰那樣的信念。」

She was faced with a dilemma that led to her resignation... I understand some of you might wonder was this worth it? The price to pay for climbing the mountain... lose a job and she only stood there for ten minutes....

　　她面臨了進退兩難的困境，這也導致她遞出辭呈...我了解到你們有些人會想，這樣到底是否值得呢？付出這樣的代價去爬山...失去一份工作，而且她僅站在山頂上面十分鐘而已...。

字彙輔助

1　trigger 觸發、引起　　　　2　climber 攀登者、登山者
3　accomplish 完成、實現　　4　motivation 刺激；推動
5　enhance 提高、增加　　　　6　psychology 心理學；心理
7　aimless 沒目標的、無目的的　8　conviction 確信、信念
9　dilemma 困境、進退兩難　　10　resignation 辭職；放棄

But the most important thing is in the last paragraph... **"Part of the realization had to do with her new definition of success. For Rebecca, success is the achievement of whatever it is you set out to do."**

但是最重要的是在最後一個段落...「部分的體認跟她新定義的成功有關係。對蘿貝卡來說，不管是什麼事情，你開始實現的事情就是成功。」

Once you have a precise goal, like Rebecca's, you are heading in a certain direction... you won't feel aimless... your devotion to the goal will eventually lead you to the exact place... that's also growth...

一旦你有著精確的目標，像是蘿貝卡那樣的目標，你已經朝著特定的方向進行了...你不會感到漫無目的...你對於目標的全心全意最終都會導致你到達確切的地方...那也等同於成長...。

Rebecca's definition helps those who are adrift and uncertain... to collect their strength and eventually do something big for themselves... eventually find the life meanings. That's also a life lesson for those who have endured so much pain... hopefully, this story can motivate some of you who don't know who you truly are and have always followed the advice given by your teachers and parents to embark on a journey of your own and find out what you truly want in life or eventually learn what is the most important thing to you... and certainly fame and money are not on the list for those who have climbed a high mountain or even the Mount Everest.... and coming up we are going to talk about Chapter 7...

蘿貝卡的定義幫助那些毫無目標且感到不安的人…集聚他們的力量並最終找到對他們來說更偉大的目標…最終找到生命的意義。對那些飽受許多痛楚的人來說，那也是個生命的課程…希望此故事可以激勵你們其中一些還不知道自己真實面容且總是追隨師長和父母們所給予的忠告的人，展開自我的追尋之旅並且找出在生命中你真實想要的東西或是最終學習到對你來說什麼才是最重要的事情…，反而名聲和金錢不在那些已經攀爬高山，甚至是聖母峰的人的清單上了…而接下來，我們要討論的是第七章的部分…。

字彙輔助

1. realization 現實；體現
2. definition 定義；釋義
3. achievement 達成；完成
4. aimless 無目的的
5. devotion 獻身；奉獻
6. adrift 漫無目的的
7. embark 從事、著手
8. fame 聲譽、名望

▶▶ 試題聽力原文

1. What can be inferred about Fran?

2. What do Gaby and Fran have in common despite how things eventually turn out?

3. Listen again to part of the lecture. Then answer the question.

   ... but it's true that if you truly want to accomplish something... a certain risk is required... climbing the mountain might be the motivation to enhance the psychology inside them, so that a certain goal can be achieved.

   Why does mountain climbing have anything to do with goal accomplishment?

4. Listen again to part of the lecture. Then answer the question.

   To her, it was more than writing a story... like what we have stated so far... she falls into the category of being aimless in life... she said "I had never sought out anything with such conviction as I did to climb Everest."

   What can be inferred about Rebecca's viewpoint about climbing Everest?

5. Listen again to part of the lecture. Then answer the question.

   Rebecca's definition helps those who are adrift and uncertain... to collect their strength and eventually do something big for themselves... eventually find the life meanings.

Why does the professor mention Rebecca's definition?

N O T E

▶▶ 記筆記與聽力訊息

| Instruction | MP3 006

　　新托福聽力與其他聽力測驗不同，可以於聽力的紙上記筆記，除了寫試題外，更重要的一點是訓練自己能夠在聽完一段訊息後，將重要的聽力訊息都記下。也可以將自己聽到跟記到的重點訊息跟試題做比對，因為試題考的就是長對話跟講座中出現的重點，能修正自己選取聽力訊息重點的能力。

| 聽力重點 |

- 記筆記有很多方式，包含符號跟自己習慣的縮寫字等等，可以找出最適合自己的模式，一定要自己重複聽音檔作練習數次。
- 這篇是關於商業概念和心靈成長，**主題也很能引導人思考並找到目標，當中要注意一些隱晦的表達，**這樣就可以不管題目怎麼換都不影響答題。

NOTE

▶▶ 參考筆記

Main idea ❶

Desperate Housewives/Fran	● her husband suddenly lost a job and followed by a cancer ● an accident or a tumor can turn you into waiting in line for a free soup
Desperate Housewives/Gaby	husband went blind and they were nearly broke, and still they made it back...

Main idea ❷

fickleness of the life	● start a journey ● there's always a story behind

Main idea ❸

Success on Your Own Term/ Rebecca	● *Financial Times* assignment triggered her to find out why those climbers would dare to take such a risk to go there ● climbing the mountain might be the motivation to enhance the psychology inside them, so that a certain goal can be achieved ● "I had never sought out anything with such conviction as I did to climb Everest."

	• For Rebecca, success is the achievement of whatever it is you set out to do.
Main idea ❹	
Rebecca's definition	helps those who are adrift and uncertain... to collect their strength and eventually do something big for themselves

N O T E

▶▶ 填空測驗

| Instruction | `MP3 006`

　　現在請再聽一次音檔，並做下列的測驗，檢視自己能否完成此填空測驗和強化自己聽力能力和拼字能力，降低自己漏聽到聽力訊息的機會，大幅提升應考實力。

　　In *Desperate Housewives*, Gaby wants to teach her children to be **1.** _____, so she takes them to a **2.** _____ shelter, only to find her friend, Fran, is waiting in line for a free soup. After the encounter, she then discusses with her husband as to why Fran can be in that kind of situation... she was so wealthy and had so many tiffany Chinas... and of course Gaby makes numerous **3.** _____, such as gambling problems, but those do not seem convinced by her husband... eventually, her increasing **4.** _____ drives her to the shelter house. There she finds Fran, and Fran responds, I'm still poor...

　　Gaby finds a not so direct way to **5.** _____ into the reason behind her **6.** _____... Fran recalls her husband suddenly lost a job and followed by a cancer... and they were **7.** _____ wiped out. Then Fran answers, an accident or a **8.** _____ can turn you into waiting in line for a free soup. However, Gaby doesn't buy what she says... so she counters with her **9.** _____ by saying that her husband went blind and they were nearly broke, and still they made it back...

To this day, this **10.** _____ still has a lot for me to think about... not just about saving money or a **11.** _____ researched retirement plan... but more about life. Anything can happen and all of a sudden... it's been taken away... truly... an **12.** _____ crash takes the life of your loved one, who claims that he or she is going to spend the rest of his or her life with you for better or for worse... the **13.** _____ of the life actually makes those who have suffered to start a **14.** _____ to find themselves... or a person who feels adrift... and that's why people would often say... there's always a story behind those who choose to climb the highest **15.** _____ ... their purposes are **16.** _____ not for showing off... and they all have undergone a lot; therefore, they have a lot of things to share... some are truly **17.** _____ ...

And let's cut to the chase... back to our textbook... *Success on Your Own Terms*... It's in chapter 5... Rebecca goes on a **18.** _____ of climbing Mount Everest... to find who she is... it's also one of the reasons why people would like to go on such a journey... to find who they are...

It all started when she worked for the *Financial Times*... the assignment **19.** _____ her to find out why those climbers would dare to take such a risk to go there... but it's true that if you truly want to **20.** _____ something... a certain risk is required... climbing the mountain might be the **21.** _____ to enhance the **22.** _____ inside them, so that a certain goal can be achieved.

To her it was more than writing a story... like what we have stated so far... she falls into the category of being aimless in life... she said "**I had never sought out anything with such 23.** _____ **as I did to climb Everest.**"

She was faced with a **24.** _____ that led to her **25.** _____ ... I understand some of you might wonder was this worth it? The price to pay for climbing the mountain... lose a job and she only stood there for ten minutes....

But the most important thing is in the last paragraph... "**Part of the 26.** _____ **had to do with her new definition of success. For Rebecca, success is the achievement of whatever it is you set out to do.**"

Once you have a precise goal, like Rebecca's, you are heading in a certain direction... you won't feel aimless... your devotion to the goal will eventually lead you to the exact place... that's also growth...

Rebecca's definition helps those who are **27.** _____ and uncertain... to collect their **28.** _____ and eventually

文學跨領域

商管跨領域

其他

do something big for themselves... eventually find the life meanings.

That's also a life lesson for those who have endured so much pain... hopefully, this story can motivate some of you who don't know who you truly are and have always followed the advice given by your teachers and parents to **29.** _____ _____ on a journey of your own and find out what you truly want in life or eventually learn what is the most important thing to you... and certainly **30.** _____ and money are not on the list for those who have climbed a high mountain or even the Mount Everest....

│ **參考答案** │

1. grateful	2. homeless
3. conjectures	4. curiosity
5. probe	6. destitution
7. completely	8. tumor
9. situation	10. scenario
11. meticulously	12. airplane
13. fickleness	14. journey
15. cliff	16. definitely
17. heartbreaking	18. journey
19. triggered	20. accomplish
21. motivation	22. psychology
23. conviction	24. dilemma
25. resignation	26. realization
27. adrift	28. strength
29. embark	30. fame

NOTE

▶▶ 摘要能力
| Instruction | MP3 006

　　除了閱讀測驗外，其實培養能在聽完一大段訊息後，口述剛才聽到的聽力訊息是學習語言和表達很重要的一件事，讓自己養成並具備這樣的能力，除了能在聽力測驗中獲取高分外，也能在新托福寫作跟口說的整合題型上大有斬獲喔！所以快來練習，除了書中提供的參考答案外，自己可以試著重新聽過音檔一遍後，摘要出英文訊息並朗讀出來。

NOTE

▶▶ 參考答案

The professor uses the sitcom as a way to introduce the concept. Anything can happen and all of a sudden... it's been taken away. The fickleness of the life actually makes those who have suffered or who are adrift want to start a journey to find themselves.

Rebecca's journey of climbing Mount Everest in *Success on Your Own Terms* helps her find out her own definition of success. Climbing the mountain might be the motivation to enhance the psychology inside them, so that a certain goal can be achieved. She said **"I had never sought out anything with such conviction as I did to climb Everest."** For Rebecca, success is the achievement of whatever it is you set out to do."

Once you have a precise goal, like Rebecca's, you are heading in a certain direction... you won't feel aimless... your devotion to the goal will eventually lead you to the exact place... that's also growth...

Rebecca's definition helps those who are adrift and uncertain to collect their strength and eventually do something big for themselves... eventually find the life meanings.

商管＋心靈成長

▶▶▶ **聽力試題** MP3 007

1. Listen again to part of the lecture. Then answer the question.
   (A) Bestsellers are not reliable.
   (B) Interviewees need straightforward answers.
   (C) Those numbers on the resume are cold and cannot move the interviewers.
   (D) Interviewees need to avoid using listing patterns.

2. Listen again to part of the lecture. Then answer the question.
   (A) to validate the importance of the trash can
   (B) to show the significance of complimenting someone
   (C) to demonstrate the hiring decision is in the hands of the head guy
   (D) to further illustrate how luck plays a role in the hiring process

3. Listen again to part of the lecture. Then answer the question.
   (A) to criticize the idea of maintaining a small number of close friends
   (B) to demonstrate negative emotions can harm one's health

(C) to contrast with making new friends

(D) to show that one needs more normal friends

4. Listen again to part of the lecture. Then answer the question.

(A) Because they insist on maintaining a close relationship with friends

(B) Because they know the fortune-tellers to do the magic

(C) Because one needs to break the existing circle to create luck

(D) Because they always have other options

5. Listen again to part of the lecture. Then answer the question.

(A) More evidence is needed to prove that luck isn't sufficient.

(B) Those millionaires are inherently rich.

(C) There are other factors that influence how the wealth is going to last.

(D) Those millionaires want their luck to last.

▶▶ 新托福聽力解析

1. 從 not compelling 中可以回推出 Those numbers on the resume are cold and cannot move the interviewers，故答案**要選 C**。

2. 教授提到的主因是 to further illustrate how luck plays a role in the hiring process，以講述幸運的功用，故**要選 D**。

3. 教授提到的主因是 to contrast with making new friends，其他選項都是干擾選項，故**要選 C**。

4. C 選項中的 one needs to break the existing circle to create luck 就是答案，因為本來固有社交圈很難有新的機會，要有新的機會和創造幸運，只能藉由認識更多的人以獲取更多的資訊等等，這些弱連結反而握有你所需要的幸運，故**要選 C**。

5. 聽力訊息中有提到 pure luck isn't enough to make it last，故要排除 A。僅提到 they have been lucky in life，無法判定是否是 inherently rich，故要排除 B。也無法判定 those millionaires want their luck to last，故也要排除 D。但從 It's an indication that pure luck isn't enough to make it last，得知 luck 無法使財富 last，故可以反推出還有其他因素影響財富的 last，也有提到富翁將其歸咎於個人特質，答案為**選項 C**。

....

答案：1. C 2. D 3. C 4. C 5. C

影子跟讀練習 MP3 007

做完題目後，除了對答案知道錯的部分在哪外，更重要的是要修正自己聽力根本的問題，即聽力理解力和聽力專注力，聽力專注力的修正能逐步強化本身的聽力實力，所以現在請根據聽力內容「逐個段落」、「數個段落」或「整篇」進行跟讀練習，提升在實際考場時專注聽完每個訊息、定位出關鍵考點和搭配筆記回答完所有題目。Go!

Most graduates misconstrue that listing several certificates and having a fancy degree are enough for their job search, but it is just for the first screening. In one of the bestsellers, *The Defining Decade*, it sets interviewees straight. **"Resumes are just lists, and lists are not compelling."** Those accomplishments listed on the resume only get HR personnel intrigued or meet the major criteria. Interviewees still need to go through the written and several interviews to get the offer. During these processes, anything can happen, and hiring can be more complicated than we imagine. There are multiple factors that will influence how one gets hired, including luck.

許多畢業生誤解了，列出證照和有亮麗的學歷對於他們找工作就足夠了，但是這僅是對於初次篩選。在其中一本暢銷書中，《20世代，你的人生是不是卡住了》，它導正了面試者們的觀念。「履歷僅是清單，而清單一點都不引人注目」。那些列於履歷表上的成就僅能讓人事專員感到有興趣或是達到主要的標準。面試者仍需要經歷過筆試和幾次的面試才能獲得錄取通知。在這些過程中，任何事情都可能發生，而雇用比我們想像中更為複雜，有著眾多因素會影響一個人如何獲得錄取通知，包含幸運。

字彙輔助

1. misconstrue 誤解
2. fancy 愛好；迷戀
3. compelling 引人入勝的
4. intrigued 感到有興趣
5. complicated 複雜的
6. multiple 多樣的
7. influence 影響、作用

In *"How Luck Happens"*, the managing director at Goldman Sachs says that **"you are going to need luck to get a job"**, and it is true that luck does play a huge role in whether a person will get the job or not. As we often hear what others say **"create your own luck"**. Most graduates just don't know how, and doing something is better than doing nothing. In *Desperate Housewives*, season 1, Tom compliments the picture of the boat on the principal's table, although doing this does not move the principal (at least he does something). In *The Success Equation*, the author accolades the executive's taste in trash cans. Luck does work in his favor, and later one of the leaders told him **"the six interviewers voted against hiring you"**, but **"the head guy overrode their assessment and insisted we bring you in."**

Of course, there are more than complimenting things that we can do.

在《幸運的科學》，高盛公司的總經理說到「你必須要擁有幸運才能拿到工作」，而這是千真萬確的，幸運確實在一個人能否獲取一份工作中扮演了重大的角色。如同我們常聽到其他人說的「創造屬於你自己的幸運」，大多數的畢業生卻不知道要從何下手，做點事比起什麼事都不做好多了。在《慾望師奶》第一季，湯姆讚美了校長桌上的一張船的相片，儘管這個舉動並沒有打動校長（至少他做了些什麼）。在《成功的方程式》，作者讚美高階主管對於垃圾桶的品味。幸運確實站在他那邊，而在稍後，其中一位領導人告訴他「有六位面試官在僱用時對你投下了反對票」，但是「主要決策者的決定壓過了他們的評估並堅持我們要僱用你」。當然，比起讚美事情，我們還有很多事情可以做。

字彙輔助

1 compliment 恭維；敬意　　2 principal 校長；社長

3 taste 品味　　4 overrode 優先於；壓倒

5 assessment 評價；估計　　6 insist 堅持

Luck can also be the personality and charm that you exude. Sometimes in a more casual interview, nothing professional is involved. Showing the best side of you or discussing your hobby can sometimes be the click to interviewers. Like, I cannot believe that we went to the same golf club or we both love A team.

Sometimes it is related to your childhood. Any bad or sad memory can be the click to someone who is about to make the hiring decision, but do not pretend to be someone who is clearly not you because often there is a background check that follows right after the interview.

幸運也可以是你所散發出的個性和魅力。有時候在更隨意一些的面試中，沒有任何專業知識牽涉在其中。展現你最好的一面或是討論你的嗜好有時候可以是打動面試官的一擊。像是，我不敢相信我們去同間高爾夫球俱樂部或是我們都同樣喜愛 A 隊伍。有時候與你的童年有關係。任何糟的或傷心的記憶也可以是打動即將要僱用你的人的決定，但是別假裝成顯然不是你本身的人，因為通常在面試後通常都會有背景調查。

However, luck has also been linked to wealth, and other aspects, not just looking for a job. One's friendship is important in our career development. That also means more opportunities and more money. To understand more, we need to delve into close friends and weak ties, and many aspects.

然而，幸運也與財富和其他面向緊密相連，不僅是在工作上。一個人的友誼對於我們的職涯發展是重要的。這也意謂著能獲取更多的機會和金錢。為了瞭解更多面向，我們需要探討親密友人和弱連結以及許多層面的東西。

Maintaining friendship with friends over a long period of time can be rewarding sometimes since you have a group of friends who understand you and support you along the way, but it can sometimes be quite harmful.

長時間與朋友們維持一段友誼可能有時候是具有報酬的，因為你在一路上有一群瞭解你和支持你的朋友，但是這也可能是相當具有傷害性的。

字彙輔助

1. personality 個性、性格
2. exude 流露出來、顯露出來
3. casual 碰巧的；隨便的
4. hobby 業餘愛好、癖好
5. pretend 假裝
6. background 背景
7. delve 探究、鑽研
8. weak ties 弱連結

In life, we all want our friendship to last long and enduring, but life just not works out that way. Ending a long, lasting friendship can harm a person for quite some time. You might isolate yourself from other people for a while, and that will damage the proper function of your body.

在生活中，我們總是想要我們的友誼能夠長久且持續，但是生命卻不是這樣發展的。結束一段長時間且持續的友誼可能對一個人來說傷害的時間相當長。你可能將自己與其他人隔離開很久一段時間，而且這會對於你身體的運作有相當的損害。

文學跨領域

商管跨領域

其他

Making new friends all the time; however, gives you the advantage of not worrying about too much since maintaining a friendship or a relationship requires a person to not give too much pressure on someone. If you are the type of person who always maintains a small number of close friends, you will encounter frustrations from time to time like why my normal friends treat me better than my close friends. These doubts and other things can be quite detrimental to one's health, but if you are the type of person who is always very open-minded and makes many new friends, you will not have a lot of worries. You are enjoying every moment you have with your friends. The good thing is that you are not pressuring them, like pressuring them to take sides or wishing them to do things for you.

然而，一直交新朋友的話給予你不用擔心太多的優點，因為維持一段友誼或感情需要一個人不要給予其他人太多的壓力。如果你是個總是能夠維持一小群親密朋友的類型的人，你會時不時遭遇著像是為什麼我的普通朋友比我的親密朋友對我更好的困擾。這些疑惑和其他事情會對一個人的健康造成相當大的影響，但是如果你是個總是心態非常開放且總是交新朋友的人，你不會有這麼多的擔憂，你會享受著你與朋友們相處的每個時刻。好處是你不會讓他們感到壓力，例如逼迫他們去選邊站或希望他們為你做什麼。

字彙輔助

1. enduring 持久的
2. isolate 使孤立；使脫離
3. damage 損害；損失
4. maintain 維持
5. pressure 壓力
6. frustration 挫折
7. detrimental 有害的；不利的
8. open-minded 心胸寬的

Another great thing about making new friends is that you will learn many things from different types of people. They are from all walks of life, and chances are that they may act as the function of **"a weak tie"**, introducing your dream job to you. This kind of thing is something your close friends cannot offer. Since your close friends and you form a tight circle, and it is just how the world works. You can always get the support from them, but you might not even have the chance of having something that your weak ties can bring to you. In the book like *"How Luck Happens"*, it discusses **"connection to other people"**. **"You and your best friends already know most of the same people - you have overlapping social circles".** It is so true that in our life our job and love mean so much to most of us. Most of the time we depend on others to introduce great jobs or amazing partners to us. Then you know someone who knows someone magic works. Lucky people are not luckier than me. They just have more new friends, so they have more opportunities.

另一件關於交新朋友的好處是，你總能從不同類型的朋友身上學習到事情。他們來自於各行各業，他們很可能可以充當「弱連結」的功用替你介紹夢想工作。這些是一些你的親密友人無法提供的。因為你的親密朋友和你形成了緊密的圈子，而且這就是世界運作的方式，你能總是獲得他們的支持，但是你卻可能毫無機會從他們身上得到弱連結朋友能帶給你的好處。在像是《幸運的科學》一書中，它探討著「與其他人的連結」。「你和你的好友已經有著大多數的共同好友，你們有著重疊的社交圈」。這是如此的真實，在我們的生活中，我們的工作和感情對我們大多數的人來說是如此的重要。多數時候，我們依賴其他人介紹工作或美好的伴侶給我們。這種你知道某人，某人又知道誰的魔法會開始運作。幸運的人並不是比我們更幸運，他們只是有著更多的新朋友，所以他們可以有更多的機會。

Aside from the friendship, inheritance is the quickest way to wealth. You will be inherently luckier than others. Inheriting a large sum of money can also be attributed to luck, but like what is stated in the book, *The Wealth Elite*, you still need the genius to harness the amount of wealth handed to you; otherwise, the depletion of wealth will soon happen. Furthermore, despite the fact that 100 millionaires interviewed by Swiss sociologists said that they have been lucky in life, scholars believe that "**Wealthy individuals tend to ascribe their wealth overwhelmingly to personal qualities.**" It's an indication that pure luck isn't enough to make it last. To the person who is not inherently wealthy, it is actually good news. If you have the rich DNA or exact personal traits, you are still able to attain wealth.

除了友誼之外，遺產是最快達到富有的方式。在先天條件之下，你就比其他人較為幸運。繼承一大筆金錢也能被歸於是幸運，但是就像是《財富菁英》這本書所述，你仍需要天賦以駕馭所遞交給你的財富，否則轉眼之間財富就會耗盡。此外，儘管瑞士社會學家們所面談的百位百萬富翁都提及，他們一生之中都一直很幸運，學者們相信「富有的人傾向將他們所擁有的財富的功勞歸咎於個人特質」。這是一個指標，單靠幸運不足以讓所擁有的財富維持下去。對於那些先天不富有的人來說，這確實是個好消息。如果你有著富有的 DNA 或是確切的個人特質，你仍舊能夠獲取財富。

字彙輔助

1. **tight** 緊密的
2. **support** 支持
3. **connection** 連結
4. **overlapping** 重疊的
5. **inheritance** 遺產
6. **attribute** 把……歸因於
7. **harness** 駕馭
8. **overwhelmingly** 壓倒性地

And after the short break, we will talk about ENVY. Highly successful people are bound to get envious of others. Do they use lucky to dilute the envy from others...?

在短暫休息之後，我們會談到「羨慕」。高度成功的人一定會受人稱羨。他們又如何使用幸運這點來淡化遭受其他人的妒忌呢？

1. Listen again to part of the lecture. Then answer the question.

    In one of the bestsellers, *The Defining Decade*, it sets interviewees straight. "Resumes are just lists, and lists are not compelling."

    What can be inferred about the statement?

2. Listen again to part of the lecture. Then answer the question.

    In *The Success Equation*, the author accolades the executive's taste in trash cans. Luck does work in his favor, and later one of the leaders told him "the six interviewers voted against hiring you", but "the head guy overrode their assessment and insisted we bring you in."

    Why does the professor mention these statements?

3. Listen again to part of the lecture. Then answer the question.

    If you are the type of person who always maintains a small number of close friends, you will encounter frustrations from time to time like why my normal friends treat me better than my close friends.

    Why does the professor mention this?

4. Listen again to part of the lecture. Then answer the question.

They are from all walks of life, and chances are that they may act as the function of "a weak tie", introducing your dream job to you. This kind of thing is something your close friends cannot offer. Since your close friends and you form a tight circle...

How can one get more opportunities from the weak ties?

5. Listen again to part of the lecture. Then answer the question.

Furthermore, despite the fact that 100 millionaires interviewed by Swiss sociologists said that they have been lucky in life, scholars believe that "Wealthy individuals tend to ascribe their wealth overwhelmingly to personal qualities." It's an indication that pure luck isn't enough to make it last.

What can be inferred about the study?

NOTE

▶▶ 記筆記與聽力訊息

　　新托福聽力與其他聽力測驗不同，可以於聽力的紙上記筆記，除了寫試題外，更重要的一點是訓練自己能夠在聽完一段訊息後，將重要的聽力訊息都記下。也可以將自己聽到跟記到的重點訊息跟試題做比對，因為試題考的就是長對話跟講座中出現的重點，能修正自己選取聽力訊息重點的能力。

| 聽力重點 |

- 記筆記有很多方式，包含符號跟自己習慣的縮寫字等等，可以找出最適合自己的模式，一定要自己重複聽音檔作練習數次。
- 這篇是關於商業概念和心靈成長，**段落中很多值得學習的論點和引述，5 題都是在檢測更高階的推測和判斷能力，而非細節考點。**

NOTE

▶▶ 參考筆記

Main idea ❶	
job search	misconceptions
The Defining Decade	it sets interviewees straight. "Resumes are just lists, and lists are not compelling."
Key factor	luck
Main idea ❷	
"How Luck Happens"	"you are going to need luck to get a job"
Desperate Housewives, season 1	Tom compliments the picture of the boat on the principal's table
The Success Equation	● the author accolades the executive's taste in trash cans. Luck does work in his favor ● "the six interviewers voted against hiring you", but "the head guy overrode their assessment and insisted we bring you in."
the click to interviewers	hobby
Main idea ❸	
Maintaining friendship	Rewarding/ harmful

Making new friends	• the advantage of not worrying about too much
	• learn many things
	• they may act as the function of "a weak tie", introducing your dream job for you.
	• *"How Luck Happens"*, it discusses "connection to other people".
a small number of close friends	encounter frustrations

Main idea ❹

the quickest way to wealth	inheritance
The Wealth Elite	• need the genius to harness the amount of wealth
	• the depletion of wealth
100 millionaires interviewed	• ascribe their wealth overwhelmingly to personal qualities
	• pure luck isn't enough to make it last
the rich DNA or exact personal traits	• still able to attain wealth

▶▶ 填空測驗

| Instruction | `MP3 007`

現在請再聽一次音檔，並做下列的測驗，檢視自己能否完成此填空測驗和強化自己聽力能力和拼字能力，降低自己漏聽到聽力訊息的機會，大幅提升應考實力。

Most graduates **1.** _____ that listing several **2.** _____ and having a fancy degree are enough for their job search, but it is just for the first screening. In one of the bestsellers, *The Defining Decade*, it sets interviewees straight. **"Resumes are just lists, and lists are not 3. _____."** Those **4.** _____ listed on the resume only get HR personnel intrigued or meet the major criteria. Interviewees still need to go through the written and several interviews to get the offer.

During these processes, anything can happen, and hiring can be more **5.** _____ than we imagine. There are multiple factors that will influence how one gets hired, including luck. In *"How Luck Happens"*, the managing **6.** _____ at Goldman Sachs said that **"you are going to need luck to get a job"**, and it is true that luck does play a huge role in whether a person will get the job or not. As we often hear what others say **"create your own luck"**. Most graduates just don't know how, and doing something is better than doing nothing.

In *Desperate Housewives*, season 1, Tom compliments the picture of the boat on the principal's table, although doing this does not move the principal (at least he does something). In *The Success Equation*, the author **7.** _____ the executive's taste in trash cans. Luck does work in his favor, and later one of the leaders told him **"the six interviewers voted against hiring you"**, but **"the head guy overrode their 8.** _____ **and insisted we bring you in."** Of course, there are more than complimenting things that we can do.

Luck can also be the **9.** _____ and charm that you exude. Sometimes in a more casual interview, nothing **10.** _____ is involved. Showing the best side of you or discussing your hobby can sometimes be the click to interviewers. Like, I cannot believe that we went to the same golf club or we both love A team. Sometimes it is related to your childhood. Any bad or sad **11.** _____ can be the click to someone who is about to make the hiring decision, but do not pretend to be someone who is clearly not you because often there is a **12.** _____ check that follows right after the interview.

However, luck has also been linked to **13.** _____, and other aspects, not just looking for a job. One's friendship is important in our **14.** _____ development. That also means more **15.** _____ and more money. To understand more, we need to delve into close friends and weak ties, and many aspects.

Maintaining friendship with friends over a long period of time can be **16.** _____ sometimes since you have a group of friends who understand you and support you along the way, but it can sometimes be quite harmful.... You might **17.** _____ yourself from other people for a while, and that will damage the proper **18.** _____ of your body.

Making new friends all the time; however, gives you the **19.** _____ of not worrying about too much since maintaining a friendship or a relationship requires a person to not give too much **20.** _____ on someone. If you are the type of person who always maintains a small number of close friends, you will encounter **21.** _____ from time to time like why my normal friends treat me better than my close friends. These doubts and other things can be quite **22.** _____ to one's health, but if you are the type of person who is always very open-minded and makes many new friends, you will not have a lot of worries. You are enjoying every **23.** _____ you have with your friends... Another great thing about making new friends is that you will learn many things from different types of people. They are from all walks of life, and chances are that they may act as the function of "a **24.** _____", introducing your dream job to you.

This kind of thing is something your close friends cannot offer. Since your close friends and you form a **25. _____** circle, and it is just how the world works. You can always get the support from them, but you might not even have the chance of having something that your weak ties can bring to you. In the book like *"How Luck Happens"*, it discusses **"connection to other people"**. **"You and your best friends already know most of the same people - you have 26. ____ _____ social circles"**. It is so true that in our life our job and love mean so much to most of us.

Most of the time we depend on others to introduce great jobs or amazing partners to us. Then you know someone who knows someone **27. _____** works. Lucky people are not luckier than me. They just have more new friends, so they have more opportunities.

Aside from the friendship, **28. _____** is the quickest way to wealth. You will be inherently luckier than others. Inheriting a large sum of money can also be **29. _____** to luck, but like what is stated in the book, *The Wealth Elite*, you still need the genius to harness the amount of wealth handed to you; otherwise, the depletion of wealth will soon happen.

Furthermore, despite the fact that 100 millionaires interviewed by Swiss sociologists said that they have been lucky in life, scholars believe that "**Wealthy individuals tend to ascribe their wealth overwhelmingly to personal 30. _____.**" It's an indication that pure luck isn't enough to make it last. To the person who is not inherently wealthy, it is actually good news. If you have the rich DNA or exact personal traits, you are still able to attain wealth.

| 參考答案 |

1. misconstrue
2. certificates
3. compelling
4. accomplishments
5. complicated
6. director
7. accolades
8. assessment
9. personality
10. professional
11. memory
12. background
13. wealth
14. career
15. opportunities
16. rewarding
17. isolate
18. function
19. advantage
20. pressure
21. frustrations
22. detrimental
23. moment
24. weak tie
25. tight
26. overlapping
27. magic
28. inheritance
29. attributed
30. qualities

| Instruction | MP3 007

除了閱讀測驗外，其實培養能在聽完一大段訊息後，口述剛才聽到的聽力訊息是學習語言和表達很重要的一件事，讓自己養成並具備這樣的能力，除了能在聽力測驗中獲取高分外，也能在新托福寫作跟口説的整合題型上大有斬獲喔！所以快來練習，除了書中提供的參考答案外，自己可以試著重新聽過音檔一遍後，摘要出英文訊息並朗讀出來。

▶▶ 參考答案

During hiring processes, anything can happen, and hiring can be more complicated than we imagine. There are multiple factors that will influence how one gets hired, including luck. How luck works in the hiring can be further illustrated in two bestsellers and the sitcom.

Luck can also be the personality and charm that you exude. However, luck has also been linked to wealth, and other aspects, not just looking for a job. One's friendship is important in our career development.

The concept of the weak tie has been revealed, and it stands in sharp contrast to that of the close friend. You need to break the status to have more opportunities. The idea can be proved in the book like *"How Luck Happens"*.

Aside from the friendship, inheritance is the quickest way to wealth. You will be inherently lucky than others. Inheriting a large sum of money can also be attributed to luck, but like what is stated in the book, *The Wealth Elite*, you still need the genius to harness the amount of wealth handed to you; otherwise, the depletion of wealth will soon happen. Furthermore, "Wealthy individuals tend to ascribe their wealth overwhelmingly to personal qualities." It's an indication that pure luck isn't enough to make it last. To the person who is not inherently wealthy, it is actually good news. If you have the rich DNA or exact personal traits, you are still able to attain wealth.

UNIT

8

▶▶ 《The Skills: from first job to dream job》想要有好工作你必須要有第一份工作的歷練、《From the Ground Up: A Journey to Reimagine the Promise of America》Howard Schultz 當初又是如何進 Xerox 呢？

▶▶ 聽力試題 MP3 008

1. How does the professor present the idea to the class?

(A) By studying critically acclaimed articles

(B) By watching the interviewers' documentaries

(C) By giving the examples of successful people

(D) By sharing her own job experiences

2. Listen again to part of the lecture. Then answer the question.

(A) They seem indecisive about making the hiring decision.

(B) They always want to hire someone who possesses a great diploma.

(C) They will have doubts about someone who finds a job for a long period of time.

(D) They do need to get acquainted with the job-seeker to know why they haven't found the job for a long time.

3. Listen again to part of the lecture. Then answer the question.

(A) You are still able to get hired by BBC without job experiences.

(B) You have to dream big to get recruited by BBC.

(C) You are capable of cutting the corner and get hired by BBC.

(D) You do need to accumulate necessary skills to get hired by places, such as BBC.

4. Listen again to part of the lecture. Then answer the question.

(A) He aimed at getting hired by Xerox after college.

(B) He didn't have much thought, and just wanted to do well for his first job.

(C) He knew superiors at Xerox wanted to poach him.

(D) APECO's work experience meant little value to him.

5. Listen again to part of the lecture. Then answer the question.

(A) to give an example of a person similar to our own

(B) to stress the significance of the innate skills

(C) to sympathize the situation of Howard Schultz

(D) to demonstrate the importance of networking in one's job search

▶▶ 新托福聽力解析

1. 教授是以兩位成功者的經驗帶領學生思考這個主題,故答案要選**選項 C**。

2. 從聽力訊息中 You might have to think of a reason to convince the next interviewer why you still haven't found the job 可以對應到選項 C 的 they will have doubts about someone who finds a job for a long period of time,故要選**選項 C**。

3. 聽力訊息中表明 Mishal Husain 當初如果僅靠亮眼的學歷是不可能進入像是 BBC 這樣的公司工作的,而是經過在 Bloomberg 的工作洗禮和累積經驗後,才進到像 BBC 這樣的公司工作,這部分對應到 you do need to accumulate necessary skills to get hired by places, such as BBC,故答案要選**選項 D**。

4. 聽力訊息中有提到 Howard Schultz 沒有任何 mentor 等等,他更沒有眼高手低,而是待在 APECO 持續做出成績後才被挖角到 Xerox,故答案要選**選項 B**,he didn't have much thought, and just wanted to do well for his first job。

5. 教授提到 Howard Schultz 所講述的這句話,很明顯是舉一個跟我們相近的例子,他也沒有任何資源等而是自己摸索出一條路,故答案為**選項 A**。

....

答案:1. C 2. C 3. D 4. B 5. A

影子跟讀練習 MP3 008

做完題目後，除了對答案知道錯的部分在哪外，更重要的是要修正自己聽力根本的問題，即聽力理解力和聽力專注力，聽力專注力的修正能逐步強化本身的聽力實力，所以現在請根據聽力內容「逐個段落」、「數個段落」或「整篇」進行跟讀練習，提升在實際考場時專注聽完每個訊息、定位出關鍵考點和搭配筆記回答完所有題目。Go!

Most of us know that first jobs are often not that great. For those who are looking for a job, they apparently don't have much experience. Lots of factors are going to influence how you choose a job, including negotiating a salary. You might have the kind of feelings that I am getting underpaid? Or I do deserve a much higher pay because I have a great education, and I have so many qualifications and certificates. But the truth is they are offering you the lowest salary range, knowing that you might want to negotiate a higher salary. There is nothing wrong if you aim to get a higher pay, but overestimating yourself can be quite a downside for someone who is looking for a job for the first time. You simply don't understand your value to the company and the salary structure in the company.

大多數的我們都知道第一份工作通常都不是那麼棒。對於那些在找工作的人來說，他們顯然沒有太多的工作經驗。許多因素都影響到你如何選擇一份工作，包括薪資協商。你可能有這樣的感覺，我是否薪資是低付了呢？或是我確實值得較高的薪資待遇，因為我受過很棒的教育，而且我有許多條件和證照。但真相是，他們提供給你的待遇落在最低薪資範圍內，了解到你可能會協商較高的薪資。你想要有較高的薪資待遇這點來說並沒有任何不對之處，但是過度高估自己可能對於初次要找尋工作的人來說是不利的。你不了解你自己對於公司的價值以及公司的薪資結構。

Some graduates have missed out on great opportunities, turning down several offers in this economy. They would rather be jobless than having a lower-than-expected salary. The point is while they are still going on a job search, their classmates have already accumulated job experiences from the first job. Even if they are getting paid less, they are learning something. For those who are too picky about jobs, they might soon realize that college diplomas soon are lackluster. Looking for a job for too long is a drawback, since there is a blank period of time that you don't have a job. You might have to think of a reason to convince the next interviewer why you still haven't found the job.

　　有些畢業生與極佳的機會失之交臂，在這樣的景氣之下，拒絕了幾個工作機會。他們寧願失業，也不願意接受低於期待的薪資。重點是，當他們仍在找工作時，他們的同學已經從第一份工作中累積了工作經驗。儘管他們薪資低付，他們還是學習到一些東西。對那些過於挑剔工作的人來說，他們可能即將了解到大學學歷馬上就失去了光環。花費太長的時間尋找一份工作是個缺點，因為那彰顯了有一段空白時段你沒有工作。你可能必須要構思一個理由去說服下個面試官，為什麼你尚未找到一份工作。

文學跨領域

商管跨領域

其他

字彙輔助

1. apparently 明顯地
2. underpaid 少付……薪資
3. deserve 應受、該得
4. qualification 資格、能力
5. certificate 證明書；執照
6. overestimating 高估
7. downside 不利
8. accumulate 累積

Furthermore, you have to start somewhere... Even if you are so lucky to have a first job without going through a long period of the job search and waiting, you will soon learn that first jobs are actually a start, and you truly need to get started right away... this leads to today's session... *The Skills: from first job to dream job*... by Mishal Husain... she has a bachelor's degree in Cambridge and her job search was smooth... almost like it was handed to her... and she didn't seem to like it... she wrote **"My heart wasn't in the financial news in which Bloomberg had made its reputation, but my time there allowed me to develop skills which I realized later would never have been possible had I gone straight from university to somewhere like the BBC."**

此外，你必須要從某個地方開始…即使你很幸運，不需要經歷過長時間的尋找和等待就有了第一份工作，你馬上就會體認到第一份

工作實際上只是個開端，而你真的需要馬上有個開始才行⋯這也導向我們今天的課程⋯米梭·蝴珊所著的《技能：從第一份工作到夢幻工作》⋯她有劍橋大學學士學位，而且她找尋首份工作之路是順遂的⋯幾乎像是工作是遞給她那樣⋯而她似乎沒那麼喜歡首份工作⋯她寫道「我所嚮往的不是從事財經新聞，一個彭博已建立起其名聲的新聞領域，但是在那裡讓我培養了技能，我在更之後了解到，我不可能從大學畢業後就直接到 BBC 那樣的公司工作。」

... I understand some of you still haven't got the book... you can see the quote from the PPT slide... I think that says it all... plus when you are looking for the next job... most of the evaluations about you stem from how well you do from your first job... you should be like a sponge... absorbing everything here and make utmost of your time... something that can take you to the next job... and hopefully getting a higher salary... this also makes us think... a great job comes from your first job... people are doing so well that they get poached by a great company in the same industry... that also reminds me of the book I read... but don't worry I'm not asking you to write a report on that book. It's true that some people get to work at a great company right out of colleges. The majority still has to be based on your first job in order to be recognized as great. And if you are so great, you will be just fine in almost every place...

⋯我了解到你們之中有些人還沒拿到書⋯你們可以從 PPT 的剪報上看到這個引述的句子⋯我認為這樣就說明一切了⋯再說，當你們在找下份工作時，大多數的評估都源於你在上份工作時的表現有多好…你應該要像個海綿一樣…在此吸收每件事，並且將你們的時間都充分使用上…一些你能帶至下份工作的經驗…並期待著能獲取更高薪資…這也讓我們思考到…一份很棒的工作源於你的首份工作…工作表現極好的人會被同產業中很棒的公司所挖角…這也讓我想起了一本我所讀的書籍…但是別擔心…我不會要你們寫關於那本書的閱讀報告。千真萬確的是，有些人畢業後就隨即進入了很棒的公司工作。你們大多數的人仍舊需要有第一份的工作表現以被認同為是優秀的。而且，如果你很棒的話，那麼你到哪裡都是一樣的…。

字彙輔助

1 financial 財政的；金融的　　2 reputation 名譽、名聲

3 evaluation 評估；估價　　4 stem 起源於

5 absorb 汲取、理解　　6 poach 偷獵；偷捕

7 majority 大多數　　8 recognized 認出、識別

Let's take a look at the first job of the previous CEO of Starbucks and what was his thinking back then when he graduated... **"I had no mentors, no role models, no network that showed me how my education and innate skills translated into a working life."** so how did he get a job at Xerox, one of the most admired companies back then... he obviously didn't get so fixated on getting hired by Xerox... he had a start at APECO, a small company, whose competition was Xerox... he had a great job performance at APECO... then was recruited by Xerox... that also corresponds to the content of our topic today.... to have a great job... you need to have the work experience of the first job... and after the break, we are having a business guest speaker at the music hall... make sure you all put your clinical masks on...

讓我們來看一下，前任星巴克執行長的首份工作，以及他回想到當初他畢業時又是如何呢？...「我沒有人生導師、沒有模範、沒有人際網以展示我，學歷和天生技能要如何轉換成工作生活。」這樣的話，那麼他又是如何進入 Xerox，在當時是間極受景仰的其中一間公司...他顯然不沉醉於被 Xerox 雇用...他的首份工作是 APECO，一間小公司，其競爭對手就是 Xerox...他在 APECO 有著傑出的表現...緊接著，他就受到 Xerox 聘僱...這也與我們今日的主題吻合...為了獲取很棒的工作...你必須要有首份工作的工作經驗...然後，在課堂休息後，我們在音樂廳會有位商業客座講者...確保你們每個人都戴上醫療用口罩...。

字彙輔助

1 mentor 導師   **2** innate 與生俱來的

3 translate 使轉化、使轉變   **4** admired 受欽佩的

5 competition 競爭   **6** performance 表現

7 recruited 聘僱   **8** correspond 符合、一致

▶▶ 試題聽力原文

1. How does the professor present the idea to the class?

2. Listen again to part of the lecture. Then answer the question.

   Looking for a job for too long is a drawback, since there is a blank period of time that you don't have a job. You might have to think of a reason to convince the next interviewer why you still haven't found the job.

   What's on the interviewers' mind?

3. Listen again to part of the lecture. Then answer the question.

   "My heart wasn't in the financial news in which Bloomberg had made its reputation, but my time there allowed me to develop skills which I realized later would never have been possible had I gone straight from university to somewhere like the BBC."

   What can be inferred about Mishal Husain's response about the job?

4. Listen again to part of the lecture. Then answer the question.

   ... he obviously didn't get so fixated on getting hired by Xerox... he had a start at APECO, a small company, whose competition was Xerox... he had a great job performance at APECO... then was recruited by Xerox...

   What can be inferred about Howard Schultz's attitude about his job search?

5. Listen again to part of the lecture. Then answer the question.

"I had no mentors, no role models, no network that showed me how my education and innate skills translated into a working life."

Why does the professor mention the saying?

▶▶ 記筆記與聽力訊息

| Instruction | MP3 008

　　新托福聽力與其他聽力測驗不同，可以於聽力的紙上記筆記，除了寫試題外，更重要的一點是訓練自己能夠在聽完一段訊息後，將重要的聽力訊息都記下。也可以將自己聽到跟記到的重點訊息跟試題做比對，因為試題考的就是長對話跟講座中出現的重點，能修正自己選取聽力訊息重點的能力。

| 聽力重點 |

- 記筆記有很多方式，包含符號跟自己習慣的縮寫字等等，可以找出最適合自己的模式，一定要自己重複聽音檔作練習數次。
- 這篇是關於商業概念和心理學，**主題中透過兩本暢銷書提供求職態度相關的看法，許多考點也需要確實理解才不會被干擾選項影響。**

▶▶ 參考筆記

Main idea ❶	
first jobs	are often not that great.

Main idea ❷	
Lots of factors	how you choose a job
Some graduates	have missed out great opportunities
their classmates	have already accumulated job experiences from the first job
college diplomas	lackluster
a blank period of time	have to think of a reason to convince the next interviewer
first jobs	a start

Main idea ❸	
The Skills: from first job to dream job / Mishal Husain	"My heart wasn't in the financial news in which Bloomberg had made its reputation, but my time there allowed me to develop skills which I realized later would never have been possible had I gone straight from university to somewhere like the BBC."
evaluations	how well you do your first job
The majority	still has to be based on your first job in order to be recognized as great

Main idea ❹

the previous CEO of Starbucks	• "I had no mentors, no role models, no network that showed me how my education and innate skills translated into a working life." • he had a great job performance at APECO... then was recruited by Xerox

▶▶ 填空測驗

Instruction MP3 008

　　現在請再聽一次音檔，並做下列的測驗，檢視自己能否完成此填空測驗和強化自己聽力能力和拼字能力，降低自己漏聽到聽力訊息的機會，大幅提升應考實力。

Most of us know that first jobs are often not that great. For those who are looking for a job, they apparently don't have much experience. Lots of **1.** _____ are going to influence how you choose a job, including **2.** _____ a salary. You might have the kind of feelings that I am getting **3.** _____? Or I do deserve a much higher pay because I have a great **4.** _____, and I have so many qualifications and certificates. But the truth is they are offering you the lowest salary **5.** _____, knowing that you might want to negotiate a higher salary.

There is nothing wrong if you aim to get a higher pay, but overestimating yourself can be quite a **6.** _____ for someone who is looking for a job the first time. You simply don't understand your value to the company and the salary structure in the company.

Some graduates have missed out on great opportunities, turning down several **7.** _____ in this economy. They would rather be **8.** _____ than having a lower-than-expected salary. The point is while they are still going on a job search, their classmates have already **9.** _____ job experiences from the first job.

Even if they are getting paid less, they are learning something. For those who are too picky about jobs, they might soon realize that college diplomas soon are **10.** _____. Looking for a job for too long is a **11.** _____, since there is a blank period of time that you don't have a job. You might have to think of a reason to convince the next interviewer why you still haven't found the job. ...

Even if you are so lucky to have a first job without going through a long period of the job search and waiting, you will soon learn that first jobs are actually a start, and you truly need to get started right away... this leads to today's session... *The Skills: from first job to dream job*... by Mishal Husain... she has a **12.** _____ degree in Cambridge and her job search was smooth... almost like it was handed to her... and she didn't seem to like it... she wrote "My **13.** _____ wasn't in the **14.** _____ news in which Bloomberg had made its reputation, but my time there allowed me to develop skills which I realized later would never have been possible had I gone straight from university to somewhere like the BBC."

... I understand some of you still haven't got the book... you can see the quote from the PPT slide... I think that says it all... plus when you are looking for the next job... most of the **15.** _____ about you stem from how well you do from your first job... you should be like a **16.** _____ ... absorbing everything there and make utmost of your time... something that can take you to the next job... and hopefully getting a higher salary... this also makes us think... a great job comes from your first job... people are doing so well so they get **17.** _____ by a great company in the same industry... that also reminds me of the book I read... but don't worry I'm not asking you to write a report on that book.

It's true some people get to work at a great company right out of colleges. The **18.** _____ still has to be based on your first job in order to be recognized as great. And if you are so great, you will be just fine in almost every place...

Let's take a look at the first job of the previous CEO of **19.** _____ and what was his thinking back then when he graduated... "I had no **20.** _____, no role models, no network that showed me how my education and **21.** _____ skills **22.** _____ into a working life." so how did he get a job at Xerox, one of the most admired companies back then... he obviously didn't get so **23.** _____ on getting hired by Xerox... he had a start at APECO, a small company, whose **24.** _____ was Xerox... he had a great job performance at APECO... then was recruited by Xerox... that also corresponds to the content of our topic today.... to have a great job...you need to have the work experience of the first job...and after the break, we are having a business guest speaker at the music hall... make sure you all put your clinical masks on...

| 參考答案 |

1. factors
2. negotiating
3. underpaid
4. education
5. range
6. downside
7. offers
8. jobless
9. accumulated
10. lackluster
11. drawback
12. bachelor's
13. heart
14. financial
15. evaluations
16. sponge
17. poached
18. majority

19. Starbucks

20. mentors

21. innate

22. translated

23. fixated

24. competition

▶▶ 摘要能力

| **Instruction** | MP3 008

除了閱讀測驗外，其實培養能在聽完一大段訊息後，口述剛才聽到的聽力訊息是學習語言和表達很重要的一件事，讓自己養成並具備這樣的能力，除了能在聽力測驗中獲取高分外，也能在新托福寫作跟口說的整合題型上大有斬獲喔！所以快來練習，除了書中提供的參考答案外，自己可以試著重新聽過音檔一遍後，摘要出英文訊息並朗讀出來。

▶▶ 參考答案

Most of us know that first jobs are often not that great. Some graduates have missed out great opportunities, turning down several offers in this economy. Looking for a job for too long is a drawback, since there is a blank period of time that you don't have a job. You might have to think of a reason to convince the next interviewer why you still haven't found the job.

Mishal Husain's example reveals the key point that you have to start somewhere. You truly need to accumulate the necessary work experience to get to the door of the great company.

It's true some people get to work at a great company right out of colleges. The majority still has to be based on your first job in order to be recognized as great. And if you are so great, you will be just fine in almost every place...

The example of the previous CEO of Starbucks corresponds to that of Mishal Husain. He had a great job performance at APECO and then got poached to one of the great companies in the world, Xerox. He didn't set his sight on Xerox. This provides a great insight for most graduates.

UNIT 9 ▶▶ 《Tip: a simple strategy to inspire high performance and lasting success》被無預警裁員後，Brian 如何突破重圍，找到事業第二春呢？

▶▶ **聽力試題** `MP3 009`

1. What is Anderson Cooper's viewpoint on getting fired?
   (A) You will learn that in advance.
   (B) You won't be featured in the news.
   (C) You have to live a luxurious life to avoid that.
   (D) You won't know when.

2. Listen again to part of the lecture. Then answer the question.
   (A) She agrees with Anderson.
   (B) Figuring out when will be fired is very important.
   (C) There is a reason behind the firing decision.
   (D) Be open to accept when the time comes .

3. Listen again to part of the lecture. Then answer the question.
   (A) They have to follow the policy of the company.
   (B) They are only thinking about what's in the best interest for the company.
   (C) They want to intimidate someone who is not valuable.
   (D) They favor firing someone unannounced.

4. Listen again to part of the lecture. Then answer the question.
   (A) to highlight how useless Brian is.
   (B) to point out how unfair the system is.
   (C) to show what drives Brain to reflect
   (D) to entice distracted students' interest.

5. Listen again to part of the lecture. Then answer the question.
   (A) to highlight her husband's expertise and contribution
   (B) to condemn her worthless husband
   (C) to refute the idea of contribution
   (D) to strengthen the importance of one's contribution to the company

文
學
跨
領
域

商
管
跨
領
域

其
他

▶▶▶ 新托福聽力解析

1. Anderson Cooper 提到 The thing with being fired is that no one tells you they are about to do it – you just get fired one day，等同選項 D 的 you won't know when，故答案要選**選項 D**。

2. 聽力訊息中教授提到 But now I think it's just partially correct... there's more to the story... people just cannot get fired one day 可以對應到選項 C 的 there is a reason behind the firing decision，故要選**選項 C**。

3. 聽力訊息中表明 since you are not going to bring any more profit or value to the company... why does the company have to pay you，這部分可以反推代表公司只想持續聘用對公司有產值的人，但聽力訊息沒有直接表達，而是比較間接的表達，這部分對應到 they are only thinking about what's in the best interest for the company，故答案要選**選項 B**。

4. 這部分有蠻多的訊息，也有提到 Brian 的貢獻，但是題目是問教授為什麼會提到這部分，主要想要說明的是也因為這樣 Brain 從自己在酒館毫無產值等，反思原來當初在當業務人員是對公司是如此毫無貢獻，這部分對應到 to show what drives Brain to reflect，故答案要選**選項 C**。

5. 教授提到 Bree 這個例子的原因是要進一步強化主題的論述（you are paid based on your expertise and contribution），也就是選項 D 的內容，故答案為**選項 D**。

答案：1. D 2. C 3. B 4. C 5. D

影子跟讀練習 MP3 009

做完題目後，除了對答案知道錯的部分在哪外，更重要的是要修正自己聽力根本的問題，即聽力理解力和聽力專注力，聽力專注力的修正能逐步強化本身的聽力實力，所以現在請根據聽力內容「逐個段落」、「數個段落」或「整篇」進行跟讀練習，提升在實際考場時專注聽完每個訊息、定位出關鍵考點和搭配筆記回答完所有題目。Go!

A recurrent scene from the news... people getting fired... most would tell you that they just don't know how... it just happened... some were promising executives with great benefits... they just don't know how to start the next chapter of their lives... and some had been living luxuriously... and you might have read something like **"The thing with being fired is that no one tells you they are about to do it – you just get fired one day."** That's awfully familiar and quite true... it's in *Getting There*... from Anderson Cooper...

新聞中重複循環出現的情景…人們遭到解雇…大多數的人會告訴你，他們不知道這個情況是如何發生的…它就是發生了…一些曾前程似錦、享有好的福利的高階主管…他們不知道如何展開他們人生中的下一個篇章…而且有些曾過著奢華的生活…然後你們可能還曾讀過像是「被解雇這件事情就是沒有人會告訴你他們正要這麼做，你就是在某一天被解雇了。」這極其熟悉且相當寫實…這來自於安德森・古柏所講的話…出自《勝利，並非事事順利》…。

I'm a fan of Anderson... But now I think it's just partially correct... there's more to the story... people just cannot get fired one day... and of course the company will not inform you so that you can get prepared... and since day one on the job you have to be always prepared... but people are falling into a circle of the job-trip mode... and they are totally unaware that they are going to be replaced by a star rookie... and many other things... getting fired is the last thing on their mind...

我是安德森的愛好者…但我現在卻認為，這句話僅部分是正確的…其背後有著更多的故事…人們不可能就這樣某一天就被解雇了…而當然公司不可能會告知你，讓你能有心理準備…而既然人們陷入了工作-旅遊的循環模式…然後他們全然沒有心理準備，他們即將要被一位表現傑出的新人所取代掉…以及許多其他事情…被解雇是他們心頭上最萬萬想不到的事情…。

字彙輔助

1. recurrent 一再發生的
2. promising 大有可為的
3. luxuriously 奢侈地；豪華地
4. awfully 非常
5. partially 部分地
6. inform 通知、告知
7. unaware 未察覺到的
8. rookie 菜鳥

In *Tip: a simple strategy to inspire high performance and lasting success,* it offers another insight to the question... people just don't get fired one day... there is always a reason... in the book, the story of a young man Brain also gets fired one day... he thinks it's totally unacceptable... he is 39 years old with two kids, living a great life, thinking that he is going to receive a paycheck next month... and probably work in the company till his retirement... the thought of getting fired gets to him... he should be well-prepared... and his superior actually points out something important... the company has to let go someone that they deem not quite valuable for the company...

在《提點：一個簡單的策略以激起高效工作和持久性的成功》中，它替這個問題提供另一種洞察…人們不是就這樣有天被解雇…總是有原因的…在書中，一位叫做布萊恩的男子也在某一天被解雇了…他認為這是全然不能接受的事情…他 39 歲了且有兩個孩子，過著很棒的生活，認為他下個月還會收到公司的薪資…還可能會在公司工作直到他退休為止…想到解雇這點使他感到擔心…他應該要做足準備的…而他的上司實際上指出了一些重要的事情…公司必須要放走一些他們認為對公司來說不具相當價值的人…。

Like what's in the news, Brain cannot believe at 39, he still has to go out and try to find a job... and he thinks he is valuable to the company... but everything happens for a reason... and one of the reasons for getting fired unannounced is that you have already been labeled as

文學跨領域

商管跨領域

其他

"valueless"... superiors and other higher-ups already know you have worked in this company for long and they know you too well... since you are not going to bring any more profit or value to the company... why does the company have to pay you? As the story fast-forwards to a much later time... Brain realizes that he always does things around average and what the company expects from an employee is definitely not average, but above average...

像是在新聞上看到的那樣，布萊恩不相信，在他 39 歲的時候，他還必須要出去並試圖找尋一份工作...而他認為自己對公司來說是有價值的...但是每件事情的發生都是有其原因的...而其中一個被無預警解雇的原因是，你已經被標示成是「不具價值的」...上司和其他高層人員已經知道了你在公司工作了多久，而且他們太了解你了...既然你並不能替公司帶來更多利益或價值的話...為什麼公司必須要支付你薪水呢?隨著故事快轉到更之後的時期...布萊恩了解到，他做事情總是達到平均左右的水平，而公司所期望員工的是，不僅是要達到平均，而是超過平均的工作表現...。

字彙輔助

1 insight 洞察力、眼光   2 unacceptable 不能接受的

3 receive 接受   4 paycheck 薪津

5 superior 上司；長官   6 valuable 有用的、有價值的

7 unannounced 未經宣布的 8 valueless 無價值的

I love the arrangement of the book that Brain eventually

has to be a bartender to earn money... although he feels reluctant at first... and he even has the feeling of thinking the job is beneath... him...

我喜愛這本書這樣的安排，布萊恩最終必須要成為吧檯員工以賺取薪資...儘管他最初很不情願...而他甚至有著這份工作配不上他的感受...。

His perception towards the value of the work has changed after working in a bar with his boss Jack and his co-worker, Kelly. The intriguing part is the company has the rule of splitting the tip in a large bucket at the end of the day... and given that Brain is too inexperienced and still in a learning phase, his contribution is basically zero or almost none... yet he still gets 1/3.

在吧檯跟他的老闆傑克和他的同事凱莉工作後，他對於這份工作的感受有了顯著的轉變。令人感興趣的部分是，公司有個規定，就是在每天最後所有員工會均分大桶子裡頭的小費...而考量到布萊恩是在學習階段，而且經驗淺薄，他對公司的貢獻基本上是零或者是幾乎是零...然而，他還是獲得了 1/3 的金額。

The story can actually assuage lots of graduates' complaints about jobs... and it is at this point that he realizes how valueless he is to his former company and the bar. He starts to realize the responsibility and values of the work.

這個故事實際上能夠緩和許多畢業生對於工作的抱怨…而且也是在這個時間點，他意識到他自己對於前雇主和吧檯來說是多麼沒有價值。他開始瞭解到工作的責任和價值。

From the company's perspective, it's always been about your contribution to the company. Just like a scene in *Desperate Housewives*, Bree tells her husband that **"you are paid based on your expertise and contribution"**. He replies, you are saying that I'm worthless. She responds... I'm just saying that you are worth less...

從公司的觀點來說，一直都是你對於公司的貢獻。就像是在慾望師奶的一個場景中一樣，當布里告訴她丈夫「你的薪資是基於你的技能和貢獻。」他回覆，妳是說我沒有價值，她回覆…我只是說你比較沒有價值…。

After working there, Brain has become a totally changed person that will benefit him in the long term for getting his desired job... and remember what we have talked about the rehearsed or memorized answers for the job interview... in the very end... Brain is able to say something that comes from his heart and that pleases his future employer... only a spontaneous answer like that will make him get hired... I'm going to leave that part for you to read... since this book is very fluent and easy to read... the deadline for the book report is next FRIDAY 6 P.M. Make sure you write at least 1,000 words... let's take a short break...

文學跨領域

商管跨領域

其他

在那裡工作後，布萊恩已經是個截然不同的人了，這也對於他長程要找到他理想中的工作是有益的...記得我們已經談論過的，在工作面試時，改述或記誦式的答案嗎...在故事最後...布萊恩能夠發自內心講述一些令他未來雇主滿意的話...也僅有像那樣自發性的答案才能讓他獲得錄取...我就把那部分留給你們自己去讀了...既然書的描述很流暢且很易讀...書籍報告的截止日期是下週五下午六點鐘。確保你至少寫一千字...讓我們短暫休息一下吧。

字彙輔助

1 bartender 酒保

2 perception 感覺；察覺

3 inexperienced 經驗不足的

4 contribution 貢獻

5 assuage 緩和、減輕

6 complaint 抱怨；抗議

7 responsibility 責任

8 expertise 專門知識

9 rehearsed 經過反覆排練的

10 memorized 記憶的

▶▶ 試題聽力原文

1. What is Anderson Cooper's viewpoint on getting fired?
2. Listen again to part of the lecture. Then answer the question.
   I'm a fan of Anderson... But now I think it's just partially correct... there's more to the story... people just cannot get fired one day... and of course the company will not inform you so that you can get prepared...
   What can be inferred about the professor's viewpoint?

3. Listen again to part of the lecture. Then answer the question.

One of the reasons for getting fired unannounced is that you have already been labeled as "unvaluable"... superiors and other higher-ups already know you have worked in this company for long and they know you too well... since you are not going to bring any more profit or value to the company... why does the company have to pay you?

What can be inferred about what's on the mind of those higher-ups?

4. Listen again to part of the lecture. Then answer the question.

The intriguing part is the company has the rule of splitting the tip in a large bucket at the end of the day... and given that Brain is too inexperienced and still in a learning phase, his contribution is basically zero or almost none... yet he still gets 1/3.

Why does the professor mention this part?

5. Listen again to part of the lecture. Then answer the question.

From the company's perspective, it's always been about your contribution to the company. Just like a scene in *Desperate Housewives*, Bree tells her husband that "you are paid based on your expertise and contribution". He replies, you are saying that I'm worthless. She responds... I'm just saying that you are worth less...

Why does the professor mention Bree from *Desperate Housewives*?

▶▶ 記筆記與聽力訊息

| Instruction | MP3 009

　　新托福聽力與其他聽力測驗不同，可以於聽力的紙上記筆記，除了寫試題外，更重要的一點是訓練自己能夠在聽完一段訊息後，將重要的聽力訊息都記下。也可以將自己聽到跟記到的重點訊息跟試題做比對，因為試題考的就是長對話跟講座中出現的重點，能修正自己選取聽力訊息重點的能力。

| 聽力重點 |

- 記筆記有很多方式，包含符號跟自己習慣的縮寫字等等，可以找出最適合自己的模式，一定要自己重複聽音檔作練習數次。
- 這篇是關於商業概念和心靈成長，**這篇也是側重推測和判斷能力，考題能鑑別出考生的程度，許多論點也很值得思考。**

Main idea ❶	
A recurrent scene	people getting fired
Anderson Cooper	"The thing with being fired is that no one tells you they are about to do it – you just get fired one day."

Main idea ❷	
Anderson	partially correct
Tip: a simple strategy to inspire high performance and lasting success	people just not get fired one day... there is always a reason
Brain's company	has to let go someone that they deem not quite valuable for the company...
reasons	have already been labeled as "valueless"
Brain's realization	doing things around average and what the company expects from an employee is definitely not average, but above average...

Main idea ❸	
Brain's perception	has changed after working in a bar

intriguing part	his contribution is basically zero or almost none... yet he still gets 1/3
Main idea ❹	
Desperate Housewives	Bree tells his husband that "you are paid based on your expertise and contribution"

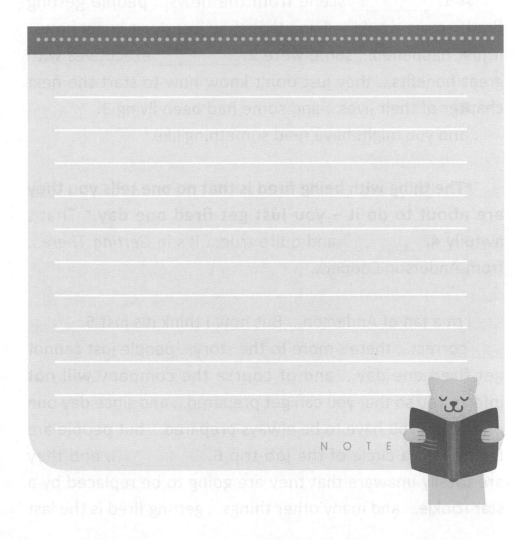

N O T E

Instruction MP3 009

現在請再聽一次音檔，並做下列的測驗，檢視自己能否完成此填空測驗和強化自己聽力能力和拼字能力，降低自己漏聽到聽力訊息的機會，大幅提升應考實力。

A 1. _____ scene from the news... people getting fired... most would tell you that they just don't know how... it just happened... some were 2. _____ executives with great benefits... they just don't know how to start the next chapter of their lives... and some had been living 3. _____ ... and you might have read something like "

"The thing with being fired is that no one tells you they are about to do it – you just get fired one day." That's awfully 4. _____ and quite true... it's in *Getting There*... from Anderson Cooper...

I'm a fan of Anderson... But now I think it's just 5. _____ correct... there's more to the story... people just cannot get fired one day... and of course the company will not inform you so that you can get prepared... and since day one on the job you have to be always prepared... but people are falling into a circle of the job-trip 6. _____... and they are totally unaware that they are going to be replaced by a star rookie... and many other things... getting fired is the last

文學跨領域

商管跨領域

其他

thing on their mind...

In *Tip: a simple strategy to inspire high performance and lasting success,* it offers another **7.** _____ to the question... people just don't get fired one day... there is always a reason... in the book, the story of a young man Brain also gets fired one day... he thinks it's totally **8.** _____ ... he is 39 years old with two kids, living a great life, thinking that he is going to receive a **9.** _____ next month... and probably work in the company till his **10.** _____ ... the thought of getting fired gets to him...

he should be well-prepared... and his superior actually points out something important... the company has to let go someone that they deem not quite **11.** _____ for the company...

Like what's in the news, Brain cannot believe at 39, he still has to go out and tries to find a job... and he thinks he is valuable to the company... but everything happens for a reason... and one of the reasons for getting fired **12.** _____ is that you have already been labeled as "**13.** _____ "... superiors and other higher-ups already know you have worked in this company for long and they know you too well... since you are not going to bring any more profit or value to the company... why does the company have to pay you?

As the story fast-forwards to a much later time... Brain realizes that he always doing things around average and what the company expects from an **14.** _____ is definitely not average, but above average...

I love the **15.** _____ of the book that Brain eventually has to be a **16.** _____ to earn the money... although he feels **17.** _____ at first... and he even has the feeling of thinking the job is beneath...

His **18.** _____ towards the value of the work has changed after working in a bar with his boss Jack and his co-worker, Kelly. The intriguing part is the company has the rule of splitting the tip in a large **19.** _____ at the end of the day... and given that Brain is too **20.** _____ and still in a learning phase, his **21.** _____ is basically zero or almost none... yet he still gets 1/3.

The story can actually **22.** _____ lots of graduates' complaint about jobs... and it is at this point that he realizes how **23.** _____ he is to his former company and the bar. He starts to realize the **24.** _____ and values of the work.

From the company's perspective, it's been always about your **25.** _____ to the company. Just like a scene in *Desperate Housewives*, Bree tells his husband that **"you are**

paid based on your 26. _____ and contribution". He replies, you are saying that I'm **27. _____**. She responds... I'm just saying that you are worth less...

After working there, Brain has become a totally changed person that will benefit him in the long term for getting his **28. _____** job... and remember what we have talked about the **29. _____** or memorized answers for the job interview... in the very end... Brain is able to say something that comes from his heart and that pleases his future employer... only a **30. _____** answer like that will make him get hired... I'm going to leave that part for you to read... since this book is very fluent and easy to read... the deadline for the book report is next FRIDAY 6 P.M. Make sure you write at least 1,000 words... let's take a short break...

| 參考答案 |

1. recurrent
2. promising
3. luxuriously
4. familiar
5. partially
6. mode
7. insight
8. unacceptable
9. paycheck
10. retirement
11. valuable
12. unannounced
13. valueless
14. employee
15. arrangement
16. bartender
17. reluctant
18. perception

19. bucket	20. inexperienced
21. contribution	22. assuage
23. valueless	24. responsibility
25. contribution	26. expertise
27. worthless	28. desired
29. rehearsed	30. spontaneous

▶▶ 摘要能力

| Instruction | MP3 009

　　除了閱讀測驗外，其實培養能在聽完一大段訊息後，口述剛才聽到的聽力訊息是學習語言和表達很重要的一件事，讓自己養成並具備這樣的能力，除了能在聽力測驗中獲取高分外，也能在新托福寫作跟口説的整合題型上大有斬獲喔！所以快來練習，除了書中提供的參考答案外，自己可以試著重新聽過音檔一遍後，摘要出英文訊息並朗讀出來。

▶▶ 參考答案

Anderson Cooper's saying makes people resonate. You just get fired, but in *Tip: a simple strategy to inspire high performance and lasting success,* it offers another insight to the question... people just not get fired one day... there is always a reason.

The company has to let go someone that they deem not

quite valuable for the company. It's a decision made by years of Brain's job performance. It's not until he works at the pub that he realizes how worthless he is to the company. What the company expects from an employee is definitely not average, but above average...

Splitting the bonus is the key for Brain to rethink about the whole thing. He starts to realize the responsibility and values of the work.

From the company's perspective, it's been always about your contribution to the company. The case can be further strengthened by a scene in *Desperate Housewives*, in which Bree tells his husband that "you are paid based on your expertise and contribution".

N O T E

▶▶ 聽力試題 MP3 010

1. Listen again to part of the lecture. Then answer the question.

   (A) The more job hops you do, the better the outcome is.

   (B) Switching a job has no relation to one's satisfaction about life.

   (C) One's attitude is very important.

   (D) The key is "but".

2. Listen again to part of the lecture. Then answer the question.

   (A) to help students get the desired salary

   (B) to practice interview skills with students

   (C) to inform students that adequate skills can be learned at school

   (D) to warn students of the potential repercussions

3. Listen again to part of the lecture. Then answer the question.

   (A) to make up for her lack of consideration

   (B) to applaud the sanctity of the freelancer

   (C) to provide insight about work

   (D) to highlight the importance of the next job

4. Listen again to part of the lecture. Then answer the question.
   (A) to show Darin Adler's remarkable ability
   (B) to show the importance of possessing the professional skills
   (C) to applaud Ken's bravery of leaving Apple
   (D) to point out the unfairness of the selection process

5. Listen again to part of the lecture. Then answer the question.
   (A) It has little effects on your next job.
   (B) Job hunters do not care about your previous job.
   (C) You don't have to do well in the current role.
   (D) Be devoted to your current job

1. 聽力訊息中沒有表明 job hop 的次數越多越好，故 A 不可以選。聽力訊息中 It's true that making a job hop can enhance the salary, leading to a more satisfying life，故 B 選項的 no relation 與聽力訊息表達不同。you should totally do it with the right mindset 中的 right mindset 對應到 attitude，故答案要選**選項 C**。有提到 there is always a "but" 但跟選項 D 的 the key 無關，也不是題目所要問的，故選項 D 亦排除。

2. 教授提到這段話的原因，不是要 help students get the desired salary，故要排除選項 A，而是要表明缺乏足夠技能的話，更難獲取理想的薪資，這部分對應到 warn students of the potential repercussions，故要選**選項 D**。

3. 教授提到 Laurel Touby 的主因是 provide insight about work，讓學生更有洞察力，故答案要選**選項 C**。

4. 教授提到 Ken Kocienda's job hop 不是要表明在蘋果的內部升遷中，Darin Adler 勝出，所以其能力勝過 Ken，故要排除 A。也不是要讚頌 Ken 的勇氣，儘管他大膽地跳脫舒適圈，且他沒有選擇離開故要排除 C。教授也不是要表明內部升遷評選的不公，且從聽力有限訊息中無法判斷，僅能知道 Ken 覺得不公平所以選擇 job hop，故要排除 D。這個段落中最主要要傳達的是，Ken 的 job hop 的大致前因後果，但這些都關乎到他的專業能力夠嗎？因為他必須具備足夠的專業能力才能獲得 Google 的錄取，這部分也是整篇所要講述的，故答案要選**選項 B**。

5. 選項 A，it has little effects on your next job 不符合，因為對下份工作是有影響的。選項 B，Job hunters do not care about your previous job 亦不符合。獵才專員會在乎你前一份工作的實際表現。選項 C 的 You don't have to do well in the current job 也是不符合，因為你必須要在現在的工作有良好表現才行，故也要排除 C。從 You have to look for the long-term，可以反推出 be devoted to your current job 也就是選項 D 的內容，故答案為**選項 D**。

答案：1.C 2. D 3. C 4. B 5. D

影子跟讀練習 MP3 010

做完題目後，除了對答案知道錯的部分在哪外，更重要的是要修正自己聽力根本的問題，即聽力理解力和聽力專注力，聽力專注力的修正能逐步強化本身的聽力實力，所以現在請根據聽力內容「逐個段落」、「數個段落」或「整篇」進行跟讀練習，提升在實際考場時專注聽完每個訊息、定位出關鍵考點和搭配筆記回答完所有題目。Go!

The biggest question that lingers in the mind of millions of graduates is the salary. A person's salary produces the gap and when it multiplies, it shows a huge difference, and this can influence a person's self-esteem and the choice of the life partner. That's why people care so much about it. And since for most people, the first salary is not usually high. They are relying on what experts' viewpoints: making a job hop...

縈繞在百萬畢業生心頭最大的問題就是薪資。一個人的薪資產生了差距而當其倍數增加時，就會顯示出顯著的差異，而這部分也影響到一個人的自尊以及擇偶的選擇。這也就是為什麼人們對薪資是如此的重視。而既然對於大多數的人來說，第一份薪資通常不太高，他們仰賴著專家們所給予的建議：跳槽...

It's true that making a job hop can enhance the salary, leading to a more satisfying life. But... there is always a

"but". Making a job hop is great, and you should totally do it with the right mindset. Most graduates have these misconceptions about making a switch of the job. Some even encounter a great hurdle during the search for a high salary. You just have to realize that all companies are built to make a profit, and no companies are philanthropic.

　　跳槽能使薪資有所增長也是千真萬確的事情，導向更令人感到滿足的人生。但是...總是有個「但是」存在。跳槽是件很棒的事情，而且你應該要抱持正確的心態去做這件事情。大多數的畢業生對跳槽都有些錯誤的觀念在。有些人在尋求高薪的過程中甚至面臨到阻礙。你就是要意識到所有公司都是以獲利為出發點，而且沒有一間公司是慈善機構。

字彙輔助

1 difference 差別、差異　　　2 self-esteem 自尊

3 viewpoint 觀點　　　　　　4 enhance 增加

5 satisfying 令人感到滿足的　6 misconception 誤解；錯誤想法

7 profit 利益　　　　　　　　8 philanthropic 慈善的

Making a job hop in exchange for a salary bump of 3000 to 5000 dollars without accumulating enough work experiences can be quite a downside. This happens often in graduates who work less than a year or without 3 years of work experience. Some just think too highly of themselves.

Without adequate experiences or professional skills that the industry is desperately in need of, it is highly unlikely that you are going to get the desired salary.

　　進行跳槽以換取台幣三千元至五千元的薪資增幅，但卻沒有累積足夠的工作經驗會是相當不利的。這個情況更常發生在工作時間不到一年或者是缺乏三年工作經驗的求職者身上。有些求職者過於自視甚高，缺乏足夠的經驗或產業迫切需要的專業技能，你不太可能獲取你所期盼的理想薪資。

In *"Mistakes I Made at Work"*, Laurel Touby shares her wisdom about work, **"Instead, you almost need to see yourself as a freelancer, building skills and capabilities to take with you to the next job and the next job."** I think Laurel is right about the attitude, and most newly recruits just cannot see things in that kind of direction. You have to realize that your next job is based on the job you are currently doing. How well you do your current job affects the return you are going to get in the salary, bonus, and the next job, so do it 100% even if you are unsatisfied with your current job. Some people who make a job hop and who get the desired salary or position are because how well they are doing in the previous job. If you do not do well in the current job, why on earth that a job hunter wants to recruit you and give you a better benefit and so on. You have to look for the long-term, not the short-term.

在《人生本來就塗塗改改》，蘿拉·圖比分享了她在工作中的智慧，「取而代之的是，你幾乎需要將自己視為是自由工作者，建立技巧和能力，讓你能帶到下份工作和下下份工作」。我認為蘿拉在態度上很正確，而大多數的新僱人員卻無法在看事情時也朝這方向思考。你必須要意識到，你的下份工作是基於你現在這份工作的表現。你在現在這份工作上做得多好影響到你在現在能拿到多少的薪資和獎金回報，以及下份工作，所以付出 100%，即使你對於你現在的工作並不滿意。有些人轉職而獲取了理想的薪資或職位，是因為他們在前一份的工作上有好的表現。如果你在現在這份工作上沒有好的表現，那究竟為什麼獵人頭公司會想要僱用你，並給你較高的獎勵等等的。你必須要看長期，而非短期。

字彙輔助

1 **exchange** 交換；調換

2 **adequate** 足夠的

3 **desperately** 迫切地

4 **desired** 渴望的

5 **wisdom** 智慧

6 **freelancer** 自由職業者

7 **recruit** 僱用

8 **unsatisfied** 不滿意的

In *Creative Selection*, we can also see how important it is to have the skills to get hired by Google. Like what I have stated... the company is not going to fritter away the money to hire someone who used to work in a big company, but in fact is just a shell in person. Ken Kocienda made his way to the top position in Apple during the Steve Job period. But there was something going on that made him look outside for other opportunities, and that led to his interview at

Google.

在《創意競擇》中，我們也能看到要能獲得 Google 的聘用，技能有多麼重要。就如同我所提到的... 公司不太可能會將錢揮霍在一位曾在一間大公司工作但能力卻名不符實的工作者。在賈伯斯時期，肯·科辛達經由一番的努力爬升至頂尖的職位。但也發生了一些事情讓他向外尋求機會，這也促成了他到 Google 的面試。

A vacancy for the Safari team manager led to his eagerness for the job. The truth was his teammate, Darin Adler also wanted the job, and eventually he didn't get the job. He thought that the decision was totally unfair, knowing that his founder's role on the job and so on. This made him want to leave Apple for Google.

蘋果的 Safari team 經理職位的空缺，讓他渴求這份工作。事實是他的團隊隊員達林·阿德勒也同時想要這份工作，最後結果是，科辛達並未獲得這份工作。他認為這個決定極不公平，有鑑於他在這份工作上有創辦人的角色等等的，這些都促成他想要離開蘋果，跳槽到 Google。

Then he had an interview at Google, where he had to answer tough questions from engineers. No mercy. He got to answer them all on a white board and on a laptop. It goes to show how important it is to have professional skills because you are going to need them to get the job. You have to earn it, and it's fair. These interviews went well and he got the job... since he was qualified for the job, Google asked him his expected salary and stock expectations... it's amazing... reading this part makes me kind of feel that it's Apple's loss... eventually, he didn't accept the offer given by Google... and I'm going to leave that part for you to read though... we're running out of time... let's jump to p132... the vacancy for manager of Sync Services... and he got the job... that totally shows **"it's not the smart who get ahead, but the bold."**... However, he was faced with another problem...

　　緊接著，他到 Google 面試，期間他被 Google 工程師們詢問了許多艱難的問題。沒有任何的寬容。他必須在白板和筆記型電腦上回答所有的問題。這些都顯示出了有著專業技能是多麼重要的事情，因為你會需要這些技能以獲取一份工作。你必須要掙得這份工作，而這樣是很公平的事。這些面試進行的很順利，而且他獲得這份工作...既然他勝任這份工作，Google 詢問他所期待的薪資和股票...這令人感到驚奇...閱讀到這部份讓我有種感覺，這是蘋果公司的損失...最後，他並未接受 Google 這份工作...而我就把那部分留給你們自己去閱讀了...我們沒什麼時間了...。讓我們跳至第 132 頁...Sync Services 經理的職缺...而他得到這份工作了...這也全然顯示出「大膽行動的人向前大步邁進，而非那些聰明的」。...然而，他卻面臨了另一個問題...。

字彙輔助

1. fritter 揮霍掉
2. eagerness 渴望
3. unfair 不公平的
4. founder 創立者

| 5 | tough 艱難的 | 6 | mercy 慈悲、憐憫 |
| 7 | expectation 期望 | 8 | vacancy 空缺 |

▶▶▶ 試題聽力原文

1. Listen again to part of the lecture. Then answer the question.

   It's true that making a job hop can enhance the salary, leading to a more satisfying life. But... there is always a "but". Making a job hop is great, and you should totally do it with the right mindset. Most graduates have these misconceptions about making a switch of the job.

   What can be inferred about the job hop?

2. Listen again to part of the lecture. Then answer the question.

   Without adequate experiences or professional skills that the industry is desperately in need of, it is highly unlikely that you are going to get the desired salary.

   Why does the professor mention this?

3. Listen again to part of the lecture. Then answer the question.

   In *"Mistakes I Made at Work"*, Laurel Touby shares her wisdom about work, "Instead, you almost need to see yourself as a freelancer, building skills and capabilities to take with you to the next job and the next job."

Why does the professor mention Touby's saying?

4. Listen again to part of the lecture. Then answer the question.

A vacancy for the Safari team manager led to his eagerness for the job. The truth was his teammate, Darin Adler also wanted the job, and eventually he didn't get the job. He thought that the decision was totally unfair, knowing that his founder's role on the job and so on. This made him want to leave Apple for Google. Then he had an interview at Google, where he was questioned by tough questions from engineers.

Why does the professor mention Ken Kocienda's job hop?

5. Listen again to part of the lecture. Then answer the question.

If you do not do well in the current job, why on earth that a job hunter wants to recruit you and give you a better benefit and so on. You have to look for the long-term, not the short-term.

What can be inferred about the current job?

▶▶ 記筆記與聽力訊息

| Instruction | MP3 010

　　新托福聽力與其他聽力測驗不同，可以於聽力的紙上記筆記，除了寫試題外，更重要的一點是訓練自己能夠在聽完一段訊息後，將重要的聽力訊息都記下。也可以將自己聽到跟記到的重點訊息跟試題做比對，因為試題考的就是長對話跟講座中出現的重點，能修正自己選取聽力訊息重點的能力。

聽力重點

- 記筆記有很多方式，包含符號跟自己習慣的縮寫字等等，可以找出最適合自己的模式，一定要自己重複聽音檔作練習數次。
- 這篇是關於商業概念和心靈成長，**要掌握核心考點，而非僅是了解文章故事內容，每個訊息點背後的意義都是考點。**

NOTE

▶▶ 參考筆記

Main idea ❶

lingers in the mind of millions of graduates	the salary
Get a high salary	making a job hop
Job hop	do it with the right mindset
truth	Without adequate experiences or professional skills that the industry is desperately in need of, it is highly unlikely that you are going to get the desired salary.

Main idea ❷

"*Mistakes I Made at Work*", Laurel Touby	"Instead, you almost need to see yourself as a freelancer, building skills and capabilities to take with you to the next job and the next job."
your next job	based on the job you are currently doing/ look for the long-term

Main idea ❸

Creative Selection/ Ken Kocienda	top position in Apple during the Steve Job period
unfairness	his interview at Google

235

Darin Adler	get promoted
interview at Google	tough questions from engineers
Main idea ❹	
These interviews	went well and he got the job

▶▶ 填空測驗

| **Instruction** | MP3 010

　　現在請再聽一次音檔，並做下列的測驗，檢視自己能否完成此填空測驗和強化自己聽力能力和拼字能力，降低自己漏聽到聽力訊息的機會，大幅提升應考實力。

　　The biggest question that **1.** _____ in the mind of millions of graduates is the salary. A person's salary produces the gap and when it multiplies, it shows a huge **2.** _____, and this can influence a person's **3.** _____ and the choice of the life partner. That's why people care so much about it. And since for most people, the first salary is not **4.** _____ high. They are relying on what experts' viewpoints: making a job hop...

　　It's true that making a job hop can enhance the salary, leading to a more **5.** _____ life. But... there is always a **"but"**. Making a job hop is great, and you should totally do it with the right **6.** _____. Most graduates have these **7.** __

_____ about making a switch of the job. Some even encounter a great **8.** _____ during the search for a high salary. You just have to realize that all companies are built to make a profit, and no companies are **9.** _____ .

Making a job hop in exchange for a salary bump of 3000 to 5000 dollars without **10.** _____ enough work experiences can be quite a **11.** _____ . This happens often in graduates who work less than a year or without 3 years of work experience.

Some just think too highly of themselves. Without **12.** _____ experiences or professional skills that the industry is **13.** _____ in need of, it is highly unlikely that you are going to get the desired salary.

In *"Mistakes I Made at Work"*, Laurel Touby shares her **14.** _____ about work, "**Instead, you almost need to see yourself as a 15.** _____ **, building skills and capabilities to take with you to the next job and the next job.**" I think Laurel is right about the **16.** _____ , and most newly recruits just cannot see things in that kind of **17.** _____ .

You have to realize that your next job is based on the job you are currently doing. How well you do your current job affects the **18.** _____ you are going to get in the salary, bonus, and the next job, so do it 100% even if you are

19. _____ with your current job. Some people who make a job hop and who get the desired salary or position are because how well they are doing in the **20.** _____ job. If you do not do well in the current job, why on earth that a job hunter wants to recruit you and give you a better **21.** _____ and so on. You have to look for the long-term, not the short-term.

In *Creative Selection*, we can also see how important it is to have the skills to get hired by Google. Like what I have stated... the company is not going to fritter away the **22.** __ _____ to hire someone who used to work in a big company, but in fact is just a shell in person. Ken Kocienda made his way to the top position in Apple during the Steve Job period. But there was something going on that made him look outside for other **23.** _____, and that led to his interview at Google.

A **24.** _____ for the Safari team manager led to his **25.** _____ for the job. The truth was his teammate, Darin Adler also wanted the job, and eventually he didn't get the job. He thought that the decision was totally unfair, knowing that his **26.** _____ on the job and so on. This made him want to leave Apple for Google. Then he had an interview at Google, where he had to answer tough questions from **27.** _____. No mercy.

He got to answer them all on a white board and on a laptop. It goes to show how important it is to have professional skills because you are going to need them to get the job. You have to earn it, and it's fair.

These interviews went well and he got the job... since he was **28.** _____ for the job, Google asked him his expected salary and stock **29.** _____... it's amazing... reading this part makes me kind of feel that it's Apple's loss... eventually, he didn't **30.** _____ the offer given by Google... and I'm going to leaver that part for you to read though... we're running out of time... let's jump to p132... the vacancy for manager of Sync Services... and he got the job... that totally shows **"it's not the smart who get ahead, but the bold."**... However, he was faced with another problem...

1. lingers
2. difference
3. self-esteem
4. usually
5. satisfying
6. mindset
7. misconceptions
8. hurdle
9. philanthropic
10. accumulating
11. downside
12. adequate
13. desperately
14. wisdom
15. freelancer
16. attitude
17. direction
18. return
19. unsatisfied
20. previous
21. benefit
22. money
23. opportunities
24. vacancy
25. eagerness
26. founder's role
27. engineers
28. qualified
29. expectations
30. accept

NOTE

▶▶ 摘要能力

| Instruction |　MP3 010

　　除了閱讀測驗外，其實培養能在聽完一大段訊息後，口述剛才聽到的聽力訊息是學習語言和表達很重要的一件事，讓自己養成並具備這樣的能力，除了能在聽力測驗中獲取高分外，也能在新托福寫作跟口說的整合題型上大有斬獲喔！

▶▶ 參考答案

The biggest question that lingers in the mind of millions of graduates is the salary. Making a job hop is one of the ways to get the high salary, but companies are not philanthropic. Without adequate experiences or professional skills that the industry is desperately in need of, it is highly unlikely that you are going to get the desired salary. Laurel Touby's insight can be helpful for those graduates to see things in the right way. You have to realize that your next job is based on the job you are currently doing. How well you do your current job affects the return you are going to get in the salary, bonus, and the next job. In *Creative Selection*, we can also learn how important it is to have the skills to job hop. Whatever the motive behind the job hop, Ken Kocienda truly possesses the skills necessary for him to survive without staying at Apple....

文學跨領域

商管跨領域

其他

UNIT 11 ▶▶ 《44 Insider Secrets That Will Get You Hired》面試到底還需要注意些什麼呢？

▶▶ 聽力試題 (MP3 011)

1. How does the professor present the idea to the class?
   (A) a combination of books and documentaries
   (B) copying the teaching materials from last semester.
   (C) inviting outside HR experts.
   (D) a combination of her own experience and other forms.

2. Listen again to part of the lecture. Then answer the question.
   (A) She wants to point out Connor's incompetence.
   (B) She wants to point out the inadequacy of preparing basic interview questions
   (C) She wants to attract student's attention by making Connor look bad.
   (D) She loves a legal thriller.

3. Listen again to part of the lecture. Then answer the question.
   (A) to strengthen the usefulness of the idea
   (B) to craft your own story
   (C) to cater to other bestsellers
   (D) to make your storytelling impeccable

4. Listen again to part of the lecture. Then answer the question.

(A) Recreating the impression is not necessary.

(B) Let interviewers know you love the job at the end of the interview.

(C) Interviewers will neglect your excitement if they like you.

(D) Interviewers are able to tell one's enthusiasm right from the start.

5. Listen again to part of the lecture. Then answer the question.

(A) You have to remain doubtful for whatever the interviewer says.

(B) Doubts will only inflict people's mind.

(C) You have to pretend that you know the secret code.

(D) Every question is designed to rule out the candidate who is not fit for the job.

▶▶▶ 新托福聽力解析

1. 教授是結合自己的經驗引入主題，之後再用其他形式的表達，故答案要選**選項 D**。

2. 聽力訊息中教授提到美劇中 Conner 的原因是要指出面試的準備工作的足夠與否，像準備基礎面試題可能就不太足夠，講述完這部分後提到 Conner 是進一步陳述 inadequacy of preparing basic interview questions，故要選**選項 B**。

3. 聽力訊息中表明 you need to craft your own story, making it flawless to the eyes of the employers... ，這部分對應到 make your storytelling impeccable，不過 B 和 D 都是干擾選項，題目是問教授為何提到 *The Defining Decade*，主因是其跟 insider secret 17 storytelling is your best defense 的論點吻合能強化本來提到這本的用處故答案要選**選項 A**。

4. 這部分要表達的是 strong excitement，從一開始就要展現熱忱，而非到最後一刻發現自己喜歡這個工作時才展現，故答案要選**選項 D**，Interviewers are able to tell one's enthusiasm right from the start。

5. 從 Each question has its meanings and gets closer to what they are looking for... or who suits the company's secret code... ，其等同於 Every question is designed to rule out the candidate who is not fit for the job（這是一個篩選機制），故答案為**選項 D**。

....

答案：1.D 2. B 3. A 4. D 5. D

影子跟讀練習 `MP3 011`

做完題目後，除了對答案知道錯的部分在哪外，更重要的是要修正自己聽力根本的問題，即聽力理解力和聽力專注力，聽力專注力的修正能逐步強化本身的聽力實力，所以現在請根據聽力內容「逐個段落」、「數個段落」或「整篇」進行跟讀練習，提升在實際考場時專注聽完每個訊息、定位出關鍵考點和搭配筆記回答完所有題目。Go!

Morning... we are going to talk about something that is quite essential to all of you... that is... interviews... we all need to get hired unless we start our own business... what's on our calendar? Right... *44 Insider Secrets That Will Get You Hired*... I'm going to ask my assistant to get the book for me... so before we start... I'm going to share something about going on a job search... I went to multiple tech firms for interviews... some were big... and there was a particular firm that I want to talk about...

早安…我們要討論個對你們來說相當重要的話題…也就是…面試…我們都需要獲得聘用，除非我們創造自己的事業…在我們議程上頭的是什麼呢？對吼…《老闆一定會雇用你的 44 個秘密》…我會要求我的助理替我去拿下這本書…所以在我們開始前…我會分享一下關於找工作的事情…我曾參加過多樣的科技公司面試…有些是大型科技公司…而有一間蠻特別的公司則是我想要談論的…。

文學跨領域
商管跨領域
其他

I was well-prepared and arrived at the gate of the company 20 minutes prior to the scheduled time... after confirming my ID, the guard let me in... still several blocks from the main building... so I hastened the speed... it was sweltering hot outside and I was sweating... wearing a business suit still made things worse... there were still 10 minutes left... so I went to the restroom to freshen up... to make sure everything... the outfit and others were just right... the strong air conditioning was like a cold breeze that made me feel better... but the feeling was soon made worse by the scene... other interviewees... everyone was good-looking... deep down I felt... it's not a modeling contest... and everyone was with a prestigious degree... it's not that I'm bad looking... but some trepidation came over me... it was a competition... everyone was with a solemn look... I could feel that everyone had the same feeling...

我準備就緒後，來到了公司大門口，面試預定時間前 20 分鐘…在確認我的身分後，警衛放行讓我進去…仍舊還需要走幾個街區才能到達主要大樓…所以我加快速度…當時外頭是異常的悶熱，然後我滿身汗…穿著西裝讓汗流得更嚴重了…不過還剩下 10 分鐘才到面試時間…所以我走向廁所去梳洗一番…以確保每件事情…服裝和其他配件都在正確的位置上…冷氣的強風就像是冷的微風般讓我感到舒暢許多…但是這種暢快感馬上就因為所目睹的情景而轉壞…其他的面試者…每個人都看起來好看極了…在內心深處覺得…這不是模特兒比賽啊…而且每個人都有名校學歷…並不是我不好看之類的…但是一些不安的感覺襲著我…這是場競賽…每個人都有著嚴肅的表情…我可以感受到大家也有同感…。

字彙輔助

1 essential 必要的、不可缺的　　2 calendar 日程

3 particular 特定的；特別的　　4 scheduled 預定的

5 confirm 確認　　6 sweltering 悶熱的

7 freshen 變得精神煥發　　8 trepidation 驚恐、慌張

9 competition 競爭　　10 solemn 嚴肅的

There was really no time for me to think about that... we were told to be seated based on the arranged seating chart... then each of us got several documents to write and multiple aptitude tests and others... it took us many hours to finish... then we were told that there was going to be a group interview... my first group interview... I was quite nervous... because I have the fear of the stage fright and not really good at talking in front of others... and I always choose the class that doesn't have to talk much... but things turned out to be quite unexpected...

　　而確實我也無暇細想這些了…我們被告知要根據安排好的座位圖表入座…然後，我們每個人都拿到幾份要寫的文件和眾多性向測驗和其他的文件…花了我們好幾個小時才完成…然後，我們被告知，緊接著將會有團體面試…也是我的首次團體面試…我當時相當緊張…因為我有上台怯場的恐懼，也不擅長在眾人面前談話…還有，我總是選修不需要講太多話的課堂…但是事情卻發展得相當令人意外…。

Perhaps I felt strangely enthralled by the surroundings... and for no reason... so when one of the interviewers... which I believe was the HR manager... asked us something do you have any questions... I could not believe what I did... I raised my hand... an act I don't usually do... and saying something like I have one... everyone was staring at me... then one question after another... I made a pretty good impression... I could see the HR manager was nodding... after that... each of us were getting asked multiple questions... and some of them were getting the hard question... it was nerve wrecking... like the bead of sweat on my forehead was going to drop... it was exhausting...

或許是我被周遭環境奇怪似地迷住了...而沒來由的...所以當其中一個面試官...我想她是人事部經理...詢問你們還有任何問題嗎?...我簡直不敢相信我接下來的舉動...我舉起手...這通常不像是我會做的事情...然後說著像是...我有個問題要問...每個人都注視著我...然後問題一個接一個...我讓面試官有相當好的印象...我可以看見人事經理點著頭...在那之後,我們每個人都被問了許多問題...而其他人都被問了很難答的問題...令人感到膽戰心驚...就像是我前額上頭的汗珠就要掉下來那樣...令人感到筋疲力盡...

字彙輔助

1. arranged 安排的
2. documents 文件
3. aptitude 傾向、習性
4. unexpected 出乎意料之外的
5. enthralled 被迷住的
6. nerve wrecking 膽戰心驚的
7. sweat 汗水
8. exhausting 令人感到筋疲力盡

So back to what we are going to talk about today... preparing for an interview is really a big thing... I know some of you have already prepared things such as 100 basic interview questions, but that's still not enough... you can still get stuck and be embarrassed at the job interview... like one of the actors in *How to Get away With Murder*... it was a hit American legal thriller... I saw some of you nodding... Connor went on a job search after the famous professor let them go... but the interview did not go well... he was told your answer sounded scripted... then eventually followed by we both know you are not getting the job... unfortunately, that's the reality... it's good that you memorize 100 basic interview questions and others... but be natural... and *44 Insider Secrets That Will Get You Hired* is the panacea for you.

回到我們今天要談論的主題...準備面試確實是個重大的事情...我知道你們之中有些人已經準備了，例如 100 個基礎面試問題，但是那樣確實不夠...你可能仍被纏住了，在面試時感到尷尬萬分...就像是在《謀殺入門課》中其中一位男演員一樣...這是部流行的美國驚悚

249

法律劇…我看到你們當中有些人點頭…康納在名教授放他們出去闖並找工作…但是面試進行的卻不順利…他被告知，他的答案像是照稿子唸的…然後，最終伴隨著的是「我們都知道你不會拿到這份工作」…不幸的是，這就是現實面…如果你背了 100 個基礎面試問題和其他的很好…但是要保持自然…而《老闆一定會雇用你的 44 個秘密》就是你的萬靈丹…。

And since we are going to have a guest speaker next week... we will jump to page 101... leave p.1 to p.100 to you... let's take a look... insider secret 17 storytelling is your best defense... this corresponds to one of the bestsellers... *The Defining Decade*... you need to craft your own story, making it flawless to the eyes of the employers... what is stating here is actually helpful... to avoid you to get attacked and use positive stories to your advantage... the key to every question... is positivity. That will make you considered... showing that you are able to work under pressure... the author has listed lots of YES and NO to contrast... it's quite useful and easily followed...

而既然我們下週會有個客座講者…我們跳至第 101 頁…留第 1—100 頁給你們自己去讀…讓我們看一下…內部秘密第 17 則說故事是你的最佳防衛…這個論點也與其中一本暢銷書吻合…《20 世代，你的人生是不是卡住了》…你需要精心編織你的故事，讓它在雇主的眼中完美無瑕…這裡所述其實是很有幫助的…避免你受到攻擊並使用正面的故事使處境轉為優勢…每個問題的關鍵…就是正向。那麼做會讓你受到考慮…顯示你是能夠在壓力下進行工作…作者已經列出了很多「該這麼說」和「不該這麼說」的比較...相當實用且很容易上手...。

字彙輔助

1 thriller 驚險戲劇

2 scripted 照稿子念的

3 memorize 記住

4 panacea 萬靈丹

5 defense 辯護

6 positive 正向的

7 positivity 積極

8 useful 有用的

Let's turn to p.224 insider secret 38 **"You dream job is here"**... it's true that excitement is the key... whether you like this job or not... show strong excitement in every job interview... the interviewer will feel that you are excited to be here... there is a good chance (like what's stated here)... you feel you like this job at the very end... but it's too late... you cannot redo the impression all over... what's also essential about this book is to clear the doubts. You have to clear all the doubts from interviewers to get to the next round of the interview and even get hired. Each question has it's own meanings and gets closer to what they are looking for... or who suits the company's secret code... that corresponds to insider secret 34 interviewers don't hear what you say... p.202... **"You must craft your answers to assuage the interviewers' fears and manage their potential interpretations."**...

讓我們翻至第 224 頁...內部秘密第 38 則你的夢想工作就在

此…千真萬確的是，興奮是個關鍵…不論你是否喜歡這份工作…在每份工作上展現出強烈的熱忱…面試官會感受到你對於在這裡是感到興奮的…有很大的機會（就像這裡所提到的）…你在面試很尾端的時候，你覺得這就是你喜歡的工作…但是卻太遲了…你無法重新製造你留下的印象…關於這本書一個也很重要的一點是消除疑慮。你必須要消除面試官們的疑慮以獲取下一輪面試，以及甚至是獲得聘用。每個問題都有其意義在，而篩選出更貼近於他們所找尋的…或是更符合公司密碼的人…這個論點也與第 202 頁上，內部秘密第 34 則，面試官沒在聽你講什麼…「你須以精心編織的答案來緩和面試官的恐懼，並且駕馭他們可能的詮釋。」…

▶▶ 試題聽力原文

1. How does the professor present the idea to the class?
2. Listen again to part of the lecture. Then answer the question.

   Connor went on a job search after the famous professor let them go... but the interview did not go well... he was told your answer sounded scripted... then eventually followed by we both know you are not getting the job... Why does the professor mention Connor from a legal thriller?

3. Listen again to part of the lecture. Then answer the question.

   insider secret 17 storytelling is your best defense... this corresponds to one of the bestsellers... *The Defining*

Decade... you need to craft your own story, making it flawless to the eyes of the employers...

Why does the professor mention *The Defining Decade*?

4. Listen again to part of the lecture. Then answer the question.

    whether you like this job or not... show strong excitement in every job interview... the interviewer will feel that you are excited to be here... there is a good chance... you feel you like this job at the very end... but it's too late... you cannot redo the impression all over...

    What can be inferred about the interview?

5. Listen again to part of the lecture. Then answer the question.

    You have to clear all the doubts from interviewers to get to the next round of the interview and even get hired. Each question has its meanings and gets closer to what they are looking for... or who suits the company's secret code...

    What can be inferred about this secret code?

▶▶ 記筆記與聽力訊息

| Instruction | MP3 011

　　新托福聽力與其他聽力測驗不同，可以於聽力的紙上記筆記，除了寫試題外，更重要的一點是訓練自己能夠在聽完一段訊息後，將重要的聽力訊息都記下。也可以將自己聽到跟記到的重點訊息跟試題做比對，因為試題考的就是長對話跟講座中出現的重點，能修正自己選取聽力訊息重點的能力。

| 聽力重點 |

- 記筆記有很多方式，包含符號跟自己習慣的縮寫字等等，可以找出最適合自己的模式，一定要自己重複聽音檔作練習數次。
- 這篇是關於商業概念和職涯規劃，**這篇也是要區隔出干擾選項並推測出語意的意思**，這篇的面試內容也很值得參考。

NOTE

▶▶ **參考筆記**

Main idea ❶	
Professor's own experience	to introduce the concept

Main idea ❷	
100 basic interview questions	not enough
How to Get away With Murder	Connor's interviews
44 Insider Secrets That Will Get You Hired	the panacea

Main idea ❸	
insider secret 17	• storytelling is your best defense • corresponds to one of the bestsellers... *The Defining Decade*... you need to craft your own story • avoid getting attacked and use positive stories to your advantage

Main idea ❹	
insider secret 38 "You dream job is here"	• show strong excitement in every job interview • redo the impression all over

clear all the doubts	interviewers don't hear what you say
insider secret 34	"You must craft your answers to assuage the interviewers' fears and manage their potential interpretations."

▶▶ 填空測驗

| Instruction | MP3 011

現在請再聽一次音檔，並做下列的測驗，檢視自己能否完成此填空測驗和強化自己聽力能力和拼字能力，降低自己漏聽到聽力訊息的機會，大幅提升應考實力。

Morning... we are going to talk about something that is quite essential to all of you... that is... interviews... we all need to get hired unless we start our own business... what's on our calendar? Right... *44 Insider Secrets That Will Get You Hired*... I'm going to ask my assistant to get the book for me... so before we start...

I'm going to share something about going on a job search... I went to multiple tech firms for interviews... some were big... and there was a particular firm that I wanted to talk about... I was well-prepared and arrived at the gate of the company 20 **1.** _____ prior to the **2.** _____ time... after confirming my ID, the guard let me in... still several blocks from the main building... so I **3.** _____ the speed...

it was **4.** _____ hot outside and I was sweating... wearing a business suit still made things worse... there were still 10 minutes left... so I went to the **5.** _____ to freshen up... to make sure everything... the outfit and others were just right... the strong air conditioning was like a cold breeze that made me feel better... but the **6.** _____ was soon made worse by the scene... other interviewees... everyone was good-looking... deep down I felt... it's not a modeling **7.** _____ ... and everyone was with a **8.** _____ degree... it's not that I'm bad looking... but some **9.** _____ came over me... it was a competition... everyone was with a solemn look... I could feel that everyone had the same feeling...

There was really no time for me to think about that... we were told to be seated based on the **10.** _____ seating chart... then each of us got several documents to write and multiple **11.** _____ tests and others... it took us many hours to finish... then we were told that there was going to be a group interview... my first group interview...

I was quite nervous... because I have the fear of the stage fright and not really good at talking in front of others... and I always choose the class that doesn't have to talk much... but things turned out to be quite **12.** _____...

Perhaps I felt strangely **13.** _____ by the surroundings ... and for no reason... so when one of the interviewers... which I believe was the HR manager... asked us something do you have any questions... I could not believe what I did... I raised my hand... an act I don't usually do... and saying something like I have one... everyone was staring at me... then one question after another... I made a pretty good **14.** _____... I could see the HR **15.** _____ was nodding... after that... each of us were getting asked multiple questions ... and some of them were getting the hard question... it was nerve **16.** _____... like the bead of sweat on my forehead was going to drop... it was exhausting...

So back to what we are going to talk about today... preparing for an interview is really a big thing... I know some of you have already prepared things such as 100 basic interview questions, but that's still not enough... you can still get stuck and be **17.** _____ at the job interview... like one of the actors in *How to Get away With Murder*... it was a hit American legal **18.** _____... I saw some of you nodding...

Connor went on a job search after the famous professor let them go... but the interview did not go well... he was told your answer sounded **19.** _____... then eventually followed by we both know you are not getting the job... unfortunately, that's the **20. _____**... it's good that you **21. _____** 100 basic interview questions and others... but be natural... and *44 Insider Secrets That Will Get You Hired* is the panacea for you.

And since we are going to have a guest speaker next week... we will jump to page 101... leave p.1 to p.100 to you... let's take a look... insider secret 17 **22. _____** is your best defense... this corresponds to one of the bestsellers... *The Defining Decade*... you need to craft your own story, making it **23. _____** to the eyes of the **24. _____**... what is stating here is actually helpful... to avoid you to get attacked and use **25. _____** stories to your advantage... the key to every question... is **26. _____**. That will make you considered... showing that you are able to work under pressure... the author has listed lots of YES and NO to contrast... it's quite useful and easily followed...

Let's turn to p.224 insider secret 38 **"You dream job is here"**... it's true that excitement is the key... whether you like this job or not... show strong excitement in every job interview... the interviewer will feel that you are **27. _____** to be here... there is a good chance (like what's stated here)... you feel you like this job at the very end... but it's too late... you cannot **28. _____** the impression all over... what's also **29. _____** about this book is to clear the doubts.

You have to clear all the doubts from interviewers to get to the next round of the interview and even get hired. Each question has its own meanings and gets closer to what they are looking for... or who suits the company's secret code... that corresponds to insider secret 34 interviewers don't hear what you say... p.202... **"You must craft your answers to 30. _____ the interviewers' fears and manage their potential interpretations."**...

| 參考答案 |

1. minutes	2. scheduled
3. hastened	4. sweltering
5. restroom	6. feeling
7. contest	8. prestigious
9. trepidation	10. arranged
11. aptitude	12. unexpected
13. enthralled	14. impression
15. manager	16. wrecking
17. embarrassed	18. thriller
19. scripted	20. reality
21. memorize	22. storytelling
23. flawless	24. employers
25. positive	26. positivity
27. excited	28. redo
29. essential	30. assuage

▶▶ 摘要能力

| Instruction | MP3 011

　　除了閱讀測驗外，其實培養能在聽完一大段訊息後，口述剛才聽到的聽力訊息是學習語言和表達很重要的一件事，讓自己養成並具備這樣的能力，除了能在聽力測驗中獲取高分外，也能在新托福寫作跟口説的整合題型上大有斬獲喔！所以快來練習，除了書中提供的參考答案外，自己可以試著重新聽過音檔一遍後，摘要出英文訊息並朗讀出來。

N O T E

文學跨領域

商管跨領域

其他

▶▶ 參考答案

The professor begins today's class by sharing her own interview experience. This can be served as a great material to link with today's session: *44 Insider Secrets That Will Get You Hired*

Preparing 100 basic interview questions is not sufficient for the job search. The example found in a legal thriller *How to Get away With Murder* can further illustrate this. Connor's interview did not go well even if he had the experience of working with a great professor.

Some concepts in the *44 Insider Secrets That Will Get You Hired* correspond to those of *The Defining Decade*. And you have to stay positive and evade getting attacked by having a great story. Furthermore, possessing strong excitement at the beginning of the interview is the key since interviews are able to sense that. Also, you have to craft your answers to make those interviewers believe whatever you say.

NOTE

03

其他

篇章概述

這個篇章涵蓋了更多的訊息區分和辨別的考題，具備良好聽力和閱讀的學習者，能夠迅速將訊息歸類並理解，強化這部分能有效提升聽力和閱讀的成績。

UNIT 12 ▶▶ 幾種蜜蜂的比較：澳洲泥蜂、道森蜂、蜜蜂和大黃蜂

▶▶ **聽力試題** MP3 012

1. The following statements list traits of dirt daubers and their category

   Click in the correct box for each category

	dirt daubers	wasps
A. desensitize the prey		
B. encounter less obstacles		
C. tunnel-shaped nests		
D. indiscriminately build the nests		

2. The following statements list traits of honey bees and hornets

   Click in the correct box for each category

	honey bees	hornets
A. paralyze the prey		
B. kill sizable insects		
C. ability to pogrom		
D. use heat to defend		

3. The following statements list traits of dawson's bees
    Click in the correct box for each category

	female	**male**
A. high competition		
B. panmictic		
C. construct the nest		
D. remain unchanged after the sexual discourse		

4. The following statements list traits of honey bees and dawson's bees
    Click in the correct box for each category

	honey bees	**dawson's bees**
A. gregarious		
B. tunnel-shaped nests		
C. kill hornets		
D. sacrifices are made during mating season		

5. Listen again to part of the lecture. Then answer the question.

    (A) to show that honeybees will pretend to be larger when attacked.

    (B) to demonstrate that physique is the key to win in the insect world.

    (C) to explain those major weaknesses are inborn.

    (D) to show that they are still capable of reversing its disadvantageous situation.

6. Why do dirt daubers have more unpleasant struggle than wasps?
    (A) because they use coloration to caution predators
    (B) because their immune system is not fully developed
    (C) because they are more predator-prone
    (D) because their nests are neighboring
7. What is the resemblance between mud daubers and female Dawson's bees?
    (A) rare instances of the cannibalization
    (B) the ability to withstand heat
    (C) an occluded home for the young
    (D) the ability to desensitize prey
8. Listen again to part of the lecture. Then answer the question.
    (A) to show why emulation in male bees has been increasingly fierce.
    (B) to demonstrate that male bees need certain physique to mate.
    (C) to pinpoint hormone fluctuations are bad for those female bees.
    (D) to show that the sexual discourse will only benefit male bees.

▶▶ 新托福聽力解析

1. 表格中 A 選項，desensitize 是聽力原文中 paralyze 的同義轉換，澳洲泥蜂也是屬於黃蜂家族，也具備癱瘓獵物的能力，所以澳洲泥蜂和黃蜂都要打勾。B 選項，聽力訊息中 the latter will encounter more hurdles 指的是澳洲泥鋒，但選項中表達的是 less obstacles，所以只有黃蜂的部分需要打勾。C 選項的 tunnel-shaped nests 指的是 Dawson's bees，故**兩者都不符合**。D 選項，indiscriminately build the nests，聽力訊息中的 randomly 換成了 indiscriminately，故要勾選黃蜂的選項。

2. 表格中 A 選項，paralyze the prey 這項能力，honey bees 和 hornets 均不符合。B 選項，kill sizable insects 是聽力訊息中 take down large insects 的同義轉換，為 hornets 的敘述。C 選項，ability to pogrom，pogrom= massacre，故要勾選 hornets。D 選項，use heat to defend 為 honey bees 的敘述，honey bees 用集體攀爬到大黃蜂身上的策略，以溫度殺死大黃蜂。

3. 表格中 A 選項，high competition 指的是 male bees，在雄性之間是高度競爭的。B 選項，panmictic，聽力訊息中所表達的是 Since Dawson's bees are panmictic，包含了 female 和 male，故**兩個都要勾選**。C 選項，construct the nest，聽力訊息中描述 Only female bees will build the nest.，故只有 female 要勾選。D 選項，remain unchanged after the sexual discourse，聽力訊息中講述到 female 在性交後體內化學物質會產生變化，故要勾選 male。

4. 表格中 A 選項，gregarious 指的是 honey bees，且聽力訊息中有表達出 dawson's bees are unique solitary nest-builders。B 選項，tunnel-shaped nests 指的是 dawson's bees。C 選項，kill hornets 指的是 honey bees，honey bees 能靠集體策略殺死 hornets。D 選項，sacrifices are made during mating season 指的是 male dawson's bees，故要選 Dawson's bees。

5. 這題要選 D，to show that they are still capable of reversing its disadvantageous situation，turn the table 指的就是能夠扭轉情勢。蜜蜂在有些情況下是能夠擊敗大黃蜂的。

6. 這題要選 D，because their nests are neighboring，因為牠們所築的巢穴太緊鄰彼此了，一旦被天敵發現就會全軍覆沒，但是 wasp 就不會有這樣的問題，因為牠們是隨機找地點築巢。

7. 這題要選 C，an occluded home for the young，occluded 等於 sealed，在前段提到 mud daubers 時有講到會提供幼蟲 a sealed home，這點跟後面提到的 Dawson's bees 之後會將巢穴密封起來是一樣的。

8. 這題要選 A，emulation 指的就是 competition，本來對雄性蜂來說競爭就很激烈了，每一個從穴中探出來的雌性蜜蜂都有很多競爭者。教授進一步指出，雌性在交配後，抑制其與雄性交配的慾望，進一步又強化了雄性間的競爭性，雄性變得要搶奪更少數的資源了。

答案： 1. A/ABD 2. D/BC 3. BC/AB 4. AC/BD 5. D 6. D 7. C 8. A

影子跟讀練習 MP3 012

做完題目後，除了對答案知道錯的部分在哪外，更重要的是要修正自己聽力根本的問題，即聽力理解力和聽力專注力，聽力專注力的修正能逐步強化本身的聽力實力，所以現在請根據聽力內容「逐個段落」、「數個段落」或「整篇」進行跟讀練習，提升在實際考場時專注聽完每個訊息、定位出關鍵考點和搭配筆記回答完所有題目。Go!

Wow what are those... eleven potatoes attached on the wall... looks like decorations from the neighborhood kids?...looks equally dark brown... but in fact, they are mud daubers. Mud daubers are also known as mud wasps or dirt daubers... You get to use these terminologies interchangeably... let's take a look at the slide here... the color actually ranges from dark brown to light yellow... it really depends on the surroundings they are in or to be more correctly the dirt they have gathered...

哇！那些是什麼啊...11 個番薯附著在牆壁上...看起來像是社區裡小孩們的裝飾？...每個看起來都同樣地暗咖啡色...但是，實際上，牠們是澳洲泥蜂。澳洲泥蜂也可以稱作是泥黃蜂或是泥汙蜂...你可以互換地使用那些術語...讓我們看一下這裡的簡報圖片...顏色範圍實際上從暗咖啡色到亮黃色都有...顏色其實是根據牠們所處的環境或是更正確地説是根據牠們所收集來的泥土...。

Witnessing their nests won't scare me at all... they are not that frightening... Mud daubers might be known for their belligerent personality, but they are quite docile if you just leave them alone.

目睹到他們的巢穴一點也不會讓我感到驚嚇…他們沒有那麼讓人畏懼…澳洲泥蜂可能以他們好戰的性格聞名，但是他們相當的溫馴，如果你不驚擾他們的話。

After building the nest, mud daubers will lay their eggs. Inside the nest, you will find the pupa and the larva, and of course around twenty paralyzed spiders for the larva to consume. The larva will have a sealed home with plenty of gourmet abundant with protein for it to enjoy.

在建造巢穴後，澳洲泥蜂會產下他們的蛋。在巢穴裡頭，你會發現蛹和幼蟲，而當然會發現的還有大約 20 隻左右癱瘓的蜘蛛以供幼蟲食用。幼蟲將會有個密封的家，有著許多富含蛋白質的美食供其食用。

字彙輔助

1 decoration 裝飾
2 terminologies 術語
3 interchangeably 互換地
4 surroundings 環境
5 belligerent 好戰的
6 docile 溫馴的
7 pupa 蛹
8 larva 幼蟲
9 sealed 密封的
10 abundant 豐富的

And it's astonishing to find that blue mud daubers feed on black widows. ... and for those of you who are having questions of how these mud daubers paralyzes the spider. We can begin by mentioning traits of these wasps. Wasps have the ability to paralyze the prey by using the sting to repeatedly sting the prey, such as tarantulas. And mud daubers also belong to the wasp's family, so they too are equipped with this ability. The injection of the neurotoxic venom on tarantula's body will only make them temporarily lose consciousness. The tarantula will be a zombie and it gets dragged to the larder of the wasp. The key difference between the wasp and the mud dauber is that the latter will encounter more hurdles. Predators are able to kill a group of the mud daubers at the same time, since the nest of the mud daubers is immensely close or adjacent to one another. Wasps, on the other hand, randomly build the larders in the habitat.

而令人感到震驚的發現還有藍色澳洲泥蜂以黑寡婦為食...然後你們之中有些人有著關於這些澳洲泥蜂是如何癱瘓蜘蛛的問題。我們可以藉由提及這些黃蜂的特性開始講述。黃蜂有個能夠癱瘓其獵物的能力，藉由使用螫針反覆地螫獵物，像是狼蛛。而且澳洲泥蜂也是屬於黃蜂家族的，所以他們也配有這項能力。注入神經毒素到狼蛛的身體將會使其短暫的失去意識。狼蛛會成了殭屍，而且被拖到黃蜂的巢穴裡。黃蜂和澳洲泥蜂最關鍵的不同在於後者會遭遇到更多的阻礙。掠食者能夠同時殺死一群澳洲泥蜂，因為澳洲泥蜂的巢穴極其靠近或是彼此緊鄰。在另一方面，黃蜂則在棲地上隨意地建構巢穴。

文學跨領域

商管跨領域

其他

字彙輔助

1 astonishing 令人驚訝的　　2 paralyze 癱瘓

3 repeatedly 重複地　　4 injection 注射

5 neurotoxic 毒害神經的　　6 venom 毒素

7 temporarily 暫時性地　　8 consciousness 意識

9 immensely 巨大地　　10 adjacent 鄰近的

In addition to the remarkable ability of wasps, the close relative of the wasp, hornets, are also fascinating. Hornets are able to take down large insects, such as mantises, which provide their offspring with a large source of protein. They contain larger venom than typical wasps. They are considered as quite incredibly cruel predators since hornets stage a large battle to other bee colonies, carrying with them larvae and adults for their young. The massacre can destroy an entire bee colony. It is not an individual fight like what a wasp does to a tarantula. The fight involves hundreds of corpses. It is the example of the cannibalization about what hornets can not only do to other insects, but species of the similar kind, such as honey bees.

除了黃蜂卓越的能力之外，黃蜂的近親，大黃蜂也是吸引人的。大黃蜂能夠打倒大型昆蟲，例如螳螂，以提供牠們後代大量的蛋白質。比起黃蜂，牠們包含較大量的毒液。牠們也被視為是相當驚人的殘酷掠食者，因為黃蜂可以策劃與其它蜂群的大型戰鬥，將牠們的幼蟲和成年蜂提供給大黃蜂幼蟲食用。此屠殺可以毀掉整個蜂群，這不只是個人戰鬥，像黃蜂對於狼蛛那般，戰鬥牽涉到幾百個屍體。這是同類相殘的例子，顯示出的不只是大黃蜂能如何對付其他昆蟲，更是牠們能如何對付如蜜蜂等的相似物種。

字彙輔助

1. remarkable 非凡的；卓越的
2. fascinating 迷人的；極美的
3. protein 蛋白質
4. contain 包含
5. typical 典型的
6. incredibly 驚人地
7. massacre 大屠殺、殘殺
8. individual 個體的
9. cannibalization 同類相殘
10. similar 相似地

Stunning as these fights are, they only tell part of the story. Honeybees are able to turn the table in some instances. What honeybees lack in physique and strength is well-known, but the number and defending strategies make up for their weaknesses. For example, when honeybees find out the scout of the hornets, honeybees do not launch an attack. Instead, they wait for the individual hornet to go inside the hive. Then the honeybees clamber all over the hornet, forming a large bee ball. The hornet obviously cannot survive under the heat, generated by hundreds of bees. While these honeybees are flipping their wings and join one another, the amount of heat is doubled, making the center increasingly heated. Increasing honeybees that enhance the temperature around a giant hornet can be quite lethal, since its body cannot endure a sudden surge of heat. The temperature has been raised to a point that the hornets cannot withstand. This happens when the attack of the hornets is very few and far between. Hornets are still notoriously hard to get rid of especially when the number of the hornets are much greater. They can facilely tear the head of the honeybees in an instant...

　　這些令人感到驚艷的戰鬥，牠們僅述説了故事的一部分。蜜蜂能夠在某些情況下扭轉情勢。蜜蜂所缺乏的體型和力量是廣為人知的，但是數量和防衛策略卻彌補了牠們的弱點，例如，當蜜蜂發現了大黃蜂的偵查兵時，蜜蜂不會發起戰鬥，取而代之的是，牠們等待個體黃蜂進到蜂巢裡，然後，蜜蜂攀爬到大黃蜂身上，形成一個大型的蜜蜂球體。大黃蜂顯然無法在那樣由數百隻蜜蜂所產生的熱度下存活。而這些蜜蜂震動牠們的翅膀並且加入其中，熱度就倍增了，導致中心的熱度不斷增加。日益增多的蜜蜂增加了大黃蜂周圍的溫度，這對大黃蜂來説可是相當致命，因為其身體無法忍受突然猛增的熱度。溫度已升至大黃蜂無法忍受的溫度。這個情況發生於當大黃蜂的數量少，而其攻擊是零星的時候。大黃蜂還是很難纏的，尤其是當大黃蜂的數量非常多的時候。牠們可以輕而易舉地撕掉蜜蜂的頭部...。

字彙輔助

1. physique 體格
2. strength 力量
3. weakness 弱點
4. scout 偵查兵
5. launch 發起
6. generate 產生
7. increasingly 日益增加地
8. withstand 抵抗

Next, I'm going to introduce bees which live underground. Dawson's bees... Dawson's bees are one of the largest Australian bees, also known as Dawson's burrowing bees, and they are unique solitary nest-builders, unlike many bees which are gregarious creatures. Only female bees will build the nest. Tunnel-shaped nests on the ground are living proof to show that those females are innately equipped with the ability to build a nest... It's also intriguing to note that female bees also cap the cell with the mud... like mud daubers...

接下來我要介紹的蜜蜂居住於地底下。道森蜂...道森蜂是澳洲最大型的蜜蜂之一，也稱作道森穴居蜂，而且牠們是獨特的獨居巢穴建造者，不同於許多社交性的蜜蜂。僅有雌性蜜蜂會建造巢穴。地面上隧道形狀的巢穴是現存的證據，顯示著那些雌性蜜蜂天生就具備著建造巢穴的能力...同樣有趣的是，雌性蜜蜂也會以泥土覆蓋蜂房的巢室...這點跟澳洲泥蜂是相同的...。

Males are competitive and combative especially during the mating season. Chemical signals emitted by females, which are about to emerge from the ground, can be a trigger for the increasingly fierce fighting... it resembles the world of the human world in that a small percentage of the male bees are getting the chance to mate with the females. Sacrifices are required if those male bees want to mate with the female. Sometimes a kill can be made before the male touches the female. Since Dawson's bees are panmictic, randomly mating with other males is common. Females might have the slightest chance to mate with several males during the mating... perhaps that will increase the diversity of the overall species and that's for the benefit of the evolution...

雄性道森蜂具競爭性和好戰性，特別是在交配季節。由即將出土的雌性蜜蜂所釋放的化學訊息可能引燃了越益激烈的戰鬥...。這跟人類世界相似，很少比例的雄性蜜蜂會得到與雌性蜜蜂交配的機會。犧牲是必須的，如果那些雄性蜜蜂想要與雌性蜜蜂交配的話。有時候廝殺在雄性蜜蜂接觸到雌性蜜蜂之前就開始了。既然道森蜜蜂有著在一個繁殖族群內會隨意交配的特徵，與其他雄性蜜蜂隨意交配是普遍的。在交配期間，雌性道森蜜蜂可能只有極小的機會與幾個雄性蜜蜂交配...可能這樣會增進整體種族的多樣性，且以演化觀點來說是有益的...。

However, it is also important to know that a change in body hormones happens right after the copulation of a female, therefore, counteracting the sexual discourse. This has a lot to do with the high competition in males as well. The chance for males to get mated has been greatly reduced...

然而，也很重要的一點是，在雌性蜜蜂交配後，體內的荷爾蒙就會發生變化，因此，抑制其接受性交。這也與雄性蜜蜂高度競爭的特性有關連。雄性蜜蜂獲得交配的機會大幅降低了...。

字彙輔助

1. solitary 獨自的
2. gregarious 群居性的
3. creature 生物
4. innately 天生地
5. combative 好戰的
6. emerge 出現
7. percentage 百分比
8. panmictic 隨意交配
9. diversity 多樣性
10. evolution 演化

▶▶ 試題聽力原文

1. The following statements list traits of dirt daubers and their category
   Click in the correct box for each category
2. The following statements list traits of honey bees and hornets
   Click in the correct box for each category
3. The following statements list traits of dawson's bees
   Click in the correct box for each category
4. The following statements list traits of honey bees and dawson's bees
   Click in the correct box for each category
5. Listen again to part of the lecture. Then answer the question.
   "Stunning as these fights are, they only tell part of the story. Honeybees are able to turn the table in some instances. What honeybees lack in physique and

strength is well-known, but the number of defending strategies make up for their weaknesses."

Why does the professor mention "Stunning as these fights are, they only tell part of the story. Honeybees are able to turn the table in some instances."

6. Why do dirt daubers have more unpleasant struggle than wasps?

7. What is the resemblance between mud daubers and female Dawson's bees?

8. Listen again to part of the lecture. Then answer the question.

However, it is also important to know that a change in body hormones happens right after the copulation of a female, therefore, counteracting the sexual discourse.

Why does the professor mention the copulation?

N O T E

▶▶ 記筆記與聽力訊息

| Instruction | MP3 012

　　新托福聽力與其他聽力測驗不同，可以於聽力的紙上記筆記，除了寫試題外，更重要的一點是訓練自己能夠在聽完一段訊息後，將重要的聽力訊息都記下。也可以將自己聽到跟記到的重點訊息跟試題做比對，因為試題考的就是長對話跟講座中出現的重點，能修正自己選取聽力訊息重點的能力。

| 聽力重點 |

- 記筆記有很多方式，包含符號跟自己習慣的縮寫字等等，可以找出最適合自己的模式，一定要自己重複聽音檔作練習數次。
- 這篇是關於生物學，**有很多表格題，對於訓練聽讀能力至關重要，要區分內文中提到的主要幾種蜜蜂和一些隱晦的訊息，綜合提到的訊息才能答對。**

NOTE

▶▶ **參考筆記**

Main idea ❶	
Mud daubers	• mud wasps or dirt daubers • belligerent personality, but they are quite docile if you just leave them alone.
the nest	the pupa and the larva
The larva	a sealed home with plenty of gourmet abundant with protein for it to enjoy
blue mud daubers	black widows
Main idea ❷	
Wasps	• the ability to paralyze the prey by using the sting • injection of the neurotoxic venom • randomly build the larders/ encounter less obstacles
hornets	• the close relative of the wasp • take down large insects, such as mantises • stage a large battle to other bee colonies/ cannibalization

Main idea ❸	
Honeybees	• turn the table in some instances • wait for the individual hornet to go inside the hive • clamber all over the hornet • cannot endure a sudden surge of heat

Main idea ❹	
Dawson's bees	• live underground • unique solitary nest-builders • females are innately equipped with the ability to build a nest • cap the cell with the mud... like mud daubers... • panmictic
Males	• competitive and combative • a small percentage of the male bees are getting the chance to mate with the females
Females	• have the slightest chance to mate with several males • a change in body hormones happens right after the copulation of a female, therefore, counteracting the sexual discourse

▶▶ 填空測驗

| Instruction | MP3 012

　　現在請再聽一次音檔，並做下列的測驗，檢視自己能否完成此填空測驗和強化自己聽力能力和拼字能力，降低自己漏聽到聽力訊息的機會，大幅提升應考實力。

　　Wow what are those... eleven potatoes **1.** _____ on the wall... looks like **2.** _____ from the neighborhood kids?...looks equally dark brown... but in fact, they are mud daubers. Mud daubers are also known as mud wasps or dirt daubers... You get to use those **3.** _____ interchangeably... let's take a look at the slide here... the color actually ranges from dark brown to light yellow... it really depends on the **4.** _____ they are in or to be more correctly the dirt they have gathered...

　　5. _____ their nests won't scare me at all... they are not that frightening... Mud daubers might be known for their **6.** _____ personality, but they are quite **7.** _____ if you just leave them alone. After building the nest, mud daubers will lay their eggs.

　　Inside the nest, you will find the **8.** _____ and the larva, and of course around twenty **9.** _____ spiders for the larva to consume. The larva will have a sealed home with plenty of **10.** _____ abundant with protein for it to enjoy. And it's astonishing to find that blue mud daubers feed on **11.** _____. ... and for those of you who are having questions of how these mud daubers paralyzes the spider.

We can begin by mentioning traits of these wasps. Wasps have the ability to paralyze the prey by using the sting to **12.** _____ sting the prey, such as tarantulas. And mud daubers also belong to the wasp's family, so they too are equipped with this ability. The **13.** _____ of the neurotoxic venom on tarantula's body will only make them **14.** _____ loose consciousness. The tarantula will be a **15.** _____ and it gets dragged to the **16.** _____ of the wasp. The key difference between the wasp and the mud dauber is that the latter will encounter more hurdles.

Predators are able to kill a group of the mud daubers at the same time, since the nest of the mud daubers is **17.** ____ _____ close or adjacent to one another. Wasps, on the other hand, randomly build the larders in the habitat.

In addition to the **18.** _____ ability of wasps, the close relative of the wasp, hornets, are also **19.** _____. Hornets are able to take down large insects, such as mantises, which provide their **20.** _____ with a large source of protein. They contain larger **21.** _____ than typical wasps.

They are considered as quite **22.** _____ cruel predators since hornets stage a large battle to other bee **23.** _____, carrying with them the larvae and adults for their young. The **24.** _____ can destroy an entire bee colony. It is not an individual fight like what a wasp does to a tarantula. The fight involves hundreds of **25.** _____. It is the example of the cannibalization about what hornets can not only do to other insects, but species of the similar kind, such as honey bees.

Stunning as these fights are, they only tell part of the story. Honeybees are able to turn the table in some instances. What honeybees lack in **26.** _____ and strength is well-known, but the number and **27.** _____ strategies make up for their **28.** _____. For example, when honeybees find out the scout of the hornets, honeybees do not **29.** _____ an attack.

Instead, they wait for the individual hornet to go inside the **30.** _____. Then the honeybees **31.** _____ all over the hornet, forming a large bee ball. The hornet obviously cannot survive under the heat, **32.** _____ by hundreds of bees. While these honeybees are flipping their wings and join one another, the amount of heat is doubled, making the center increasingly heated. Increasing honeybees that **33.** _____ the temperature around a giant hornet can be quite **34.** _____, since its body cannot endure a sudden **35.** _____ of heat. The temperature has been raised to a point that the hornets cannot withstand. This happens when the attack of the hornets is very few and far between. Hornets are still **36.** _____ hard to get rid of especially when the number of the hornets are much greater.

They can facilely tear the head of the honeybees in an instant... Dawson's bees are one of the largest Australian bees, also known as Dawson's burrowing bees, and they are unique **37.** _____ nest-builders, unlike many bees which are gregarious creatures. Only female bees will build the nest. Tunnel-shaped nests on the ground are living **38.** _____ to show that those females are **39.** _____ equipped with the ability to build a nest... It's also intriguing to note that female bees also cap the cell with the mud... like mud daubers...

Males are competitive and **40.** _____ especially during the mating season. Chemical signals emitted by females, which are about to emerge from the ground, can be a **41.** _____ for the increasingly fierce fighting... it resembles the world of the human world in that a small **42.** _____ of the male bees are getting the chance to mate with the females. Sacrifices are required if those male bees want to mate with the female. Sometimes a kill can be made before the male touches the female.

Since Dawson's bees are **43.** _____, randomly mating with other males is common. Females might have the slightest chance to mate with several males during the mating... perhaps that will increase the **44.** _____ of the overall species and that's for the benefit of the evolution... However, it is also important to know that a change in body **45.** _____ happens right after the **46.** _____ of a female, therefore, counteracting the sexual discourse. This has a lot to do with the high competition in males as well. The chance for males to get mated has been greatly reduced...

| 參考答案 |

1. attached	2. decorations
3. terminologies	4. surroundings
5. Witnessing	6. belligerent
7. docile	8. pupa
9. paralyzed	10. gourmet
11. black widows	12. repeatedly
13. injection	14. temporarily
15. zombie	16. larder
17. immensely	18. remarkable
19. fascinating	20. offspring
21. venom	22. incredibly
23. colonies	24. massacre
25. corpses	26. physique

27. defending	28. weaknesses
29. launch	30. hive
31. clamber	32. generated
33. enhance	34. lethal
35. surge	36. notoriously
37. solitary	38. proof
39. innately	40. combative
41. trigger	42. percentage
43. panmictic	44. diversity
45. hormones	46. copulation

▶▶ 摘要能力

| Instruction | MP3 012

　　除了閱讀測驗外，其實培養能在聽完一大段訊息後，口述剛才聽到的聽力訊息是學習語言和表達很重要的一件事，讓自己養成並具備這樣的能力，除了能在聽力測驗中獲取高分外，也能在新托福寫作跟口說的整合題型上大有斬獲喔！所以快來練習，除了書中提供的參考答案外，自己可以試著重新聽過音檔一遍後，摘要出英文訊息並朗讀出來。

▶▶ 參考答案

Mud daubers are also known as mud wasps or dirt daubers. Mud daubers might be known for their belligerent personality, but they are quite docile if you just leave them alone. After building the nest, mud daubers will lay their eggs. Inside the nest, you will find the pupa and the larva, and of course around twenty paralyzed spiders for the larva to consume. The larva will have a sealed home with plenty of gourmet abundant with protein for it to enjoy.

These mud daubers share the same trait with their similar cousins: wasps. They paralyze the spider. The injection of the neurotoxic venom on tarantula's body will only make them temporarily lose consciousness. The key difference between the wasp and the mud dauber is that the latter will encounter more hurdles. Predators are able to kill a group of the mud daubers at the same time, since the nest of the mud daubers is immensely close or adjacent to one another. Wasps, on the other hand, randomly build the larders in the habitat.

In addition to the remarkable ability of wasps, the close relative of the wasp, hornets, are also fascinating. Hornets are able to take down large insects, such as mantises, which provide their offspring with a large source of protein. They contain larger venom than typical wasps. They are considered as quite incredibly cruel predators since hornets stage a large battle to other bee colonies, carrying with them the larvae and adults for their young. The massacre can destroy an entire bee colony.

However, honeybees are able to turn the table in some instances. What honeybees lack in physique and strength is well-known, but the number and defending strategies make up for their weaknesses. Large bee balls can create higher temperatures that those hornets cannot stand, and therefore cook those hornets. Hornets are still notoriously hard to get rid of especially when the number of the hornets are much greater.

Dawson's bees are one of the largest Australian bees, also known as Dawson's burrowing bees, and they are unique solitary nest-builders, unlike many bees which are gregarious creatures. Only female bees will build the nest.

Tunnel-shaped nests on the ground are living proof to show that those females are innately equipped with the ability to build a nest.

Males are competitive and combative especially during the mating season. Chemical signals emitted by females, which are about to emerge from the ground, can be a trigger for the increasingly fierce fighting... Sacrifices are required if those male bees want to mate with the female. Since Dawson's bees are panmictic, randomly mating with other males is common. Females might have the slightest chance to mate with several males during the mating... perhaps that will increase the diversity of the overall species and that's for the benefit of the evolution...

Hormone changes in females will make the competition fiercer because female bees will not show the interest in mating. This will cause a reduction for male bees to get mated.

UNIT 13 ▶▶ 《Women Who Love too Much》為什麼最終如願跟第三者在一起並結婚了，彼此卻不快樂？

▶▶▶ **聽力試題** MP3 013

1. Listen again to part of the lecture. Then answer the question.
   (A) to encourage the lash out against the other women
   (B) to reduce the sense of loneliness
   (C) to further illustrate the phenomenon after the introduction
   (D) to overvalue the impending crisis

2. What can be inferred about Lucy?
   (A) She never intends to be the other woman.
   (B) She likes the feel of getting touched by Carlos.
   (C) Gaby has never had the slightest doubt about Lucy.
   (D) Her outer appearance cannot compete with Gaby.

3. Listen again to part of the lecture. Then answer the question.
   (A) Lynette has stronger intuition to be Gaby's spy.
   (B) Gaby wants to keep a watchful eye on them herself.
   (C) Gaby's instinct tells her that something is going on.
   (D) Gaby totally trusts her husband's faithfulness

4. The following list the predictions about being the other women.

Click in the correct box.

predictions
A. instinct
B. fewer candidates
C. movie's influence
D. fate
E. financial pressures
F. fastidiousness
G. heredity
H. guy's receptiveness

5. Listen again to part of the lecture. Then answer the question.

(A) Helen should take the total blame.

(B) They don't care about karma because they are westerners.

(C) Helen will be replaced by another woman in the future.

(D) Charles seduces Helen in the coffee shop.

▶▶ 新托福聽力解析

1. 教授提到這點的原因是要在引入這話題後，進一步闡明這個現象，才提到後面這幾句話，故答案要選**選項 C**。

2. 聽力訊息中無法判定 Lucy 是否是第三者，僅知道 Gaby 對她有所懷疑，故要排除 A。文中也沒有辦法判定她喜歡被 touch，故要排除 B。Gaby 對 Lucy 有所懷疑，故要排除 C，Gaby 有説 Lucy 不是 competition，故**要選 D**。

3. 聽力訊息中沒有針對 Gaby 和 Lynette 的直覺進行比較，故無法判斷，要排除 A。聽力訊息中有明確表明 Gaby 的直覺告訴她不太對，故答案要選**選項 C**。

4. **B** 的 fewer candidates 對應到符合經濟等條件的男人較少。文中沒有提到 movie's influence 故要排除 C。文中有提到可能是 **fate**，故**要選 D**。沒有提到女性有 financial pressures，故要排除 E。文中敘述中有描述到不想 settle down 等，都符合了挑選和挑剔等，這點對應到 **F**。文中沒有提到 heredity 故要排除。文中有提到男人太容易接受投懷送抱，這點對應到 **guy's receptiveness**，故**要選 H**。

5. 也沒辦法判定責任在第三者也就是 Helen 身上，故排除 A。文中有提到 karma 和跟東方人思維不同，但是沒辦法判定他們不 care karma，故排除 B。文中也沒辦法判定 Helen 在咖啡廳誘惑 Charles，故排除 D。根據敘述的部分，可以推測出 Helen 因為當了第三者，故在未來可能也面臨相同的命運，答案**要選 C**。

答案： 1. C 2. D 3. C 4. BDFH 5. C

影子跟讀練習 MP3 013

做完題目後，除了對答案知道錯的部分在哪外，更重要的是要修正自己聽力根本的問題，即聽力理解力和聽力專注力，聽力專注力的修正能逐步強化本身的聽力實力，所以現在請根據聽力內容「逐個段落」、「數個段落」或「整篇」進行跟讀練習，提升在實際考場時專注聽完每個訊息、定位出關鍵考點和搭配筆記回答完所有題目。Go!

We all want to be happy, and yet turn out to be so unhappy... and I believe that no one sets out to become the other woman or the other man... but the problem of the other woman does exist and it threatens the status of the wife... people condemn the behavior of the stealing of one's spouse so much that they are making the decision of not buying the advertised products of the star, who is cheating on his or her spouse... it's quite true that if you don't defend those who suffer, chances are that when you are in the same situation... you are alone...

我們都想要快樂，可是卻變得不快樂…而我相信沒有人會將自己設定成要變成小三或者是小王…但是小三的問題確實是存在著，而且這威脅到了正宮的地位…人們是如此譴責竊取別人配偶的行為，以致於民眾不會去購買對自己配偶不忠的明星所代言的廣告商品…相當真實的是，如果你不替那些因為受配偶外遇而苦惱的人辯護的話，很可能當這件事情是發生你在身上時...你只剩自己一人獨自面對...。

In *Desperate Housewives*, Gaby is told that her husband, Carlos is going to invite his ex-girlfriend Lucy for dinner... her antenna goes up... Gaby tells her husband... **"I will not be on board"**... to which he replies... I'm in over my head with this new job... please... I need Lucy's help... please don't be jealous... and hours later when they answer the door, Gaby is relieved to find out that Lucy is no competition. Lucy is apparently overweight. The dinner goes well till Lucy takes a phone call for business. She got a really hard-to-land guy for Carlos. And she says **"poaching is easier when you say something like we are going to double your salary..."** then Carlos touches Lucy's butt... an act that makes Gaby cast doubt on them...

在「慾望師奶」中，蓋比被她丈夫卡洛斯告知他將要邀請他前女友露西到家中晚餐...她的理智線快要斷了...蓋比告訴她丈夫...「我不會同意的」...對此她丈夫回應...這份新工作已搞得我焦頭爛額了...拜託...我需要露西的幫忙...請別忌妒...幾個小時之後，他們應門，蓋比發現露西不是對手後就鬆了一口氣。露西顯然體重過重。晚餐進行的很順利，直到露西接了一通商業電話。露西替卡洛斯挖角了一位很難獵取到的員工。然後她說道「獵人頭變得更容易，當你說著像是我們會讓你薪資加倍。」...接著，卡洛斯就觸碰露西的臀部...這個舉動讓蓋比對他們起了疑心...。

字彙輔助

1 threaten 威脅
2 condemn 譴責
3 advertising 廣告
4 product 產品
5 antenna 天線
6 jealous 忌妒的
7 overweight 過重的
8 poaching 偷獵

When people are in a relationship, people are constantly worried about getting cheated on. Women have such strong intuition that they can tell with the slightest thing that something is going on.... even in Gaby's case... she is not threatened by Lucy... yet she sends her friend Lynette to be her spy and keeps a watchful eye on them during work...

當人們在一段感情中，總會不斷地擔憂伴侶可能會外遇。女性有著如此強烈的直覺，所以他們可以察覺出細微事，當中一定有什麼事情發生了…即使在蓋比的情況中…她並不覺得露西對她造成威脅…然而，她還是派了她的朋友奈勒特充當她的間諜並且在工作期間監視他們…。

This also serves as a great opening for us to discuss today's topic about **"Charles's attraction to Helen"** why would someone want to become the other woman? Is it because at the right age especially after 30, most well-to-do men are already married, and women don't want to settle down to someone whose salary and other things are below her... great guys are too slim in pickings... or is it because things just happen? It's fate... or is it the explanation of the drama... the person who doesn't get loved is the other woman... or is it because guys will take any chance with those who come to them? And it's innate to them... or is it because being in love and being married are two different things... being in love is at the stage you get the romance and do not have other concerns, such as financial pressures... so it's relatively easy... when being married... it creates the loophole for either party to fall into others. Married people don't get admiration from their spouse but from the other woman... and that can be a problem...

　　這也充當了我們今天要談論的話題「查理斯對海倫的吸引力」很好的開端，為什麼有人會想要成為小三呢？是因為在適婚年紀，特別是過了 30 歲後，大多數富有的男性都已婚了，而女人不想要屈就薪資和其他條件都低於自己的人…條件好的男性太鳳毛麟角了…亦或是因為事情（成為小三）就這樣發生了。這是命運…又或是從電視劇中得到的解釋…不被愛的人才是小三…還是因為男人都會接受靠近自己的女性，只要有機會的話？而這是他們的天性…又或是戀愛和結婚是兩回事…戀愛是你獲取浪漫情感的階段而不用有其他考量，例如財務壓力，所以是相對簡單的…當結婚時…其對任一方產生了易於愛上其他人的漏洞。已婚者從自己伴侶身上得不到欽佩感，但是從其他女人身上卻能得到…而這樣就會產生問題了…。

字彙輔助

1 constantly 不斷地

2 watchful 警惕的；戒備的

3 explanation 解釋

4 romance 浪漫

5 admiration 欽佩

6 loophole 漏洞

Even though Charles let Helen know he was married..., he loved the appreciation from Helen.... that's the first sign that I think his marriage is not going to last... the second alarm is his attraction to his wife dwindles... but what puzzles me the most is that if he gets a divorce and eventually gets to be with Helen... and get married... pretty simple... but why can't they live happily there after...?

即使查理斯讓海倫知道他已婚了...，他喜愛從海倫那裡得到的欣賞...那也是我認為他的婚姻不會持久下去的第一個徵兆...第二個警報是他對於自己妻子的吸引力下滑了...但是令我感到困惑的是，如果他離婚了且最終能跟海倫在一起...並且結婚...相當簡單的流程...但是為什麼他們無法從此過的幸福快樂呢？

let's take a look at the analysis... it's on page... 123... **"Helen wanted only what she couldn't really have."** Only an unavailable man can provide her that kind of love... another key point that the author points out is that excitement is gone... when they are in a commitment period... that is totally a different explanation from the eastern point of view... we believe that there is karma... whatever you are getting... you are going to lose that way... that means... today... you get to be the other woman and steal your friend's husband... when the time comes... you are going to face the same fate as the ex-wife... you are going to end up getting divorced and being replaced by another woman... no exceptions... and I want you all to write about how you feel about this story... it's about time to take a break... and I'm going to take a phone call from the dean... for the next hour... you are going to write 500 words and hand it in to my assistant... Jane...

讓我們看一下解析...是在第 123 頁...「海倫只想要她沒辦法真正擁有的。」只有得不到的男人可以提供她那樣的愛情...另一個作者有指出的關鍵是在於彼此間的興奮感消失了...當他們處於承諾階段時...這解釋全然與東方的觀點截然不同...我們相信是有因果報應的...你怎麼得到的，就會怎麼失去...那也意謂著...今天...你成了別人的小三且奪取了你朋友的丈夫...當時候到的時候...你會面臨與他前妻相同的命運...你最終也會以離婚收場並且被另一個女人所取而代之...沒有例外...而現在我想要你們撰寫關於這個故事的感受...也快下課了...我要接一下院長的來電...接下來的一小時...你們要寫 500 字英文，然後交給我的助理...簡...。

字彙輔助

1 appreciation 欣賞

2 alarm 警覺

3 dwindle 減少

4 divorce 離婚

5 unavailable 得不到的　　6 excitement 興奮

7 commitment 承諾　　　 8 karma 因果報應

9 fate 命運　　　　　　 10 exception 例外

▶▶ 試題聽力原文

1. Listen again to part of the lecture. Then answer the question.

   It's quite true that if you don't defend those who suffer, chances are that when you are in the same situation... you are alone...

   Why does the professor mention this?

2. What can be inferred about Lucy?

3. Listen again to part of the lecture. Then answer the question.

   Women have such strong intuition that they can tell with the slightest thing that something is going on.... even in Gaby's case... she is not threatened by Lucy... yet she sends her friend Lynette to be her spy and keeps a watchful eye on them during work...

   What can be inferred about Gaby's response?

4. The following lists the predictions about being the other women.

   Click in the correct box.

5. Listen again to part of the lecture. Then answer the question.

... you get to be the other woman and steal your friend's husband... when the time comes... you are going to face the same fate as his ex-wife... you are going to end up getting divorced and being replaced by another woman... no exceptions...

What can be inferred about Charles and Helen's affair?

▶▶ 記筆記與聽力訊息

| Instruction | MP3 013

　　新托福聽力與其他聽力測驗不同，可以於聽力的紙上記筆記，除了寫試題外，更重要的一點是訓練自己能夠在聽完一段訊息後，將重要的聽力訊息都記下。也可以將自己聽到跟記到的重點訊息跟試題做比對，因為試題考的就是長對話跟講座中出現的重點，能修正自己選取聽力訊息重點的能力。

| 聽力重點 |

- 記筆記有很多方式，包含符號跟自己習慣的縮寫字等等，可以找出最適合自己的模式，一定要自己重複聽音檔作練習數次。
- 這篇是關於心理學，**包含了更高階的同義轉換能力和複選題，更能鑑別出考生程度，多練習幾種同義字替換等就能強化這類的答題。**

▶▶ 參考筆記

Main idea ❶	
happiness	unattainable
the problem of the other woman	does exist and it threatens the status of the wife
condemn the behavior	not buying the advertised products
don't defend those who suffer	you are alone

Main idea ❷	
Desperate Housewives	• Gaby is not threatened by Lucy • Intuition drives Gaby's inspection on Lucy and her husband

Main idea ❸	
Multiple reasons	• fewer candidates • fate • fastidiousness • guy's receptiveness

Main idea ④

"Charles's attraction to Helen"	• that's the first sign that I think his marriage is not going to last... the second alarm is his attraction to his wife dwindles... • "Helen wanted only what she couldn't really have." Only an unavailable man can provide her that kind of love...
others	• Karma/ eastern point of view

▶▶ 填空測驗

| Instruction | MP3 013

現在請再聽一次音檔，並做下列的測驗，檢視自己能否完成此填空測驗和強化自己聽力能力和拼字能力，降低自己漏聽到聽力訊息的機會，大幅提升應考實力。

We all want to be happy, and yet turn out to be so unhappy... and I believe that no one sets out to become the other woman or the other man... but the problem of the other woman does **1. _____** and it **2. _____** the status of the wife... people **3. _____** the behavior of the stealing of one's spouse so much that they are making the decision of not buying the **4. _____** products of the star, who is cheating on his or her spouse...

it's quite true that if you don't **5. _____** those who suffer, chances are that when you are in the same situation... you are alone...

In *Desperate Housewives*, Gaby is told that her husband, Carlos is going to invite his ex-girlfriend Lucy for dinner... her **6. _____** goes up... Gaby tells her husband... **"I will not be on board"**... to which he replies... I'm in over my head with this new job... please... I need Lucy's help... please don't be jealous... and hours later when they answer the door, Gaby is **7. _____** to find out that Lucy is no **8. ____**

_____. Lucy is apparently **9.** _____.

The dinner goes well till Lucy takes a phone call for business. She got a really hard-to-land guy for Carlos. And she says "**10.** _____ **is easier when you say something like we are going to 11.** _____ **your salary...**" then Carlos touches Lucy's butt... an act that makes Gaby cast doubt on them...

When people are in a **12.** _____, people are constantly worried about getting cheated on. Women have such strong intuition that they can tell with the slightest thing that something is going on.... even in Gaby's case... she is not **13.** _____ by Lucy... yet she sends her friend Lynette to be her spy and keeps a **14.** _____ eye on them during work...

This also serves as a great opening for us to discuss today's topic about "**Charles's 15.** _____ **to Helen**" why would someone want to become the other woman?

Is it because at the right age especially after 30, most well-to-do men are already **16.** _____, and women don't want to settle down to someone whose salary and other things are below her... great guys are too slim in pickings... or is it because things just happen?

It's fate... or is it the **17.** _____ from the drama... the person who doesn't get loved is the other woman... or is it because guys will take any **18.** _____ with those who come to them? And it's innate to them... or is it because being in love and being married are two different things... being in love is at the stage you get the **19.** _____ and do not have other concerns, such as **20.** _____ pressures... so it's relatively easy...

when being married... it creates the **21.** _____ for either party to fall into others. Married people don't get **22.** _____ from their **23.** _____ but from the other woman... and that can be a problem...

Even though Charles let Helen know he was married..., he loved the appreciation from Helen... that's the first sign that I think his marriage is not going to last... the second alarm is his attraction to his wife **24.** _____

... but what puzzles me the most is that if he gets a **25.** _____ and eventually gets to be with Helen... and get married... ... pretty simple... but why can't they live happily there after...?

let's take a look at the analysis... it's on page... 123... **"Helen wanted only what she couldn't really have."** Only an **26.** _____ man can provide her that kind of love...

another key point that the author points out is that **27.** _____ _____ is gone... when they are in a **28.** _____ period... that is totally a different explanation from the **29.** _____ point of view...

We believe that there is **30.** _____... whatever you are getting... you are going to lose that way... that means... today... you get to be the other woman and steal your friend's husband... when the time comes... you are going to face the same fate as the ex-wife... you are going to end up getting divorced and being replaced by another woman... no exceptions...

and I want you all to write about how you feel about this story... it's about time to take a break... and I'm going to take a phone call from the dean... for the next hour... you are going to write 500 words and hand it in to my assistant... Jane...

| 參考答案 |

1. exist
2. threatens
3. condemn
4. advertised
5. defend
6. antenna
7. relieved
8. competition
9. overweight
10. poaching
11. double
12. relationship

13. threatened

14. watchful

15. attraction

16. married

17. explanation

18. chance

19. romance

20. financial

21. loophole

22. admiration

23. spouse

24. dwindles

25. divorce

26. unavailable

27. excitement

28. commitment

29. eastern

30. karma

NOTE

| Instruction | MP3 013

除了閱讀測驗外，其實培養能在聽完一大段訊息後，口述剛才聽到的聽力訊息是學習語言和表達很重要的一件事，讓自己養成並具備這樣的能力，除了能在聽力測驗中獲取高分外，也能在新托福寫作跟口說的整合題型上大有斬獲喔！所以快來練習，除了書中提供的參考答案外，自己可以試著重新聽過音檔一遍後，摘要出英文訊息並朗讀出來。

▶▶ 參考答案

Happiness in a marriage is not easy. The problems of the other woman or man can be the decisive factor in determining whether the marriage lasts or not. The condemnation of this behavior helps maintain people's morality.

The professor uses Gaby and Carlos' marriage to further illustrate the phenomenon. Women's intuition serves as the defense for Gaby to guard her marriage. She uses her friend Lynette to spy on Carlos and Lucy even though Lucy is not attractive as she is.

The example also links to today's topic: "Charles's attraction to Helen" There are numerous reasons for a

文學跨領域

商管跨領域

其他

woman to be the other woman. In Charles and Helen's situation, Charles enjoyed the admiration from Helen. It got worse when his love for his wife dwindled. What Charles fails to understand is that his unavailable status is what attracts her, so when they are together, the intimacy is gone.

NOTE

Unit 1	
Frankenstein	"ten innocent should suffer than that one guilty should escape."
Frankenstein	"As I fixed my eyes on the child, I saw something glittering on his breast. I took it; it was a portrait of a most lovely woman. "
Frankenstein	"Thanks to the lessons of Fliex and the sanguinary laws of man, I had learned how to work mischief."
Frankenstein	"I believe that I have no enemy on earth, and none surely would have been so wicked as to destroy me wantonly."
Unit 2	
The 1,000,000 Bank Note	."Enclosed you will find a sum of money. It's lent to you for thirty days, without interest."
Mark Twain	"Clothes make a man."

文學跨領域

商管跨領域

其他

Storynomics	"consumers only debate brands in the mental minute just before they make purchase."
Unit 3	
The 30,000 Bequest	"Vast wealth, to the person unaccustomed to it, is a bane; it eats into the flesh and bone of his morals."
The 30,000 Bequest	"Money has brought him misery, and he took revenge upon us."
Unit 4	
Gone with the Wind	"she could see so clearly now that he was only a childish fancy, no more important really than her spoiled desire for the aquamarine earbobs she had coaxed out of Gerald."
Gone with the Wind	"Do you think Pa is a pauper? He's got all the money I'll ever need and then I have Charles' property besides."
Gone with the Wind	"Yes, I want money more than anything else in the world."

Gone with the Wind	"but there is a penalty attached as there is to most things you want. It's loneliness."
Gone with the Wind	"you forget Ms. Wilkes" "I dare say she'd approve of anything you did, short of murder."
Gone with the Wind	"she's even approved of murder."
Gone with the Wind	"We haven't lost each other and our babies are alright and we have a roof over our heads."
Gone with the Wind	"she stayed with me through the whole siege when she could have gone home, when Aunt Pitty had run away to Macon..."
Gone with the Wind	"she had relied on Melanie, even as she had relied upon herself, and she had never known it."
Unit 5	
Success on Your Own Terms	"Today's success currency isn't about what you have achieved in the past; it's about your capacity to learn and grow in the immediate future."

文學跨領域

商管跨領域

其他

Unit 6	
Success on Your Own Terms	"I had never sought out anything with such conviction as I did to climb Everest."
Success on Your Own Terms	"Part of the realization had to do with her new definition of success. For Rebecca, success is the achievement of whatever it is you set out to do."

Unit 7	
The Defining Decade	"Resumes are just lists, and lists are not compelling."
How Luck Happens	"you are going to need luck to get a job."
The Success Equation	"the six interviewers voted against hiring you"
The Success Equation	"the head guy overrode their assessment and insisted we bring you in."
How Luck Happens	"You and your best friends already know most of the same people - you have overlapping social circles."

The Wealth Elite	"Wealthy individuals tend to ascribe their wealth overwhelmingly to personal qualities."
Unit 8	
The Skills: from first job to dream job	"My heart wasn't in the financial news in which Bloomberg had made its reputation, but my time there allowed me to develop skills which I realized later would never have been possible had I gone straight from university to somewhere like the BBC."
From the Ground Up: A Journey to Reimagine the Promise of America	"I had no mentors, no role models, no network that showed me how my education and innate skills translated into a working life."
Unit 9	
Getting There	"The thing with being fired is that no one tells you they are about to do it – you just get fired one day."

Desperate Housewives	"you are paid based on your expertise and contribution"

Unit 10

Mistakes I Made at Work	"Instead, you almost need to see yourself as a freelancer, building skills and capabilities to take with you to the next job and the next job."
Rich Dad Poor Dad	"It's not the smart who get ahead, but the bold."

Unit 11

44 Insider Secrets That Will Get You Hired	"You dream job is here."
44 Insider Secrets That Will Get You Hired	"You must craft your answers to assuage the interviewers' fears and manage their potential interpretations."

Unit 13

Desperate Housewives	"I will not be on board"
Desperate Housewives	"Poaching is easier when you say something like we are going to double your salary..."
Women Who Love too Much	"Helen wanted only what she couldn't really have."

文學跨領域

商管跨領域

其他

國家圖書館出版品預行編目(CIP)資料

魔鬼特訓：新托福聽力120 / 韋爾著-- 初版.
-- 新北市：倍斯特出版事業有限公司, 2021.
12 面；公分. --（考用英語系列；035）
ISBN 978-986-06095-9-2（平裝）
1.托福考試

805.1894   110019252

考用英語系列　035

魔鬼特訓－新托福聽力120（附QR Code音檔）

初　　版	2021年12月	
定　　價	新台幣520元	

作　　者	韋爾
出　　版	倍斯特出版事業有限公司
發 行 人	周瑞德
電　　話	886-2-8245-6905
傳　　真	886-2-2245-6398
地　　址	23558 新北市中和區立業路83巷7號4樓
E - m a i l	best.books.service@gmail.com
官　　網	www.bestbookstw.com
總 編 輯	齊心瑀
特約編輯	郭玥慧
封面構成	高鍾琪
內頁構成	菩薩蠻數位文化有限公司
印　　製	大亞彩色印刷製版股份有限公司

港澳地區總經銷	泛華發行代理有限公司
地　　址	香港新界將軍澳工業邨駿昌街7號2樓
電　　話	852-2798-2323
傳　　真	852-3181-3973